# THE TROUBLE WITH MIRACLES

## The Organ Grinder Factor

*A 3-D printer that replaces human organs
    without the need for surgery
    . . . but even miracles can kill*

**Other Book by Stephen Steele**

**The Trouble with Miracles** *series*
Book One: *The Cannastar Factor*
Book Two: *The Organ Grinder Factor*

**COMING SOON!**
Book Three: *The Fusion Factor*

# THE TROUBLE WITH MIRACLES

## The Organ Grinder Factor

*A 3-D printer that replaces human organs
without the need for surgery
. . . but even miracles can kill*

### Stephen Steele

SPEAKING VOLUMES, LLC
NAPLES, FLORIDA
2021

The Organ Grinder Factor

Copyright © 2021 by Stephen G. Mitchell

Cover design by Hannah Linder

All rights reserved. No part of this book may be reproduced or transmitted in any form or by any means without written permission.

This is a work of fiction. Names, characters, organizations, places, events and incidents are either products of the author's imagination or used fictionally.

ISBN 978-1-64540-558-0

*For Beverly
forever and always*

# Preface

*The Organ Grinder Factor* is the second volume in a 3-volume series entitled *The Trouble with Miracles*. The first volume, *The Cannastar Factor*, is a timely thriller about an alarming issue of today: how money runs the medical world.

Filled with mystery and suspense, *The Cannastar Factor* revolves around the heartfelt passions and resolute courage of Alex Farmer, M.D. and Cyd Seeley. Alex is a former drug addict trying to put his tortured life behind him. Cyd is a brilliant botanist and rancher in dire financial straits. They are inadvertently thrown together when a mutual friend is murdered after developing an inexpensive, organically grown cure for viral diseases. The miracle plant is called Cannastar, and it cures all manner of viruses from coronavirus and cancer, to HIV and herpes. Cannastar costs next to nothing to grow and returns the hopelessly ill to good health. Big Pharma will stop at nothing to keep it off the market.

The very existence of this new miracle drug threatens to bankrupt the pharmaceutical industry by making many of their patented drugs—drugs that generate billions of dollars in annual profit for them—worthless and obsolete. Wielding their vast political influence, Big Pharma manages to have Cannastar declared a Schedule I drug, lethal as fentanyl, addictive as heroin and cocaine.

Cyd and Alex, aided by faithful Native Americans from the Flathead Indian Reservation in Montana and the Navajo Nation in Arizona, fight to grow Cannastar and provide it to a desperate world. Their perilous journey draws them into the dangerous world of notorious drug dealers in a harrowing adventure that ranges from the Rocky Mountain wilderness, to the political corruption of Washington D.C., to the jungles of Mexico, to the deserts of the Southwest.

*The Cannastar Factor* is at heart an evolving love story between Alex and Cyd, how they learn and grow from the horrific challenges they face, how they are forever changed by their efforts to put a permanent end to viral disease. The first of three volumes ends as they flee the U.S. aboard Alex's sailboat, one step ahead of the Federal authorities who are intent on their capture.

Among the friends they are forced to leave behind is Otis Appleseed. Otis is a rotund former mortician with a green thumb who is now in charge of the clandestine Cannastar growing operation that Alex and Cyd helped establish on the vast Navajo reservation in Arizona.

Safely stored aboard their sailboat are bags of Cannastar seed that they intend to use to start a 'Grow' in another country as far away from the ruthless reach of Big Pharma as possible. In this new country, wherever it turns out to be, they hope to grow enough Cannastar to supply the entire world with their medical miracle. The last sentence in *The Cannastar Factor* reads:

"They were in the wind, they were on the wind, reaching for a distant shore, for a place unseen, unknown and yet to come."

# Prologue

Escaping California one step ahead of the authorities, Cyd and Alex embark on a desperate journey down the coast of Mexico and Central America in their sailboat, putting into port only when they need supplies. Arriving in Panama, they learn that the Canal Authority requires smaller boats to be lashed to the sides of much larger ships for journeys between the Pacific and Atlantic oceans. Their trip through the Panama Canal with their forty-eight-foot cutter lashed to the side of a gigantic cargo ship feels like being lashed to the leg of an elephant for a run through the jungle. They just hope the elephantine ship doesn't make any sudden moves sideways. Ten hours and fifty miles later, they enter the Caribbean with their bags of "illegal" Cannastar seeds still safely stowed aboard their boat. Here, for the first time in a long time, they are able to breathe a sigh of relief and finally feel safe.

In a kind of waking, floating dream, Cyd and Alex spend the next year and a half randomly crisscrossing the Caribbean exploring one hot, dusty, tropical island after another. The calamities and near-disasters that they survive—the sudden squalls, the boat-killing reefs and coral heads, the drug pirates who try to rob them, the vacant-eyed port authorities with their infuriating fees and regulations, the desperately broken equipment that has to be repaired on the spot with no clue how to do it—this is all the stuff of grand adventure, the halcyon days of love and magic they will always remember with a sigh and a smile.

While visiting Grand Cayman, they open a bank account at one of the one hundred and fifty-eight international banks on the island. After that, Otis has a place to send their share of the profits from the clandestine Cannastar Grow back on the Navajo reservation in Arizona. Surprisingly, the deposits that Otis sends keep getting larger every month. Their big disappointment comes when they can find no place in the Caribbean that is remote and secluded enough to throw out their anchor and start another Cannastar farm. In Bridgetown, Barbados, while waiting for a new generator to arrive so they can install it, the idea of going to Africa first occurs to them. And once it does, they can't wait to get there.

The books in their sailing library all warn that crossing a major ocean is not the same as island hopping. Anxious hours are spent preparing for and anticipating the worst that Mother Nature can throw at them. Happily, in the end, their Atlantic crossing is peaceful and uneventful.

Scudding along beneath the wind and a relentless sun, they dream and plan. Otis's ongoing success with the Cannastar Grow they left behind encourages them to think they can easily establish a similar plantation on one of Africa's vast savannah plains. All they need to find now is a remote country with friendly locals and an abundant water supply.

# Chapter One

## ANY WAY THE WIND BLOWS

The millions of stars that crowded the African sky off the Guinea coast—so many pinpoints of light there was hardly any room for the dark—all went out at once. Cyd and Alex were too absorbed in one another to notice. She lay stretched out in the cockpit of their sailboat with her head resting in his lap, her pale blue eyes looking up at him in peace and contentment as he lazily steered the boat with his knee. He gazed down at her lightly freckled face, marveling at her beauty. The wonder in his eyes was for her alone, not for the unimaginable canopy of stars that had just disappeared overhead, not for the mysteries of the dark continent that lay just ahead somewhere off their bow.

Cyd's shining dark hair had grown shoulder length in their year and a half at sea. The rigors of sailing, combined with a steady diet of fish, fruits and local vegetables, had toned and toughened their bodies. Buttered in sunscreen and browned to perfection, they looked like they had been sunbathing naked their entire time at sea—which wasn't far from the truth.

The tall, lanky doctor bent to kiss the face that was smiling up at him. "Happy birthday," he said.

She avoided his lips. "Are you going to get tired of me now that I'm old? Tell the truth."

"Thirty isn't old."

"Seriously, Alex."

"Seriously, I'll probably get tired of breathing first."

"Prove it."

"Prove it?"

"I can't remember the last time you made love to me."

"You can't remember as far back as this morning?"

She sighed. "I must be getting old."

They were about to kiss when the wind shifted direction. Their cutter quickened its pace, then shuddered and slowed as the wind shifted again. It was coming from straight over their bow now, and the sails flapped loudly.

Sitting up, they looked around in mild alarm. Alex checked his compass and fell off to the south. Cyd trimmed the jib and sheeted the main. The boat shot forward into the rising waves, and the windspeed indicator spun higher.

"Cyd, take the helm!" Alex shouted, diving below through the companionway to check for a weather update. "Weatherfax said it would be a calm night, last time I checked."

Minutes later he was back to find Cyd struggling with the helm.

"We've got too much sail up!" she cried. The wind tore the words from her mouth and sent them flying. "What did the Weatherfax say?"

"Freak storm!" he yelled. "Sudden dip in the African easterly Jetstream caused by melting polar icecaps. Never happened before. Dry air from the Sahara Desert is colliding with the moist humid air rising up from the Pacific and making it spin. They're forecasting a possible typhoon."

The storm broke with the fury of war guns. Thunder woke the gods and lightening scared the angels. The deafening explosion sent Cyd and Alex's sailboat flying from wave to wave like a cork shot from a champagne bottle.

Cyd fought the wheel with a pounding heart. "Alex, I don't know if I can hold it!"

## The Organ Grinder Factor

Clinging to anything he could grab, the thirty-nine-year-old doctor made his way forward along the wet, heaving deck. "Head her up! Got to douse the main!"

He freed the halyard and hundreds of square feet of sail came crashing down in a soggy, billowing pile. Making his way back to the cockpit to furl the jib, he heard the headsail blow out. It sounded like a bomb had hit the boat. Fragments of sailcloth flapped from the headstay like shredded laundry in a cyclone.

When the mainsail came down, the mainsheet broke loose and sent the heavy boom sweeping wildly across the deck. The boat pitched and rolled, and with each sweep of the boom Alex had to duck to keep from getting his skull caved in.

Cyd screamed in warning as he reached the cockpit, and this time they both had to duck. "I tried to start the engine!" she shouted in his ear. "It's flooded!"

A wave caught the boat sideways and broke over the top of them. The crashing water threw them to the floorboards choking and spitting. The sudden storm had taken the seasoned sailors completely by surprise. Deafening noise made it impossible to think. Lightening flashed, and through the driving rain they saw waves, white and foaming, crashing on the nearby rocks. A terrible grinding sound reached their ears, the boat lurched to a halt and waves of fear washed through them.

They were aground, listing to one side. Looking up in terror, they saw a mountain of water towering over them. The foaming curl hung suspended . . . then broke all at once, crushing their helpless craft under the weight of tons of water. One minute Cyd was standing on the slanted deck, the next she was gone, washed overboard, swallowed by the sea.

Alex stared in horror at the empty, flooded place where she had been, then coiled and sprung, launching himself over the side after her just as the boom swept back across the deck . . . and everything went black.

A peaceful calm came over him, and in the soothing stillness he felt the current pulling him under.

*** 

By morning, the sun had come out and the African easterly jet had straightened back out, sending the typhoon on its way along the normal hurricane track to the Caribbean.

Alex woke with his face buried in sand and the surf lapping gently at his bare feet where the storm had torn his shoes off. He sat up slowly, shaking his throbbing head to try and clear it while spitting out sand from between his cracked lips. His mind began to clear and a desolate beach came into focus. Bits and pieces of their sailboat's hull and rigging, along with remnants of their tattered belongings, were strewn about the sand in either direction, some of it awash in the surf.

His hand went to the back of his head, grasping at his wound. His fingers came away sticky with blood. He didn't need a mirror to know he had an open gash in his scalp that needed cleaning out and probably stitching up. He also didn't have to be a doctor to guess that he'd had a concussion.

He didn't care.

Where was Cyd? He had to find her!

Staggering to his feet, he stumbled desperately up the beach too terrified to face the possibility that she was lost. *If I survived, she survived,* he told himself. He just had to find where she had come ashore, that's all. Clumsily, violently, impatiently, he searched among the ruins of what had been their entire world. Half of the boat's hull lay a short distance away looking like a shark had chewed it in two. He ran toward it, and frantically peered inside.

Nothing. A hollow shell of frayed and ragged fiberglass. Further on, he came upon the soggy remains of his favorite baseball cap, a torn shirt, the binoculars Cyd was so fond of using smashed and covered in sand. One or two sacks of Cannastar seed had washed up on the beach still sealed in their waterproof bags, and looking like big, black balloons.

He didn't care.

He picked up his broken laptop, saw the screen was shattered, and threw it aside. Cyd's halter top and a tennis shoe, a lifejacket, a smashed cooking pot were all jumbled together in a sandy pile. Suddenly, up the beach, he caught a glimpse of what looked like the twisted limbs of a body wedged behind some rocks. He broke into a panicked run, lurching and stumbling toward it . . . but it was only a tangle of seaweed and driftwood that had caught his eye. A desperate cry escaped his lips and he staggered on.

Then further on, half-buried in a pile of something smelly and slimy and swarming with buzzing sandflies, he saw a bright red ribbon. The same red ribbon he had so often admired in her dark hair. He untangled it from the remains of a dead fish, held it in his shaking hands, and fell to his knees as tears burned his cheeks.

A howl of anguish came out of his throat, and from the nearby jungle something wild returned his call. The sound roused him, and he stared out to sea. A point of land ran out into the surf. A short distance from the beach he could see the current dividing itself in half and splitting around the point. One part of the ocean went one way, the other part the other. This was where she had gone, he was sure of it! Cyd was just around that point!

Scrambling to his feet, he ran on.

# Chapter Two

## FAT MAN AND LITTLE BOY

Storm debris littered the west African beaches of Guinea-Bissau where the wayward hurricane had briefly visited the night before, wreaking havoc and driving Cyd and Alex's sailboat onto the rocks. It was still early morning, but even with the ocean breezes the temperature was already approaching a humid eighty degrees.

Along one of these deserted stretches of Bissau beach, Fat Man and Little Boy were taking their morning constitutional. Nicknamed after the only two atomic bombs ever used in combat, their real names were Avi Ben-Haim and Ashraf Shaviv respectively—although no one ever really called them that. Even they usually referred to one other by the names that best described their rather volatile natures and startling difference in size. The difference in their appearance was further accentuated by Fat Man's head which was too small for his oversized body, and Little Boy's feet which were unnecessarily large for such a small man.

Stepping over and around broken tree limbs and trash, the two hapless curmudgeons were arguing loudly as usual. Both wore yarmulkes on the backs of their heads, both had the same birthday, both were fifty years old. Listening to their constant bickering, it was sometimes difficult to tell that they were the best of friends who loved each another like brothers.

Water, of course, was the basis of their conjoined life. The very mention of it was likely to stop any argument in mid-sentence and send them into a frenzy of enthusiasm and excitement over how to achieve the most retrieval and flow from the most unlikely of sources, and how to deliver it to the most unlikely of places.

Fat Man mopped at his sweaty brow. "I should never have let you talk me into this," he complained.

Little Boy was perplexed. "How did I talk you into it when it was you who insisted we take this job in the first place? You want to be mad at somebody, be mad at yourself."

"And it's me, I suppose, who's refusing to do the job now that we're here? Me who's going to get us sent home in body bags if they find out we absolutely won't build it?"

"I came here to help these people who are starving to death in the middle of the worst drought in African history," his small companion insisted. "Little did I know."

Fat Man swelled with indignation. "Little did I know what a putz you'd turn into the minute we got here. May I remind you, dear friend, our company is paying us to be engineers, not to take sides in local politics."

"Avi, do you really want to make it easier for Guinea-Bissau's cocaine cavalry to grow their drugs and make even more money than they already do? Do you really want to help these homicidal drug barons lounge around beside their oversized swimming pools with their expensive girlfriends while people are starving and dying from lack of water? While Africa dries up and blows away? I won't do it, I tell you. I won't build it."

"We're going to die here because of you, I hope you know that."

"These are violent criminals, Fat Man! Where's your sense of decency? We do what they're demanding of us, and we're no better than they are."

"We build it and we go home, Ashraf! Murder is a national pastime with these people, or hadn't you noticed?"

"Exactly my point. This isn't Africa we're in. This isn't even a country. It's a narco-state! You know as well as I do, no matter how much water we create for them, not a single drop of it will go to the people, their crops or their animals."

"Ah, but what if you're wrong?" Fat Man pleaded. "Such a wonderful design we've created! It's revolutionary, Little Boy. It's brilliant. And I couldn't have done it without you."

"Such a mensch, you are. It is brilliant what we've designed. It would be the beginning of a new day for Africa, a path forward into 21$^{st}$ century. But not here, not for these gaudy Columbian drug thugs who . . ." Little Boy stopped in mid-sentence and stared up the beach. "Do you see what I'm seeing? Oh, my God . . .!"

They broke into a run, Fat Man looking like a jelly donut rolling along the sand and Little Boy beside him looking like a popsicle stick with churning legs.

Up the beach a wild-eyed girl in torn clothes with her hair full of sand was frantically pulling floating bags that looked like black balloons out of the surf and piling them on the sand just out of the reach of the tongues of waves that were washing gently in and out. Judging from the way she was acting, muttering to herself and working with the frenzied movements of someone pulling bodies out of the surf, the girl was delirious. It wasn't until the pair of Israeli engineers were a few feet away that they could hear what she was actually saying.

"Alex will want these . . . glad that I saved them . . . want to know they're safe . . . he'll see when he comes . . . he'll know we saved the only thing that matters . . . have to get them all in before…"

Fat Man reached out to her and she jumped back, bracing herself against the piled bags of seed like a feral cat protecting her kittens.

"Cyd?" A distant voice. "Cyd!"

Fat Man and Little Boy looked up to see a tall, ruddy-skinned man rounding the point, running toward them, waving his arms and calling at the top of his lungs.

"Stay back, the both of you," Alex cried, rushing up and gathering Cyd in his arms. "Can't you see she's in shock?"

"Alex?" Cyd's voice was distant, disoriented, disconnected. "Alex, where have you been? The seeds, I saved them. They're all safe . . ." She felt at his face like a blind woman trying to confirm his identity. "Your head, darling, it's bleeding. You're hurt. Why . . .?" And with that she went limp in his arms.

"Out cold," Fat Man observed. "Maybe we should . . ."

Alex looked incredulously from the big one to the little one standing there in their wrinkled linen suits and white shirts and bowties and cried "Hospital! We need a hospital!"

"Not far," Little Boy rushed to assure him. "Only a little way."

"Let me help you," Fat Man offered, working his way under Cyd's limp arm and lifting her on one side while Little Boy helped prop her up on the other. "It's just through the jungle there and up the street a bit."

Alex grabbed her away from them. Lifting and cradling her in his arms, he staggered off through the wilted, battered undergrowth in the direction they were pointing. "Hurry up then! Let's go!"

\*\*\*

Bissau, the capital city of Guinea-Bissau, was at best a slum. The beach trail where Alex burst out of the trees with Cyd in his arms and Fat Man and Little Boy scrambling to keep up was in one of the worst sections of town.

Shirtless teenagers lounged arrogantly in the doorways of buildings ravaged by years of civil war. Faded walls, once colorfully painted, were riddled with bullet holes and broken by bombs. Everything was so damaged and littered with garbage it was impossible to tell what part of the destruction was a result of the hurricane and what part was just the way things were.

Vendors were busily setting their tents back up along both sides of the rutted dirt street, and a growing crowd of brightly dressed women were flooding out of their huts and hovels to do their daily shopping. Smiling black faces of poverty-stricken children with huge, innocent eyes and great white teeth looked on with genuine curiosity as the tall white man carrying the limp white woman in his arms staggered up the bustling thoroughfare followed by two other white men, one fatter than an elephant and the other smaller than a monkey.

Alex shifted Cyd's weight in his arms as a brand-new Mercedes SUV honked its way through the throngs of locals with its speakers booming Spanish rap music so loud it shook the ground. A brown Columbian arm hung out the driver's window adorned with a solid gold, diamond encrusted Rolex.

As the vehicle made its way slowly past, weaving to avoid the potholes, Alex couldn't help noticing the black haired, light skinned woman with European features in the passenger's seat. If she wasn't Ms. Columbia, she should have been. To the teenagers in the doorways, the scantily-clad woman in the Mercedes looked like the kind of young lady that is adorned with a staple in her navel in certain popular magazines. The driver, cold and indifferent, seemed to regard his beautiful passenger as merely another accouterment of endless wealth: an expensive horse, an expensive car, fast and flashy and easy to ride.

Fat Man, with Little Boy close on his heels, wheezed loudly as he tried to keep up. Alex, hurrying along with his awkward burden, turned and gave them a questioning look as the Mercedes boomed past through the teeming crowd.

Fat Man shrugged indifferently.

"*Narcotraficantes,*" (drug traffickers) Little Boy muttered bitterly. "Our delightful employers."

Fat Man pointed a chubby finger. "Up ahead," he wheezed. "Just there on the other side of that open sewer. The big tent with the open flaps."

"Hospital?" Alex demanded anxiously.

"If you could call it that," Little Boy replied. "Catholic missionaries run it."

Cradling Cyd in his arms, Alex ran toward a ramshackle building with a rusted tin roof, canvas sides, a wide veranda and a small wooden chapel attached to one side.

\*\*\*

The overhead paddle fans in the canvas-walled infirmary squeaked loudly but did little to move the hot, sticky air, or remove the smell of disinfectant from the stifling enclosure. Two long rows of hospital beds ran down the makeshift ward partially filled with black bodies in various states of agony and distress.

Cyd lay motionless on one of the beds with Fat Man and Little Boy watching over her like worried parents. The elderly priest in the dirty black cassock who had received them with such compassion and concern stood taking her vitals. Alex sat on the bed next to Cyd while a white nun in a soiled white uniform cleaned out his headwound with antiseptic soap and a stiff brush. Every time she scrubbed too deep, he winced and tried to pull away, but his eyes never strayed from Cyd's comatose form.

"You wish not for an infection, *Monsieur*, you will kindly stop squirming." The nun's air of authority suggested she was the mother superior. "I stitch now, so no movement, please."

Cyd's chest rose and fell with even breaths. The priest stepped back to study her a moment, relieved that her blood pressure and temperature had returned to normal. Fat Man's metal folding chair creaked under his weight as he leaned forward to lovingly touch her hand. Little Boy rose and carefully readjusted her bedding. From their solicitous attentions it was clear they had both fallen in love with her.

"Wonder Woman, she looks like," Fat Man sighed.

"Sleeping Beauty," Little Boy countered softly.

Fat Man gave him a look of exasperation. "Such a schmuck, you are. At least Wonder Woman is a brunette—and from Israel."

"Schmuck yourself," Little Boy persisted before lowering his voice. "Wonder Woman is an Amazonian. Do you think those black bags she was trying to rescue are full of drugs?"

Fat Man rolled his eyes. "An idiot I have for a partner! You think a girl like this could be a drug smuggler?"

"How should I know? Did you remember your mosquito repellent? You know how you are."

"So now you're my mother, too?"

"Somebody has to be." Little Boy's face darkened. "I hope you didn't hurt your back again trying to lift her. It would be just like you to hurt yourself at a time like this."

"Alex . . ." Cyd rasped dryly from the bed. "Alex?"

"She's waking up, she's waking up!" the pair cried excitedly, waving their arms to get everyone's attention.

Alex shook off his seamstress and leapt to Cyd's side. If she had risen from the grave, he couldn't have been more relieved. "You had us worried there for a minute, old girl."

She smiled up at him weakly. "How's the boat?"

Heart bursting, he gently brushed her cheek with the back of his hand. "Worse off than you are, I'm happy to say."

"Did you find the seeds I saved? I don't know if I got them all . . ." He didn't respond, and she struggled to sit up. "Alex, where are they? Don't you have them?"

"They're still on the beach. Now lie still."

"Well go and get them, for heaven's sake! What are you thinking? We can't just leave them there . . .!"

Alex's nurse impatiently stuck her suture needle and thread in her lapel and brushed Alex aside. "You will all of you please stop bothering my patient!"

Another nun appeared with a tube of disinfectant, pulled back Cyd's sheet and began to gently rub the numbing, healing salve on Cyd's battered and bruised arms and legs.

Cyd lifted her head to see what was going on, saw that her limbs and torso were covered in long red scrapes and scratches. "I look like I lost a fight with a belt sander," she observed in mild amusement before falling back exhausted onto her pillow.

Sounds of a commotion came from outside, growing louder as a dozen black men in blood-soaked combat uniforms burst into the tent supporting and dragging one another along. The old priest rushed to their side and bustled them into his surgery, which was nothing more than a second tent attached to the first by way of a rusted, tin-roofed breezeway.

Alex automatically leapt to his feet to help, then remembered Cyd and quickly sat back down.

"Go on," she urged him weakly. "Help the others. I'll be fine."

"You sure? I don't want to . . ."

She smiled at the mismatched pair of men who were watching over her so closely. "I think I may have some new friends to look after me."

Alex nodded with an anxious look back and hurried into the other tent where he started examining the wounded patients. Both the priest and the nun that had stitched his head told him to stay back, that they would handle this.

"I'm a doctor," he announced curtly. "Army. Two tours in the Middle East. I was also an emergency room doctor in South-Central Los Angeles. I think I know a little something about bullet wounds."

Alex worked alongside the priest and his staff all day and into the night performing emergency surgery and tending to the bullet wounds of the insurgents. One man's leg was mostly blown off below the knee, and all Alex could do was cut it the rest of the way off and stop the bleeding. By midnight he was covered in blood himself, but all the soldiers were alive, in relatively stable condition and recovering in their beds in the main ward.

Alex stood beside the bed of their leader, Zamora Diallo, checking under his bandage. He had been shot in the arm, and the bullet had gone straight through. The wound wasn't that serious, but Alex was concerned about infection. The veteran fighter looked to be in his late forties with thick lips, a broad nose and skin so black it seemed to absorb the light. A shaggy black beard covered the lower half of his face except where crisscrossed scars wouldn't allow the hair to grow.

"For the sake of my men, I thank you," Zamora told Alex in an African voice accented in the country's official language of Portuguese.

"I would have done the same for whoever shot you," Alex informed him evenly.

"Not if you knew them as we do."

The priest overheard the conversation and came over to stop it before it got out of hand.

Zamora held up a hand. "It's alright, Father José. I can see in his eyes that this is a good man. The doctor has a good heart."

Alex ignored the acknowledgement. "Who are you?"

"I command a hundred and fourteen men." Zamora paused sadly. "Less than a hundred after today."

"Who are you fighting?"

"We fight our corrupt president and his corrupt army who take everything for themselves. We fight the drug dealers who bribe them. We fight the chaos and evil that has overtaken Guinea-Bissau, and we fight for our people who live in some of the worst poverty on earth."

Alex was overwhelmed by his courage.

"Also, we fight for revenge."

"How long has this been going on?"

"Guinea-Bissau won its independence from Portugal in 1974. Fifteen thousand of our people died in that war. We have had coups and civil wars ever since."

"Working out well for you, is it?"

"It would have stopped long ago if the people knew how to be free. They only know how to be victims. I fight for the heads of my enemies that I keep under my bed."

Alex laughed and realized he was deeply fond of this man. "It must be getting a little crowded under there by now. Why go on?"

Zamora was silent a moment. "It is better to die fighting than to live without hope."

## Chapter Three

### NO EXIT

Alex sent Fat Man and Little Boy to retrieve the black bags of Cannastar seed from the beach and spent what was left of the night in one of the metal chairs beside Cyd's bed. The next morning, she woke with an appetite, ate a simple but hearty breakfast prepared by the kindly nuns and walked out of the hospital on Alex's arm. She was a bit wobbly and battered. Otherwise, she was recovering nicely.

They stood on the hospital's rickety wooden veranda looking out as a burning sun rose over the red dirt street in front of the hospital that was already filling up with its daily swarm of colorful vendors, shoppers, women balancing overloaded baskets on their heads, squealing children and worthless idlers. Coming up the street toward them was a new shiny black Cadillac Escalade that was hitting every other pothole and giving its occupants a rather uncomfortable ride.

The huge Cadillac, strangely out of place in this land where the clocks had somehow managed to stop around the time man was learning to walk upright, pulled up and stopped in front of the hospital. Cyd and Alex stared. Inside, grinning up at them through the windshield and motioning to them to get in, was Fat Man and Little Boy.

"Nice ride," Cyd remarked as they climbed into the back seat.

"You two decide to become narcos overnight?" Alex asked.

"As favored employees of the Columbians, at least for the moment, we get certain perks," Little Boy replied indifferently. Unable to look over the steering wheel, he looked through it instead and accelerated away.

"Watch out for that woman!" Fat Man cried. "You trying to kill us? Slow down!"

Little Boy seemingly had gone deaf. Minutes later, his erratic driving on unpaved streets brought them to the outskirts of town where the road wound past a scattering of magnificent Spanish haciendas sequestered behind high walls and partially hidden by jungle landscaping that looked dried and limp.

Cyd suddenly remembered her black bags from the beach. "My seeds, where are they?" She was frightened. "Do you have them?"

"In the back," Little Boy replied, giving her a reassuring smile in the rear-view mirror. Grim men with automatic weapons were patrolling one of the largest estates as they passed, and he gave them a halfhearted salute. "We could only find two of the bags. The tide had washed the rest out to sea."

Cyd nodded and sighed. "We've started with less."

Fat Man turned and handed Alex a large, water stained, clear plastic pouch. "We searched through what was left of the debris on the beach. Wasn't much after the tide came in. Found this buried in the sand. It must have floated ashore when your boat broke up."

Alex quickly opening the pouch and searched its contents. He pulled out two passports and with great relief saw that they were only slightly water damaged. "We'd be in big trouble without these. Thank you."

Little Boy slowed the SUV as they approached a smaller, vine-covered villa that looked like it might be the guest house of the big hacienda they had just passed. Turning into a gravel drive, he pulled up and stopped.

A very black woman wearing a very white turban opened the big wooden front door and stood attentively as the new arrivals got out of the car. Cyd went around to open the tailgate and retrieve her bags of seed but was assured by Little Boy that they would be safe where they were.

Curious and not a little confused by her surroundings, she followed Alex and their hosts into the house, stopped and stood looking around at the cool, tile-floored interior of the mini hacienda.

Coming in from the steaming humidity outside made her shiver and she rubbed her bare arms. Through sliding glass doors that opened onto a large outdoor patio with a high wall around it, she saw a lush, flowered garden that filled the room with a fragrant scent. Carved wooden beams in the high wood ceiling caught her attention and she turned in a circle admiring the expensive Spanish-style furnishings.

Fat Man addressed the woman in the white turban. "Mariama, will you kindly take our friends to the guestroom so they can refresh themselves? We'll have our lunch on the patio today."

The stoic head housekeeper led the way down a wide, airy hallway, opened the door to a spacious guestroom with a huge four-poster bed and bowed them inside. "You will in the dresser fresh clothes find," she informed them in a haughty Portuguese accent. "Shower is through there, as you see. You will please not waste the water."

"Drought that bad?" Alex asked.

Mariama bowed herself out. "Lunch in an hour… Senhor e Senhora (Mr. and Mrs.)."

Alex turned to Cyd the moment she was gone. "What the hell is going on here? Who are these guys? *What* are these guys?"

Cyd smiled. "I think they're cute, whoever they are."

They entered the outdoor patio to find the center of the dining table piled high with a mountain of fresh fruit. Highbacked chairs were pulled out for them by silent black men who looked more like armed guards than servants. Through open French doors to an office, they could see a cluttered drafting board with rolls of working drawings spread out amid piles of scribbled calculations.

Fat Man and Little Boy were already seated and waiting for them. They smiled with delight at their guests but seemed reluctant to speak until the help had left the room. The moment they were gone, they lowered their voices.

"As you can see, we are prisoners here," Little Boy whispered hurriedly.

"Could have fooled me," Alex remarked.

Fat Man glared angrily at Little Boy. "Our so-called escape is scheduled for tonight . . . thanks to him."

Cyd looked from one to the other. "What on earth are you talking about?"

"I've been in contact with our company," Little Boy whispered. "I insisted they get us out of here before it's too late."

"Too late for what?" Alex asked in confusion.

Fat Man again glared at his friend. "Ask him, why don't you."

"Plane will be here at midnight," Little Boy went on. "I strongly suggest the two of you be on it with us."

Cyd looked at Alex in alarm.

"We'll be returning to Israel," Little Boy added. "To Tel Aviv. From there you can catch a flight to wherever you like."

Alex was more confused than ever. "I thought you said you were prisoners?"

Dark rings had formed under Fat Man's armpits. "They find out what we're up to, and we'll be dead prisoners."

"Who's they?" Cyd insisted.

Fat Man looked left and right for eavesdroppers. "The Columbians, who do you think? This is the most lawless place on earth. You do as they say, or they kill you."

Little Boy put a reassuring hand on his friend's broad shoulder. "Stay if you like, Avi, but when they find out we've only been pretending to work on a project we have no intention of building, I suspect they'll cut us up in little pieces and feed us to one of those awful creatures we hear screeching and howling in the jungle at night."

"How do you mean lawless?" Alex persisted.

Little Boy smiled nervously. "You do know that Guinea-Bissau is a failed country run by Columbian drug lords? The locals here are all destitute. Most of them can barely afford food, let alone electricity. Decades of civil war led to decades of a Marxist-Leninist dictatorship. The institutions, the officials, especially the army, they're all bought off. Law enforcement is almost nonexistent. It's a drug trafficker's dream. The ideal transit hub for moving cocaine from Latin America to Western Europe."

"I suppose there is a bit of a drug trade here," Fat Man admitted.

"*Roaring* drug trade," Little Boy amended. "The heads of the military are all on the U.S. government's list of major drug traffickers. An estimated one ton of pure Columbian cocaine leaves Guinea-Bissau daily on its way to Europe."

"And what exactly are the two of you doing here?" Cyd asked weakly.

Little Boy shook his head in despair. "Making water to grow their coca plants so they won't have to go to the risk and expense of transporting it across the Atlantic. As of now, their boats can only travel at night and have to stay motionless by day under blue tarpaulins so the airplanes can't see them."

Fat Man counted on his fingers. "Crops are failing, people and animals are dying, the land is cracked and broken, and swarms of desert locusts are ravaging the grazing land. Ashraf here, he wants to abandon the African people in the middle of the worst drought in centuries when we could so easily solve their problem for them." He turned indignantly to his best friend. "I hope you're proud of yourself."

"How do you make water in the middle of a drought?" Cyd was genuinely fascinated.

Fat Man's indignation turned to pride. "Little Boy here is one of the world's leading experts in RO engineering."

"RO?"

"Reverse Osmosis."

Little Boy blushed. "My associate exaggerates. Avi is every bit as good of an RO engineer as I am. We helped our company build Israel's state-of-the-art desalination plant in Tel Aviv. He and I were part of the lead SWRO team that designed it."

Cyd raised her eyebrows at Little Boy. "SWRO?"

"Salt Water Reverse Osmosis," Fat Man replied impatiently. "We turn sea water into potable water by the millions of gallons at very little cost."

"Thanks in no small part to our efforts," Little Boy went on, "our arid homeland now has virtually unlimited drinking and irrigation water forever. Crops are flourishing, the Israeli people are thriving. We thought we were coming here to do the same for Africa."

"We still could if you weren't so pig-headed," Fat man complained miserably.

The botanist in Cyd couldn't resist. Her curiosity wasn't intentional, it was just a part of who she was. "You say your Colombian employers want to grow coca in Africa. Northern Africa is sub-Saharan desert, am I right? Central and southern Africa are tropical, but almost all of it has a monsoon season. The coca plant would like all this humidity, but it also likes altitude, nutrient-rich soil and a one-season climate. This last is most important. Where do these drug runners of yours think they're going to grow it?"

"They claim to have found the perfect place," Little Boy answered, nearly as miserable as Fat Man. "We were going to have to pump the water hundreds of miles though." He looked at his guests and tried to smile. "Enough about us. What about you two? Not to pry, but what are those big bags of seeds for that had you so worried?"

Just then the servants came in carrying steaming platters of freshly baked fish ringed in vegetables and decorated with small flowers. The diners waited in silence until they were served and the equally soundless help had left the room.

Little Boy turned to Cyd waiting for an answer.

"We're drug dealers, as well," she replied evenly. "We're wanted fugitives."

Fat Man's hands flew in the air and Little Boys' eyes grew huge.

"Back in the States," Alex added, "we have a growing operation on an Indian reservation that supplies North and South America through a Mexican cartel. We're here in Africa to start a planation that will do the same for the rest of the world."

"If you intend to help us," Cyd said, "you should know the truth."

Fat Man slammed down his knife and fork. "I knew something wasn't right with you two, I just knew it!"

Little Boy's tiny face had turned red. "Out!" he cried, jumping to his feet. "Out of this house this instant!"

Alex didn't move. "The difference," he explained calmly, "is that the drug we grow actually saves lives instead of destroying them. Unlike cocaine, it cures people instead of killing them."

Little Boy sat back down with an open mouth.

"It's called Cannastar," Cyd went on quickly. "It cures viral disease. Everything from cancer and epidemics of flu, to HIV and herpes. Big Pharma made certain it was illegal so they could keep selling their expensive drugs, and it wouldn't put them out of business." She smiled bitterly. "Which is the reason we're fugitives in the first place. If you still want us to leave, we will."

Little Boy and Fat Man's shock had turned to fascination as their adoration for Cyd overrode their suspicion.

"So, it actually exists?" Fat Man was incredulous. "Cannastar is a real drug?"

"We've heard about it," Little Boy admitted. "Personally, I thought it was too good to be true. Were you the ones who invented it then?"

"The inventor is dead," Alex replied bluntly. "We're just the farmers."

"Unlike coca," Cyd added, "Cannastar will grow almost anywhere. All it needs is lots of water. Which is why I'm so terribly disappointed to hear that Africa is in the middle of a terrible drought, and so impressed that you can make water."

Fat Man gave his diminutive friend an accusatory glance. "We're sorry we doubted you."

"At least let us help you get out of this terrible hellhole," Little Boy begged. "Guinea-Bissau is no place you want to be, let alone any place you want to try and grow your Cannastar."

Cyd grimaced. "All good things must come to an end, I suppose."

"And we were having such a good time," Alex added.

\*\*\*

It was a long wait watching the clock move slowly toward midnight. Cyd and Alex sat dressed and alert in their room while Fat Man and Little Boy went nervously about the house trying to decide what they dared to take with them without alerting the household staff.

When it came time to go, Fat Man knocked on Cyd and Alex's door and announced a little too loudly that they were taking their new friends out to what was left of a nearby watering hole so they could observe the different kinds of animals that congregated there at night. Then quickly, the four of them piled into the big Cadillac SUV and headed for the airport. Little Boy drove, Fat Man was in the passenger seat complaining constantly about Little Boy's driving and Cyd and Alex sat in the back getting bounced around.

Bissau's relatively modern Osvaldo Vieira International Airport, dark and deserted at this hour except for the tiny landing lights that lit the runway, had been built decades ago before the UN abandoned their mission in Bissau and the US abandoned their embassy. Little Boy pulled up and stopped just off the tarmac, doused his lights and switched off the engine. A wild and foreign darkness closed in around them, and they sat in silence as if in fear of disturbing whatever might be hiding beneath its cloak.

Then out of the night sky small lights appeared, and a sleek, modern, twin-engine turboprop whistled in and lightly touched down with two small squeals of its tires. Little Boy flashed his lights, and the engines wound up again as the aircraft taxied toward them.

Alex and Cyd started to get out so they could retrieve their bags of Cannastar seed from the back—just as a loud explosion shattered the calm. They looked up to see a blinding streak of light, a distant burst of flame, and the newly-arrived airplane disappear in a volcano of smoke and fire.

The four escapees sat stunned as flames lit the night sky and a tank rumbled out of the jungle with a long smoking gun. Helmeted soldiers dressed in camouflage and draped in cartridge belts ran alongside the tank on either side carrying rifles and rocket propelled grenade launchers.

Cyd took one look and screamed.

"Drive!" Alex yelled at Little Boy who was fumbling with the ignition. He managed to start the engine and the SUV rocketed away, throwing its passengers back in their seats.

Battered pickup trucks full of black shouting faces appeared out of nowhere and swarmed the Cadillac before it had gone a hundred yards. Little Boy slammed on the brakes, pounding the steering wheel as the soldiers piled out of the pickups with triumphant cries of glee.

In the back of the SUV, Alex bent over and stuffed something under the driver's seat.

"What are you doing?" Cyd cried.

"Hiding our passports. The military gets their hands on them and turns us over to the American authorities, we're screwed. We're still wanted back in the states."

Rough hands reached in, pulled Cyd and Alex out of the car and lined them up against a nearby rock wall. Other soldiers pulled Fat Man and Little Boy out, quickly searched them, found their passports in a pocket sewn into the waistband of Fat Man's pants, and threw the two of them into the back seat of the Cadillac.

Cyd and Alex stood facing the rock wall and didn't see what was happening until they were abruptly turned back around and marched to the rear of the vehicle.

The tailgate stood open and they stared in shock.

"Oh, no . . . Oh, no!" Cyd protested, backing away. "Those aren't ours! No way!"

Alex flared. "You can't be serious!"

Fat Man and Little Boy craned their necks to see what was going on and were ordered to keep their eyes forward. Continued denials from Cyd and Alex fell on deaf ears. In among their two black bags of Cannastar seed, scattered about as if carelessly thrown in, was a pile of Russian and Chinese made automatic weapons.

# Chapter Four

### KIDNAPPING THE KIDNAPPED

Cyd and Alex watched as Fat Man and Little Boy were driven away in the Cadillac with Fat Man busily accusing his miserable little friend of trying to get them killed.

"They didn't do anything!" Cyd screamed after them as she and Alex were manhandled into a camouflage-painted military vehicle. "Where are you taking them?"

The armed guards ignored Cyd's demands and drove them off in the opposite direction.

The military headquarters where they were taken were in a former government administration building. Only one side of the structure remained intact. The other side had been torn away by a long-ago bomb that left ragged walls and interior floors fully exposed.

Cyd and Alex were marched down to the basement where they were interrogated throughout the night. Had they anything to confess, they surely would have confessed it in light of the repeated threats of torture they were promised. Alas, they could only profess their innocence—which was no defense at all given the gravity of their crime. Guinea-Bissau had a zero-tolerance policy against gun smuggling.

By dawn, their interrogators were no closer to discovering the truth about the guns found in the back of the Cadillac SUV, or what Cyd and Alex intended to do with them, than they were when they started. Bored, tired and hungry, the officers all went home for a well-deserved rest.

\*\*\*

## The Organ Grinder Factor

The inside of the jail was hotter than the inside of a bread oven with the sun beating down. Cyd and Alex were handed over to a sleepy, gray-haired African jailer named Fernando who was seventy years old if he was a day. The armed guard that brought them there yawned and turned to leave with the reminder that gun running in Guinea-Bissau carried a mandatory sentence of ten years.

The jail itself was a one-story building that looked ready to collapse under its own weight. Its blue paint was faded almost to white and patches of it had peeled away in ragged circles exposing the weathered plaster underneath. Inside, there was no electricity, no running water and no beds. Instead, filthy mattresses with filthy bedding lined the walls of a large common room where a despondent collection of African prisoners lounged about talking, smoking and playing cards. The sky was visible through holes in the roof, the floor was littered in trash and the stench from the open toilet along the back wall turned Cyd's stomach.

She paced angrily back and forth coughing at the smell. Alex followed her with his eyes, keenly alert to the dangers of being the only two white prisoners in a room full of black criminals.

"We don't even get a goddamn phone call?" she fumed. "These people are animals! I take that back. Animals are more civilized. This is crazy, Alex! It's insane! Where are our seeds? What are we even doing here?" He took her in his arms and she began to weep. "This place makes the Santa Fe jail I was in back in New Mexico look like a five-star hotel!"

As the day wore on, the room grew even hotter until they could barely breathe. They found a corner where they could sit with their backs against the wall. Exhausted as they were, they didn't dare close their eyes, and it was too hot to sleep anyway. An old black prisoner approached and stood over them, silently holding out his hand.

*He can't possibly be asking for a handout,* Cyd thought, frightened at what he might do when he learned she had nothing to give him.

He opened his fingers and she saw he was offering her a rock-hard crust of bread. Stunned at his generosity, unwilling to take the last of his food, she shook her head in refusal. The old man pressed his offering into Cyd's hand with gentle insistence. She took it graciously, smiling affectionately as he hobbled back to his mattress.

Fernando the jailer brought in a bucket of water with debris and insects floating on top and set it down with a loud expulsion of breath. He had apparently expended great effort to bring water to his prisoners. The inmates all fell on the bucket, carefully ladling out an equal share for each, saving the last two shares which they offered up to Cyd and Alex. They were a family of the damned, a community of felons who shared a common bond.

By sunset, the heat in the jail had reached a level approximately equal to the surface temperature of the sun. Its two white inmates were ready to faint. Fernando appeared once more, turned with a meaningful look, and shuffled out again leaving the barred door standing wide open behind him. Cyd and Alex watched in stunned disbelief as the prisoners all scrambled to their feet and began to shuffle out.

The old man who had given Cyd the crust of bread stopped by their corner as he followed the others to the exit. "We go home now to dinner," he informed them in broken English. "Fernando, he will be back at dawn. Be sure you are back by then or Fernando, he get angry."

Baffled, stunned, not a little confused, the two white prisoners scrambled to their feet and followed their fellow prisoners out the door. No one seemed to be in any particular hurry. Emerging into a beautiful African evening, they saw peacocks landing in the trees and taking their assigned places along their particular branches with loud, repeated, screeching calls—a ritual repeated at sunset in this magical land since the dawn of time.

Cyd and Alex stood blinking in the twilight, not quite believing or trusting in their good fortune. What kind of country lets their criminals go home to dinner? From up the street came a loud honking and they turned toward the sound. A dirty, dented pickup truck was coming toward them. Inside, through a filthy windshield, they could see a man in a military uniform behind the wheel. The truck pulled up and stopped.

"Zamora!" Alex cried in sudden recognition. "What the hell . . .?"

"Get in," the bearded rebel leader commanded. "Hurry."

Alex opened the door for Cyd and slid in after her. "Why aren't you in the hospital where you belong?" he asked as they drove away.

The battle-scared commander held up his arm where the bandage on his bullet wound was already soiled and falling off. "All healed," he grinned with crooked teeth. "Thanks to you, doctor."

"How did you know where to find us?" Cyd asked, squeezed between the two men.

"We have our own people in the army. They tell us everything."

Cyd shook her head. "This place gets more amazing all the time."

Zamora sobered. "You need to get out of the country. Right now. Tonight."

Cyd stiffened with fear. "Not without Fat Man and Little Boy. Where are they? What have they done with them, do you know? Are they alright?"

"They are back in their guest house," Zamora replied. "Under heavy guard." He was making lefts and rights through the poverty-stricken streets, checking constantly in his rearview mirrors to make certain they weren't being followed.

"Guest house?" she persisted. "Why there? What for?"

"The narcos have made it perfectly clear. If your friends ever want to see Israel again, they need to finish whatever it was they came here to do."

"We can't just leave them." Her anger made her forget her fear. "We have to help them!"

"Us and what army?" Alex argued.

"You go if you want, but I'm not leaving without them."

"We're only two people, Cyd. There's no way . . ."

Zamora stopped him. "You are more than that now. You are one hundred."

Alex leaned forward to look across Cyd at their driver. "Why would you want to help us? These are drug smugglers. Dangerous criminals. This isn't your fight."

Zamora stared ahead through the dirty windshield adroitly avoiding the potholes. "This is Africa, Dr. Farmer. The Columbians are invaders, just like the Portuguese that we drove out were invaders. How can you say this isn't my fight?"

"I see his point," Cyd agreed.

"You helped my men," Zamora went on. "Some of them would have died without you. You come as a friend; you will leave as a friend. These Israelis. You say they are your friends?"

"They are," Alex said.

"Then they will leave with you, as well."

Cyd's eyes filled with tears. "How can we ever thank you?"

"You already have," Zamora replied.

The truck arrived at one of Zamora's safe houses in the jungle, and he escorted them inside. An hour later, they had taken sponge baths and been given fresh clothes. They sat at a crude wooden table where they were served steaming bowls of rice and fish by a large, friendly African woman who smiled at them with yellowed teeth. When they could eat no more, they were encouraged to rest on clean cots.

It was well after dark when Zamora came to wake them. "It's time," the veteran guerilla fighter whispered, shaking Alex gently by the shoulder.

Cyd stirred on the cot beside him as Alex opened his eyes and tried to focus. "For what?"

"To go and get the fat one and the little one."

Alex swung his feet to the floor and shook himself awake. "You got that right."

Zamora handed him an automatic rifle and leaned another against Cyd's cot. "You'll be wanting these."

***

Truckloads of militiamen laden with weapons, some of them fresh out of the hospital where Alex had tended their wounds, drove without lights along rutted jungle roads that had to be followed more from memory than sight in the dark. At a small clearing they stopped, the men got out and silently huddled together at the edge of the jungle. Zamora motioned for them to spread out and enter the thick undergrowth at different points, then turned to Cyd and Alex. "Through here," he whispered, leading the way into the jungle along a separate route.

Cyd and Alex trailed dutifully behind carrying their rifles, blindly stepping where the guerilla leader stepped, and each time finding themselves on a thin, worn, animal path almost invisible to the naked eye. The howling, screaming, furtive jungle fell silent as the small army of rebels moved through it in the dark.

"Back home in Montana," Cyd whispered nervously, swatting at a bug that bit her neck as she scrambled to keep up, "we hunted in the fall to have meat for the winter. I've never hunted men before."

"Same difference," Alex whispered back. "Just pretend your life depends on it, and you'll be fine."

Cyd failed in her attempt to smile. "I'll try and remember that."

Zamora turned and shushed them both. In the dark, the only things visible in the black commander's face were the whites of his eyes and the flash of his ivory teeth.

A hundred yards further on they came to the edge of a road. Beyond the road and off to the left was the huge walled hacienda of the drug traffickers who had kidnapped Fat Man and Little Boy. Straight across the road from them was the mini hacienda where the two Israelis were supposedly being held captive. Warm yellow lights glowed in the windows of both homes, and armed men, grim and alert, patrolled the exterior.

Alex turned to Zamora. "You forgot to mention this was a suicide mission," he murmured. "How the hell do we get past all those guards?"

"Diversion," Zamora murmured back, just as a horrendous explosion rocked the earth. Missiles launched from shoulder mounted rocket launchers streaked out of the surrounding jungle, sailed over the walls of the big hacienda like Roman candles and landed on the narcos' lavish estate. It looked like both the bombs that Fat Man and Little Boy were nicknamed after had exploded at once. Fire and flames rose into the sky until the area was lit up like a sports arena. Panicked shouting and yelling could be heard coming from the compound along with the staccato sound of automatic weapons being fired in the air in random bursts.

The two men guarding Fat Man and Little Boy inside the guest house came rushing out and were immediately mowed down in a hail of bullets from the jungle. Zamora quickly led Cyd and Alex across the road in a crouch. At the front door they were joined by four of his rebel fighters.

Zamora motioned for Cyd and Alex to enter. "Go," he whispered. "You have one minute. You're not out with your friends in exactly sixty seconds, were leaving."

Fat Man's and Little Boy's expressions of alarm turned to surprise and then delight when they saw it was Cyd and Alex who had burst into their living room.

Alex put a finger to his lips to keep them from crying out. "Saddle up, boys. You're going home."

Little Boy jumped to his feet. "You see, Fat Man? What did I tell you? I told you we'd be rescued."

"You haven't been rescued yet," Alex advised. "Come on!"

"Yes, yes," Fat Man agreed. "Let's leave this place immediately." He lurched to his feet and started for the other room. "I just have to pack a few things first . . ."

Alex grabbed him by the collar. "Out! Now! Let's go!"

By the time they made it back through the jungle and reached the clearing where the trucks were parked, Fat Man was so drenched in sweat he looked like he had swum the entire distance underwater. He tried to get into the back of Zamora's pickup but was too exhausted, and Cyd and Little Boy had to help him.

Alex walked over to the rebel leader who was busy gathering his men. "This may be a silly question," he said, "but with the military after me and Cyd, and the Columbians after Fat Man and Little Boy, how in hell do we get out of this country?"

"I might have an answer for you," Zamora replied. "You're not going to like it. Can you take a look at this man's leg first? A bullet may have bit him."

\*\*\*

The foulest smelling truck imaginable, a great lumbering thing with high wooden slats for sides, a canvas roof and a narrow, single-seat cab with a hard bench for the driver rumbled north out of Bissau on its way to the Senegal border. In the back, crowded in among a squirming mass of grunting hogs, and standing ankle-deep in dung, mud and slop, were Alex, Cyd, Fat Man and Little Boy. The pigs appeared to be the only ones content with the arrangement.

"How is this supposed to get us across the border?" Fat Man whined, casting about miserably at the rotund creatures that were crowding him on all sides.

Little Boy grinned. "Would *you* come anywhere near the back of this truck if you didn't have to?" he asked, reaching up and wiping a bit of dung off his friend's face.

Fat Man shook his head in misery.

Little Boy smiled encouragingly. "It's not so bad if you breathe through your mouth."

Up ahead was the border between Guinea-Bissau and Senegal. A wooden railroad type crossing barrier was across the road. A pair of African border guards lounged outside a guard shack smoking and talking. At the sound of the truck, they struggled to their feet.

The hog truck driver turned and called back to his passengers. "Get down!" he rasped in barely recognizable English. "Keep low!"

The warming day was warming the stench coming from the hogs. Cyd stood with Alex holding onto one of the slats. A fat sow was rubbing contentedly against her leg. She looked down at the disgusting ooze sloshing around her feet that she had been trying to ignore, then back up at Alex. "Get down?" she asked in horror. "Keep low?"

The truck brakes screeched loudly as it came to a halt. The driver handed his papers out through the window to one of the guards who recoiled from the smell. The other guard, clipboard in hand, started toward the rear of the truck, halted and threw his arm over his mouth. "*Aller! Aller!*" he shouted, waving the truck on. "Go! Go!"

The driver nodded in dutiful silence, retrieved his papers, ground the truck into gear and lurched ahead. Loud grunts and wheezes could be heard coming from the rear of the lorry.

Three hours passed as the hog truck wound its way through the southern region of Senegal. To the passengers in the back, it felt like three days. The small, dusty, mostly poverty-stricken towns of Kolda, Velingara and Manda came and went, and they were once again out on the open plains. The larger, more prosperous city of Tambacouda, the driver's final destination where he would deliver his hogs, was still another thirty minutes away. His passengers would have to find their own way from there. Until then, they had no choice but to stand there and enjoy the ride.

Fat Man looked ready to faint, and probably would have fainted from the ordeal, had it not been for the jovial chatter of his small companion. Cyd and Alex leaned wearily against the side of the truck nearby. The hog that had been rubbing up against Cyd's legs had apparently decided that Cyd was its mother because it kept looking up at her with loving eyes.

She reached down and tried gingerly to divert the hog's head, then straightened in distress as she remembered something. "Alex, the Cannastar seeds! They're gone! What are we going to do?"

Alex gazed out through the slats at the parched countryside, flat and dry as sandpaper. "I wouldn't worry," he said. "If Otis can send us money, he can certainly send us more seeds when we're ready for them."

"You're right," she sighed. "I should have . . ." Another thought occurred to her, and she flushed in panic. "We are so screwed! Our passports, Alex! We can't just waltz into an American embassy and apply for new ones without alerting the authorities and telling them where to find us. Even if we could, to replace a passport you need a birth certificate, and we don't have those either. How do we even get money from our bank account in Grand Cayman if we don't have an ID to show?"

Fat Man overheard, reached inside his voluminous pleated pants and pulled out two small, thin booklets. "You looking for this?" he asked, holding up two American passports with a broad grin.

Alex stared in disbelief. "Where the hell . . .?"

"I grew up in a family of diamond merchants," Fat Man explained proudly. "From the time I was in long pants I had a pocket for a diamond wallet sewn inside my waistband. I was supposed to go into the family business along with my brothers and all my cousins. When I announced I was going to engineering school instead, my father never spoke to me again." He sighed sadly and handed Cyd their passports. "I still miss him."

Her eyes widened in delight. "That still doesn't explain . . ."

"After the army blew up our getaway plane and grabbed us up at the airport," Fat Man bragged, "their only instructions were to return me and Little Boy to the Columbians. We had no idea where they were taking you two, or even if we'd ever see you again. As soon as they shoved us into the back of the SUV, I saw your passports sticking out from under the front seat. When the soldiers searched us, they found our passports in my inside pocket. Since it was empty, I put yours down there." He swelled with self-important satisfaction. "It never occurred to them to search me again."

"So much for us," Alex said. "What are you two going to do without passports?"

Fat Man waved away his concern. "All we have to do is get to the Israeli embassy in Dakar, the capital, contact our company and they'll arrange to get us new ones."

Cyd smiled adoringly. "You're amazing, Fat Man. You really are."

"I'm always telling him that," Little Boy agreed. "Aren't I always telling you that, Avi?"

Alex was still marveling at the passports they'd been handed. "I never knew diamond merchants kept their diamonds in their pants."

They rode on in silence, but their mood had changed. Somehow their hope had been restored, and with it their confidence. Alex looked out through the slats of the truck as a broad savannah teeming with wildlife came into view, its waving grasslands brown and dry against the backdrop of a snowcapped volcano in the far distance. His eyes swam in awe of the magnificence he was witnessing, a landscape vast as space and mysterious as an alien world.

"Africa, Cyd. Isn't it beautiful?"

She sighed and laid her head against his shoulder. "Yes," she smiled. "I suppose it is."

# Chapter Five

## ROAD TO DAKAR

Before their hasty departure from Bissau, Zamora, the rebel leader who arranged their escape to Senegal, handed Alex a little traveling money. It was enough that they could afford a hotel, at least for one night.

In America, *Le Hôtel Relais Tamba* would have been a forgotten motel on some two-lane blacktop that the Interstate had bypassed decades ago. To the four weary travelers from the hog truck, *Le Hôtel Relais Tamba*, located in the city of Tambacouda amid a sea of squaller, was as welcome and luxurious a sight as any 5-star hotel. The one-story structure had clean, whitewashed rooms with tall, carved wooden entry doors that surrounded a swimming pool on all four sides. Tall palms and blue umbrellas shaded the clear pool during the day and at night provided a softly lit backdrop to an oasis of tranquility.

It was after dark. They had eaten a good meal together in the hotel dining room, after which Fat Man and Little Boy went directly to their room in a state of exhaustion. Cyd and Alex sat out alone by the pool in lounge chairs. They had thrown away their dirty clothes when they got there, taken brief-but-wonderful showers to wash off the smell of pig, and put on the new t-shirts, shorts and sandals they bought in town after the hog truck dropped them off.

Cyd felt remarkably refreshed now that she was clean and well fed. She looked out from her lounger admiring her surroundings and enjoying the solitude. "How can they have a swimming pool full of all this delightful water in the middle of such a horrible drought?"

"I don't know," Alex replied sleepily, "but I'm not going to be the one to tell them to drain it."

She leaned over on one elbow and touched his face in concern. "Are you alright? You look tired."

"A good night's rest and I'll be fine."

Cyd looked up at the sky and took a deep breath of night air. "There's something about Africa that smells so . . . eternal." Hearing no response, she glanced over and caught him staring at her. "What?"

"How can you have gone through everything you just went through and still look so beautiful?"

"Enjoy it while it lasts," she warned. "Thirty years from now you might not be thinking the same thing."

"Thirty years from now, I'll still be seeing the real you."

She brightened and said slowly, "Speaking of thirty years, with the hurricane and losing our boat and both of us almost drowning and all, my birthday celebration got totally spoiled."

"I'm sorry, Cyd." It pained him to disappoint her. "How can I make it up to you?"

"You can give me my present."

"Present?"

"You know. Same as last year."

He feigned confusion. "Same as . . . ?"

"You don't remember?"

"You'll have to remind me."

She leaned over and brought her face close to his and slowly they kissed and Africa fell away and the world fell away and what was left was joy and love.

\*\*\*

In the morning the four travelers met rested and refreshed in the hotel dining room for breakfast. The city of Dakar was still far to the west, and Cyd was adamant about not leaving Fat Man and Little Boy until she had seen them safely delivered to the Israeli embassy there. Alex had no objection since he was certain they could easily get money wired to them from their Grand Cayman account once they reached the capital. The hotel desk clerk told him the bus for Dakar was leaving in an hour and called a cab to take them to the bus station. After paying their hotel bill, he had barely enough money left for their four bus tickets—which the desk clerk was able to sell him as well.

The early morning light was just turning the red dirt road in front of the hotel from dull gray to dull orange as a horse-drawn cart pulled up. A sign in French on the side of the cart read *Taxi*. Its passengers climbed happily aboard. After their long ride in the hog truck, the horse cart seemed like luxury transportation.

The bus station itself was another matter. It was a fallen-down shack that looked to be in worse shape than the Bissau jail. "A self-respecting rat wouldn't be seen dead in there," Cyd remarked in disgust.

A small bus parked in front of the station was already jammed with passengers. African arms and faces hung out of window frames that presumably had once held glass. The bus itself leaned to one side and looked like a crushed and battered coffee can shot through with holes. It was painted so many faded colors it was no color at all. Stacked on the roof was an immense pile of teetering boxes and crates tied down with crisscrossed ropes.

"There must not be any bridges over the highways in Senegal," Alex observed. "If there are, I don't see how that bus is going to get under any of them with that load."

Cyd stared at the bus in horror. "I hope you're not expecting me to get on that thing! It isn't safe!"

"Dakar is almost three hundred miles from here," he argued. "That bus is the only . . ."

"You go on." She turned away in disgust. "I'll walk."

Just then a modern bus approximately the size of a small cruise ship pulled in and stopped with a loud exhale of its air brakes. The shadow of its massive yellow body, highlighted in red and green to match the colors of the Senegalese flag, completely blanketed the local bus. Above the driver's towering windshield was a destination sign that read "Dakar". In this land where time had lost its watch, the enormous bus looked like it had just arrived from Mars.

There was no shortage of passengers for Dakar. Fat Man and Little Boy managed to find seats together near the back of the coach, but Cyd and Alex had to sit across the aisle from one another. Cyd fell into the plush luxury of her red velvet seat and leaned back, relishing the air conditioning.

***

The yellow bus had been barreling west on uneven roads for about four hours now and still had another three or four hours to go before it reached Dakar. The passengers who weren't sleeping or reading gazed out through the tinted windows with dull eyes at the barren, sunbaked countryside flashing past. A French built railroad track that once ran east and west the full length of Senegal lay rusted and abandoned beside the road.

Cyd sat chatting amicably with her seatmate, a petite French woman named Juliette Cohen who lived part time in Paris and part time in Senegal. Middle aged with bobbed brown hair, her fading good looks suggested she had once been a striking beauty. A certain sensuality still defined her, a coquettishness, as though the skin in which she was comfortably burrowed was electric. Her English was clearly spoken in a vibrant French accent that made the words sound almost delicious rolling off her tongue. She was clearly a woman of wealth, though there were no pretentions of wealth about her. Passion ruled Juliette's life with feelings that ruled out any attempt at reflection or introspection. She was, quite simply, a kind and generous woman of boundless emotion and energy.

Cyd happened to glance out the window as the bus was going down a lane flanked on either side by trees that stood like tall brown carrots a hundred feet tall and thirty feet around with no vegetation on their trunks, and only a small display of stubby limbs at the top. Ever the curious botanist, she asked Juliette what they were.

"Baobab trees," the French woman explained in her delightful accent. " 'The Tree of Life' or the 'Upside-down Tree' they're called. Some are thousands of years old. They are the world's largest succulent and hold I-don't-know-how-many hundreds of gallons of water. The fruit of the baobab is considered a superfood, and the elephants love its bark. They remove it with their tusks and trunks all the way around and it still grows back."

Cyd looked again. "They look like they're from another world," she marveled.

The sun hung low over the western ocean by the time the bus entered the sprawling coastal city of Dakar. Alex stood restlessly to stretch his long legs, anxious to get to wherever they were going so they could figure out what to do and where to go next.

Cyd was staring out the window again, this time in distress. Barefoot boys in shorts and t-shirts with athletic logos on them swarmed the streets. They looked horribly poor, and each one carried an empty tomato can or a plastic bowl. "All those children," she exclaimed. "What are they doing?"

"Begging," Juliette replied sadly. "Their mothers have them and can't take care of them or feed them, so they are sent to religious schools called *daaras* here in Dakar where their teachers force them to beg. If they do not meet a quota of money, rice or sugar they are beaten. The number of boys suffering this kind of abuse and living in filth and squaller is staggering."

Cyd was appalled.

"Forced begging is the most common form of human trafficking in Senegal," Juliette went on, "but there are others far worse."

"Worse?"

"Slavery today is a thriving business in Africa, especially here in Senegal. Far more than in the old days. Child sex slaves are in big demand throughout the Middle East."

Cyd turned away feeling sick to her stomach, then quickly looked back. "Isn't there anything anybody can do?"

"A few of us are trying. I for one am helping a wonderful local man build a school and dormitory for boys who run away from the *daaras*. We will only be able to take in a hundred at a time to start. It's a drop in the ocean, but it is better than nothing." Juliette saw tears forming in Cyd's eyes and smiled bravely. "There is hope, *chèrie*. His name is Nelson Abdoul Slade. He is the former Minister of Hydraulic Engineering and Electricity, and he is running for president."

"I didn't think half the people in this country even had water and power."

"They don't. Senegal is ninety-eight percent Muslim, so nothing ever changes. Nelson Slade is the illegitimate son of the existing president. For the longest time he was considered a joke, a wealthy playboy with too much money and too much time on his hands. He was so much of an embarrassment that his father long ago cut him off completely."

"And this is your great white hope?"

"Black hope. His mother only was white. He has forsaken his dissipations suddenly and turned into this firebrand politician with promises to end child trafficking and child slavery forever."

"And the people believe him?"

"Believe him? They absolutely worship him! Past presidents have all promised to end slavery, but nothing was ever done. Nelson, he is different. Not like the others. You should hear him speak. He is finally the leader Senegal has been waiting for. Only . . ."

"Only what?"

Juliette's face fell. "The problem is the people have heard it all before. His words are happy drugs that wear off quickly. Slavery has been going on in Africa since before recorded history. It is so ingrained in the Senegalese culture that nobody actually thinks it will ever end. His promises to end slavery are sadly not enough to get him elected. His family, the Slade family, they have run things for generations. Their grip on power is . . . *inexorab*?"

"Inexorable?" Cyd interpreted.

"*Oui.* They have such a strong grip on everything that if he wasn't the president's son, illegitimate or not, he would have disappeared without a trace long before now."

"What are his chances then?"

"*Mince et aucun, mon cher* (slim and none, my dear). But he is our best hope, so we must fight and keep on fighting for him any way we can, *non?*"

Cyd was skeptical. "How is he paying for it? Does he have the money for a real campaign?"

"I do what I can to help, but he has *beaucoup* money of his own. Nobody knows where it comes from. He is mounting a lavish crusade in every corner of the country, not just Dakar. I am just now returning from helping him set up rallies in some of the eastern cities."

"It all sounds . . . wonderful." Cyd's voice trailed off thinking it all sounded pretty hopeless.

"I just love him," Juliette enthused, pointing at something outside Cyd's window. "He is so good looking, don't you think?"

Cyd turned and saw they were passing a giant billboard. Around the base of it were more child beggars holding out their cans and pails to passersby. On the billboard was the handsome face of a thoughtful, light-skinned African with slightly European features. His hair was black and wavy, and he seemed to be smiling without smiling in a way that implied strength and inspired confidence. It was impossible to tell what was behind the sunglasses he wore, but judging from what was visible one could easily assume that the eyes were as brave and intelligent as the rest of the face. Below the image in bold yellow, red and green letters were the words *Sénégal Libre!*

"Free Senegal?" Cyd asked.

"Free Senegal!" Juliette repeated passionately.

"Why is he wearing those dark glasses?"

"He claims the light hurts his eyes, even indoors. He is six feet, six inches tall if you can imagine." Her sigh sounded more like a swoon.

Dakar's jumbled confusion of homes, shops and low-rise structures gave way to modern, high-rise office and apartment buildings as they entered the center of the city.

"Where are you staying?" Juliette asked.

"Nowhere until we can get money wired to us from our Caribbean account," Cyd answered despondently. "Until then, we're penniless. We'll probably end up sleeping in the street tonight along with those boys."

Juliette was appalled. "*Pourquoi? Comment?*" (Why? How?)

"We shipwrecked off Guinea-Bissau, then nearly got killed trying to rescue two friends we just met from the Columbian drug dealers."

"Friends? Drug dealers? *Je ne comprends pas.*" (I don't understand.)

"A pair of delightful Israeli engineers." Cyd motioned with her head toward the back of the bus. "A little eccentric—a lot eccentric, I suppose—but I absolutely adore them. They're sitting in back there somewhere. They need to contact their company for money and passports before they can leave the country."

Juliette clapped her hands in delight. "It's settled, then! You are all staying with me!"

"We couldn't," Cyd protested. "We wouldn't want to impose . . ."

"Nonsense! I have plenty of room. And you are my friends now and I must hear the stories of your other friends, and your most amazing adventures. Won't you please stay?"

"Thank you," Cyd smiled in relief. "You can't know what this means to us."

## Chapter Six

### FOR THE CHILDREN

Juliette Cohen's residence was the entire top floor of one of the Dakar's newest high-rises. The elegant forty-five hundred square foot condominium had tall ceilings, intricate moldings and an outdoor roof garden and aviary that would not have been out of place on New York's Central Park South or Paris's Avenue Montaigne. Daker's entire population of a million-plus people could be seen coming and going at one time or another from one of her lofty balconies.

Cyd and Alex stood at one of the balcony railings with cups of coffee in hand, looking out and admiring the view. Brown and dry, Dakar was a city of contrasts, the past at war with the present, with images of a modern world imposed over a Stone Age landscape. A gigantic Islamic mosque the size of a small city boasting five towering minarets, nine large domes and costing some $50 million dwarfed the international chemical companies and textile factories that surrounded it. A soaring bronze statue intended to inspire patriotism and hope rose five hundred feet above the city from another distant location. It cost $33 million to build and stood as a monument to the excess of a corrupt government to a resentful population making less than $2 a day. And everywhere there was poverty and squaller.

Juliette, dressed in a slightly wrinkled white blouse and shorts and wearing no makeup, opened the sliding glass door and came out to join them. "There you two are," she smiled happily. "You slept in."

"It was heaven," Cyd replied. "I can't thank you enough." She pointed out to sea where their view of the North Atlantic would have included the Caribbean islands were the world not round. "Do you know what that little island is out in the bay?"

"Gorée Island," Juliette answered sadly. "*La Maison des Esclaves* (The House of Slaves) is there."

"Is that where 'The Door of No Return' is?" Alex asked.

Juliette nodded and sighed. "Many argue Gorée Island was not an important place of departure in the Atlantic slave trade. Others claims hundreds of thousands of slaves were shipped from there to the British, French, Spanish, Dutch and Portuguese colonies in the Americas. To me, it is a symbol of the centuries of Africans enslaving Africans."

Cyd shuddered and changed the subject. "Have you seen Fat Man and Little Boy? They were gone by the time we got up."

Their hostess brightened. "We have been up since dawn talking, the three of us. You were right about them. They are amazing, and so is their work with… *osmose inverse d'eau salée et saumâtre*?

"SWRO," Cyd translated, taking her clue from the context and sounds. "Salt and Brackish Water Reverse Osmosis. Fascinating, right?"

"More than that, perhaps. They were anxious to see about new passports, so I had my driver take them over to the Israeli embassy. Speaking of such things, would you like me to set it up with my bank so you can get your money transferred?"

"Thanks," Alex said. "Soon as it comes in, we'll get out of your hair."

"We don't want to wear out our welcome," Cyd added.

"*Absurdité* (nonsense)! You are welcome here as long as you like. We have so much to talk about. Come inside and I will have my cook make you some breakfast."

They gave their breakfast order to Juliette's French chef and followed her out to her roof garden aviary where they sat at a table under a large, screened-in enclosure full of leafy green plants and noisy birds of every color and description.

"Fat Man and Little Boy told me a little about this Cannastar of yours," Juliette said. "How did you ever get involved in such a thing, and is it really the miracle cure they say?"

For the next two hours, in the filtered light of the flying, fluttering solarium, Cyd and Alex answered questions about their Arizona Grow and the cure for viral disease that had turned them into fugitives.

When their diminutive hostess could think of nothing more to ask, she sat thinking. "And you say this Cannastar cures HIV?

"HIV is a virus," Cyd replied confidently, "so yes, it cures HIV."

"Did you know," the French woman agonized, "that almost eighty percent of people worldwide who are living with HIV live in Africa?"

"I'd heard it wasn't as bad in Senegal as in other parts of Africa," Alex said.

"It's bad enough," Juliette replied. "Can you imagine how absolutely wonderful it would be if all of Africa had a cure for AIDS?"

"I can," Cyd answered. "Easily."

Juliette nodded thoughtfully. Clearly, she had more in mind than she was saying. "No doubt you are anxious to get your money transferred. I grew up poor, so I know what it's like to be broke. Shall I call my banker and tell him you'll be down to see him today?"

"That would be great," Cyd said with a puzzled look.

Juliette smiled. "I can see by your face that you're wondering how I came by all of . . ." She gestured around her. "This."

"It's none of my business."

Juliette waved away her concern. "My ex-husband owned commercial property in downtown Paris. Quite a lot, actually. It had been in his family for generations. When he died of the cancer, it all came to me."

She reached in back of her, took a framed picture from a sideboard and showed it to them with pride. "This is us in happier days."

The photograph was of a beautiful young French girl and a handsome older man with curly black hair streaked in grey who was wearing thick glasses. The smiling couple wore safari clothes and were holding hunting rifles. Clustered around them and grinning broadly were a group of African bearers and guides. "We were very much in love, Jean-Luc and I. He brought me to Africa on our honeymoon. He adored hunting. Me, I took one look at Africa and never wanted to leave."

Cyd tried to conceal her repulsion. "You spent your honeymoon killing animals?"

"Not really," Juliette laughed lightly. "Jean-Luc couldn't hit an elephant if it was standing on his chest. He was terribly nearsighted, you see. I, on the other hand, am a terrific shot. I could shoot the freckle off a frog at a hundred meters. When we hunted, I would always miss on purpose. He thought I was a worse shot than he was, which was fine with me. Truth is, I can't stand the thought of killing anything. And besides, I didn't want to show my husband up. At the end of the day, the only thing we ever killed was a bottle of wine." Her smile faded. "When he died, I couldn't bear to get rid of his guns. He'd spend hours cleaning and fondling the awful things. If I sold them, it would be like selling a part of him."

\*\*\*

Fat Man and Little Boy telephoned their company in Tel Aviv from the Israeli embassy in Dakar. Their superiors were greatly relieved to hear from them and horrified at hearing all they had been through. The director of the company, Arie Nakash, came on the line to say how sorry he was for their troubles. "We'll try and hurry things along," he promised his two engineers, "but it could be three weeks before we can get you new passports." The silence on the other end of the line prompted him to add, "Until then, I want you both to enjoy a stay at the best hotel in town. The company will pay for everything."

When Juliette heard that two of her guests were moving to a hotel, she wouldn't hear of it. "You're staying right here with me," she insisted, "and that's final." As a result, they were five for breakfast the next morning in the aviary—not counting the birds.

"You know, Ashraf," Fat Man complained to Little Boy, ducking as a wayward bird swooped low over his head, "if you hadn't insisted on leaving Bissau in such a hurry, we wouldn't be sitting here on our hands right now with nothing to do."

"If you sat on your hands, you'd never find them again," Little Boy countered.

"And if you sat on your head, it would finally be in the right place . . ."

Little Boy touched his friend's arm in concern. "Did you remember to take the new allergy pills we got for you yesterday?"

Juliette turned to Cyd. "Are they always like this?"

"Pretty much," Cyd smiled.

Fat Man turned to Cyd and Alex. "We told the director of our company everything you had done for us to save our lives. He said if you ever needed anything, anything at all, you were just to ask."

"Appreciate it," Alex replied.

"I was thinking," Juliette began, speaking up to be heard over all the racket the birds were making. Her guests waited politely while dozens of African Grey parrots entertained them with a rather extensive vocabulary of French words and phrases. Though loudly and intelligently spoken nobody, not even Juliette, knew exactly what it was they were saying. "Fat Man, Little Boy," she went on, "you came to Africa to build an osmosis plant, am I right? Do you care where you build it?"

"Not in the least," Little Boy replied as Fat Man rolled his eyes.

"Cyd, Alex, you came to Africa to start a Cannastar plantation. Do you care where you establish it?"

"Not really," Alex answered.

"Anywhere we can get the water," Cyd added.

"*Très bon!* (very good)," Juliette exclaimed. "Because I have a plan. What do you think would happen if a candidate running for president of Senegal could add to his anti-slavery platform the promise that he would provide the country with unlimited water forever *and* deliver a permanent cure for AIDS?"

"He'd probably be elected president of Africa for life," Alex ventured.

"And it wouldn't be empty promises he'd be making, either!" Cyd cried.

"Madam," Fat Man announced in his erudite voice, "you are brilliant."

"Indeed, she is," Little Boy echoed.

Juliette smiled. "I will call Nelson's office today then and set up a meeting. You will for certain come?"

"You know this Slade character personally?" Alex asked.

"She works for his campaign," Cyd answered.

"Money buys access anywhere," Juliette laughed. "You didn't know that?"

Cyd, intrigued by the idea, told Juliette she'd love to meet the next president of Senegal. Juliette looked to Alex, waiting for a response.

"Sure," he said. "Why not?"

Juliette clapped in delight. "*Magnifique*! Meanwhile, you would like to see, perhaps, the children's home I am building for runaway boys?"

"Not I," Fat Man responded. "There is much work to be done."

"He's right," Little Boy agreed. "We have to start scouting locations for the new RO plant so we sound like we know what we're talking about when we meet your Mr. Slade."

"I'll go," Cyd offered. "I wouldn't mind seeing something hopeful for a change."

"What kind of medical attention are these street kids getting?" Alex asked, hoping to hear that there were free clinics around the city at least.

Juliette shook her head. "None whatsoever."

\*\*\*

Cyd and Alex followed Juliette down a pathway between two ruined cinderblock walls that was so narrow they had to turn sideways to get through. "You should see the reality these boys are living with before you see the new children's home," she told them over her shoulder.

They came out in a square enclosure roughly the size of a large house. The cinderblock walls were the only thing left standing; there was no roof, only sky. Garbage littered the ground and human feces was lumped against one wall in a stinking pile.

Cyd covered her nose. "This is the most disgusting place I've ever seen."

In the shade against the far wall sat a man with buck teeth that crowded his mouth like ivory dominoes. He wore a dirty blue kaftan and a religious skullcap, and was addressing a dozen or so ragged, barefoot boys who sat at his feet with shining black faces turned up to their teacher in rapt attention. Above the teacher's head, affixed to the wall like some sort of all-seeing eye, was the medallion of a snake. The roped coils of the serpent's body were covered in black shining scales, and a long black tongue stuck out of its smiling mouth.

"This is the typical *daara* or religious school," Juliette explained to her appalled companions. "Those boys you see there are *talibés* or students of the Quran. The one in the blue robe sitting on the gas can is their Quranic teacher or *marabout*. The *marabout* holds classes three times a day, and afterward the boys are sent back out to beg for food and money. At night they return here to sleep under newspapers and trash on the open ground. There are literally hundreds of these *daaras* all over Dakar."

"What happens to the money they collect?" Cyd asked in disgust.

"They are allowed to keep none of it," Juliette replied sadly. "Some, a small percentage, goes to the *marabout*. It is how he makes his living. Another percentage, a larger one, goes to the brotherhood of imams who run the big mosque you saw downtown. Everyone pays the imams."

"And the rest?" Alex asked. "Do the boys get to keep anything for themselves?"

"The rest goes to the Black Mamba."

"Africa's deadliest snake?" Cyd was confused.

"Worse," Juliette replied. "Black Mamba is the slaver who runs the child slave trade in Senegal. No one has ever seen his face. He is ruthless, clever, dangerous."

Alex was furious. "What's his symbol doing here?"

"The snake is everywhere you look," Juliette sighed. "Black Mamba is the ghost that haunts the streets. He sees everything."

Alex marched across the square for a closer look.

"Alex," Cyd hissed, hurrying to catch up, "don't make a scene!"

The *marabout* went on reciting the Quran without looking up to acknowledge his visitors. His students didn't dare look up. Alex bent, took the arm of one of the smaller boys who was faithfully mouthing the words of his teacher, and examined it. "Some of these boys have bruises on them!" he announced, sickened at what he was seeing. "This boy looks like he has cigarette burns all over him!"

"He has not been meeting his quotas," Juliette whispered cautiously.

The *marabout* muttered some sort of conclusive words. The boys all knelt in a row and put their heads to the ground, then jumped to their feet, grabbed their tomato cans and plastic pails and ran squealing out of the *daara*.

"Translate for me," Alex told Juliette while glaring angrily at the *marabout*. "What are you doing to these boys? Why do they have bruises and burns all over them?"

Juliette dutifully translated his questions. The *marabout* answered with a passive smile and a few muttered words. Alex continued to glare. "What did he say?" he demanded.

Juliette shook her head. "He says the boys are lying if they say they are beaten. He claims they are clumsy and sometimes fall down. Some are learning to smoke and don't know how."

Alex was so mad that Cyd was afraid he might do something rash. "Alex," she said, grabbing his arm, "this isn't our world. Let's get out of here."

"She's right," Juliette urged. "We should go."

Alex reluctantly let himself be led away. "And the government just lets this guy get away with it?"

"The *daaras* are not regulated by the government," Juliette answered, walking ahead so he could not see her face. "The *marabouts* are the intermediaries between the people and Allah. To try and tell them what to do would be to try and tell God what to do."

"I've never seen anything so horrible in my life," Cyd remarked. "Is there nothing anybody can do?"

Juliette turned, and they saw tears streaming down her cheeks. She smiled weakly at their compassionate expressions. "Never mind. I always cry when I come here. And yes, there is something we can do. We can help the people of Senegal elect a new president."

*** 

The public street outside *Maison d'Enfants* (Children's Home) was a chaotic confusion of noisy traffic and crowds of pedestrians in colorful dress going about the business of their daily lives. Behind a broken-down gate that opened onto the street was a small stone courtyard, and behind that a building that was in no better shape than the gate. Attached to one side of the decrepit building was the school and dormitory that Juliette was funding—a new two-story structure still under construction.

The director of *Maison d'Enfants*, Malick Mbaye, met his guests at the gate and gave Juliette a warm hug that she enthusiastically returned. Cyd and Alex were introduced as friends who had come to Senegal "to help the people." Malick asked humbly if they would care for a tour of the facility. Cyd said they very much would like to see it and the visitors followed him through the gate.

Looking back, Cyd noticed that affixed to a wall across the street was a medallion of the Black Mamba exactly like the one she had seen at the *daara*. The thought crossed her mind that the coiled black reptile with the long tongue and smiling mouth looked like it was watching the gate. It gave her the chills.

The original school and rescue mission that Malick started on his own five years earlier had a cluster of battered school desks in the center of a big, airless room with bunk beds pushed up against bare, splintered walls. *At least it's clean and has a roof*, Cyd thought. They were ushered out a side door where Malick proudly showed them the new facility that he and Juliette were building.

"All this is for the kids that run away from the *daaras*?" Alex asked.

Malick smiled and nodded that it was. He was a tall and slender African of some thirty-five years with a long and narrow face, and a high forehead wrinkled in permanent concern for all the boys he couldn't help. His pants and shirt and scarf were all of a different shade of orange. His nose was flat and wide, and his hair hung down in the kind of matted ropes worn by the Rastafarians in Jamaica. But it was the sadness in his voice and the kindness in his eyes that most impressed his guests.

"Over a hundred thousand kids are exploited in Senegal every day," he explained in surprisingly good English. "More and more, they come to the cities now with so many starving from the drought. Most end up in the *daaras* where they are sent out each morning to beg with no breakfast and no bath and must return with money twice a day or else. What is worse is they are always disappearing."

"The Black Mamba?" Cyd asked, still appalled at the name.

"The ghost," Malick lamented. "Sometimes he takes a dozen at a time."

They were escorted back inside, and invited to sit at a small, rickety table in a kitchen with mostly bare cupboards. "Everybody knows where they go," Malick said as he poured out cups of a purplish red drink to which he added mint leaves before passing the cups around. "They go to be sex slaves in other Muslim countries. The Senegalese people, they say nothing. They only let it happen."

Alex was livid. "This gets worse by the minute."

"Child sex slaves are one of Senegal's major exports—along with peanuts," Malick remarked. "It is like fishing: you don't have to grow them; you only have to harvest them in your net. Child fish are in big demand; a delicacy to the Arabs."

"I can't believe it." Cyd railed. "It can't be that bad."

"Westerners are naïve," Juliette said harshly. "These people still hide their women under bedsheets. Can you imagine the domination, the sexual repression, the hidden perversions that go on in a culture like this?"

"I don't know what I imagined," Cyd admitted. "Civilization? Progress? Humanity?"

"Are all the *daaras* as bad as the one we saw today?" Alex asked.

"Some *daaras* are good," Juliette replied. "Most are not."

"The orphans, they need a fresh start," Malick agonized. "This school and shelter we are building; it will hopefully be a new beginning for them."

"I can help him, so I am," Juliette added in her lilting accent.

*It all seems so hopeless,* Cyd thought.

Malick smiled, proud and humble. "When I see boys that I have helped who are grown and getting paid for work they are proud to be doing, that is like a victory. My wish is for the day no child is forced to beg in Senegal."

\*\*\*

Cyd and Alex stood on one of Juliette's balcony's looking out at the sprawling sub-Saharan city and enjoying the evening. She slid her hand into his back pocket. Her touch was electric, and a shiver went through him. They had each other in this strange and foreign place, and it made everything else exciting.

Below was a park with parched grass and tall trees that was rapidly filling with a raucous, shouting mob of Africans. So many dark faces were pressing in together that they were spilling out into the street. Chants and cries filled the night, and handmade signs, too far away to read, bobbed up and down in the crowd.

Juliette came out on the balcony to join them. "We have a meeting set up with Nelson Slade for tomorrow morning at ten," she announced happily.

"What's going on down in that park there?" Cyd asked. "It looks like it could turn into a riot at any minute."

"Nelson is going to speak at a rally," Juliette replied. "Those are some of his supporters."

Cyd turned her head trying to hear. "What are they chanting?"

"*Senegal libre!* and *Plus d'esclavage!* 'Free Senegal!' and 'No more slavery!' It is written on their signs as well."

"They sound angry," Alex remarked.

"They know what's coming, I'm afraid," Juliette replied. "Nelson's father, President Léopold Slade, he has banned all political rallies until after the election."

"He can do that?" Every time Cyd learned something more about this country she became more appalled.

"He does as he pleases," Juliette said. "Many of his relatives, Nelson's uncles and cousins, they keep getting thrown in jail for corruption, and he keeps letting them out and reappointing them to the same offices they were expelled from when they were arrested."

"What's going to happen to those people down there?" Alex asked with growing concern.

Juliette pointed. "See the police forming up around the perimeter? As soon as Nelson starts to speak, they will shut the whole thing down."

Just then a roar came up from below, and a tall man in a business suit and dark glasses stepped out onto a makeshift stage that had been set up at the edge of the park. For a minute or so there was too much noise for him to speak. When he did, his words did not reach all the way up to Juliet's balcony, but they could hear the mighty cheers and roars that followed every other sentence. The candidate was clearly loved.

Slade hadn't been talking more than a few minutes when more police came pouring out of the side streets armed with shields and clubs. Teargas was fired, billowing clouds of smoke enveloped the scene and a melee ensued. The rising smoke burned the eyes of the spectators watching from Juliette's balcony. Through the haze they saw bodyguards appear and whisked the speaker away to safety.

The riot was over almost before it started. The park was cleared and an eerie quiet fell over the scene. All that remained were burning tires and a few lifeless bodies that littered the ground, barely visible in the dark.

# Chapter Seven

## NELSON ABDOUL SLADE

Nelson Slade's offices were on the second floor of a commercial building on a busy, downtown street that was more or less permanently gridlocked with snarls of traffic and swarms of pedestrians. Cyd, Alex, Fat Man, Little Boy and Juliette sat in Slade's noisy outer lobby as campaign workers made posters, stapled flyers, answered phones and hurried past on urgent errands.

At ten minutes past the hour, the door to an inner office opened and an old Arab was pushed out in a wheelchair. He wore a flowing cotton *disdasha* (white robe) with a red and white checked headcloth ringed in a black band. Pushing the wheelchair was a dark-haired young man in a sweatshirt with the logo of the Italian sportscar maker Ferrari emblazed on the chest. From the young man's casual, arrogant demeanor one could surmise that he was probably a close relation to the man in the wheelchair. Seeing them out was a tall, handsome, light-skinned African in a business suit and dark glasses who filled the room with his presence. "*Ma'a as-salama* (go in peace)," he said to the Arab in the chair with his hand over his heart. The gruff Arab held five fingers up to the sky in a cupped hand to indicate it was up to God to decide his fate and motioned for the young man to keep pushing.

Nelson Slade turned his attention to his next visitors. "Juliette!" he cried, towering over the petite French woman with his six-foot six-inch frame. "How is the home for runaway boys coming? It is going to be the beginning of the end of child slavery for all Senegal, I know it." His almost-perfect English was flavored with just the trace of a French accent.

Juliette lowered her eyes. "From your lips to Allah's ears."

"You are a champion of the people," he assured her. "The Joan of Arc of Senegal!"

"I hardly think so," Juliette blushed. "I only wish I could do more."

Nelson glanced over at the other newcomers. "The citizens of Senegal thank you. Now who are these people I absolutely must meet with today, and why is it so important? I only have a few minutes, I'm sorry. I am very busy . . ."

"You might want to clear your schedule," Alex said. "We're here to get you elected."

Nelson turned abruptly to face him. "And you are?"

"Alex Farmer, M.D."

"From America, from the sound of it." He shook Alex's hand warmly. "We can always use another good doctor in Senegal."

Alex motioned with his head to indicate Fat Man and Little Boy. "You can use two these guys a lot more than you can use me. They're Israeli water engineers, and they can make your dreams come true."

"Water engineers?" Slade exclaimed, suddenly intrigued. "I too am a water engineer. Master's degree in hydrology from University of Arizona. Come in all of you. And welcome."

Cyd followed the others into his office feeling like the odd man out.

The moment Slade learned that Fat Man and Little Boy had been the lead engineers on the SWRO plant in Tel Aviv, he couldn't stop asking questions. For the next twenty minutes, he grilled them enthusiastically about their accomplishment.

Cyd and Alex sat looking around his office. It was decorated in an extensive collection of erotic African art. Primitive sculptures filled the shelves, many of them renditions of the male sex organ. Other statues depicted naked natives in various positions of sexual intercourse. The brown and ebony art was old, undoubtedly valuable—and vaguely disturbing to look at.

Slade listened intently as Fat Man and Little boy described the perfect location for a RO plant they had found on the coast just outside of Dakar. Despite his charm and charisma, Cyd found his air of absolute authority somewhat intimidating. Something about him frightened her.

"A RO plant for Senegal!" Nelson cried when Fat Man and Little Boy stopped long enough to take a breath. "Praise Allah!"

"It takes money," Little Boy cautioned. "It cost nearly half a billion dollars to build the one in Israel."

"Allah will provide! You have brought me a victory!"

"Part of a victory anyway," Alex said.

Slade sobered. "I beg your pardon?"

"Hear him out," Juliette urged. "Have you ever heard of Cannastar?"

"Oh, my God!" Nelson cried. "Are you the criminals from America? I heard you were in Africa, but I had no idea you were here. Last year when I was in America, Cannastar was all everyone was talking about. What brings you to Senegal?"

"Hoping to start a Cannastar plantation," Cyd replied.

Slade turned as if he hadn't realized she was in the room.

"If we can get the water we need," she added

Nelson turned back to Alex and directed his questions to him. How was it developed, this Cannastar? Who developed it? How is it grown? What does it cure, exactly? If it's all you say it is, why has the U.S. criminalized it? Is there any validity to the reports that people are dying from taking it?

Alex answered in medical and scientific terms to sound as credible as possible. Cyd was ready to tell him how she cured her own cancer with Cannastar, but every time she started to speak, Slade cut her off. Half an hour later he was pacing the floor in excitement. "America sent us this

HIV virus! It is only right that Americans should come to Africa to end it!"

Cyd and Alex exchanged a look of incredulity. *Is this guy for real?*

"Senegal will become the envy of all!" the presidential candidate enthused. "A reverse osmosis plant to forever end drought and a Cannastar farm to forever end AIDS! My election is guaranteed!" Gesturing about as he spoke, Slade exposed his forearms.

Cyd stared. *Is that a tattoo of a coiled snake on his arm?*

Slade mistook Cyd's look of shock for doubt and added fervently, "Of course, as president, I will then have the power to put an end to the abomination of child slavery that plagues Senegal. Allah be praised, this is a miracle! The people must hear of it immediately!"

Cyd nodded numbly but couldn't get the image of his tattoo out of her mind.

\*\*\*

That evening they all celebrated over a bottle of wine in Juliette's aviary. The birds had quieted down for the night and stars could be seen twinkling like fireflies through the overhead screen.

Alex raised his glass. "To RO plants and Cannastar plants in Africa!"

Three glasses clinked with his. Cyd's remained on the table. "Did anybody besides me happen to notice the tattoo on Slade's arm?" she asked. They all shook their heads. "Maybe it was just my imagination." She started to take a sip of her wine and stopped. "Not that it's any of my business, and not that I care, but you guys do know that Nelson Slade is gay."

"What makes you say that?" Alex scoffed.

"A woman can sense these things."

Juliette sighed. "I don't get any sexual energy coming from him, either."

"Not to mention the fact that he hates women," Cyd added.

"I did kind of notice that," Alex admitted.

Juliette put both hands flat on the table. "All that matters to me is that he helps the poor children."

"And helps us bring water to Africa!" Fat Man exclaimed. Ever since the meeting, he had been so excited he hadn't been able to sit still.

"Not to mention bringing Cannastar to the million-plus Africans a year who die from AIDS," Little Boy added. "As far as I'm concerned, Nelson Slade is the best news since Moses climbed Mount Sinai and got handed the ten commandments."

Cyd took a sip of her wine. "Let's hope Slade has read them."

# Chapter Eight

## THE BURNING SKY

Senegal lay scorched and dry under a boiling African sun. The election was just thirty days away, and the political fervor around Nelson Slade's revitalized presidential campaign had risen to a fever pitch. What started as rallies of no more than a thousand or so supporters in parks and fields had swollen to tens of thousands pouring into the streets and filling town squares across Senegal. The candidate's emphatic vow to end Senegal's long history of child slavery once and for all, together with his promises of unlimited water and lifesaving Cannastar, had voters in a frenzy. His rhetoric inspired the nation, and the riots turned deadly.

The military was called in to control the violence. At first, the government was winning—and then they weren't. The soldier's efforts to curtail the fighting were beginning to result in a lopsided body count of more uniforms on the ground after a bloody melee than bodies of impassioned citizens. The officers changed their tactics. Armed forces began surrounding Nelson's rallies with orders that under no circumstances were they to lift their weapons or wade in and start a fight; they were merely to stand there looking grim and determined. This was fine with the soldiers on the front line. After listening to so many of Nelson Slade's speeches, they too were beginning to believe he really was the savior Senegal was looking for.

It was around this time that Slade's father, President Léopold Slade, magnanimously lifted the ban on political rallies and decreed instead, in the interest of public safety, that he alone could give political speeches. Anyone standing up at a public gathering and pretending to know more about the affairs of state than the existing President would be arrested. Not surprisingly, his impudent son was immediately thrown in jail. The good citizens of Dakar, inspired by hope and inflamed by hate, protested the jailing of Nelson Slade by trying to burn the city down.

Nelson was released from prison the next day, and the burning abruptly stopped. The international press reported that President Slade, confident of his reelection, had thrown his unruly son in jail merely to teach him a lesson. "Illegitimate or not," Léopold Slade proclaimed, "he is still my boy, and a father's love knows no bounds—even for a juvenile delinquent. The public can rest assured that a free and open election will proceed in Senegal as it always has."

\*\*\*

Juliette was spending more and more time as Nelson Slade's tireless campaign worker. Between helping Malick Mbaye put the finishing touches on his sanctuary for runaway boys and crisscrossing the country with the presidential candidate to help coordinate his rallies, she was getting little, if any, sleep. Late one evening, Cyd found her slumped in a chair in her aviary staring at an untouched glass of wine. She sat down next to the French woman watching her with concern.

Juliette turned with overbright eyes and smiled weakly. "I have never been more excited in my life, Cydney. We're doing something really important here."

"I don't know how you do it," Cyd replied. "You look exhausted."

"The children! We are going to save them. This endless atrocity of child slavery is about to come to an end. It is a great day for Senegal, for its people, for the future!"

"I wish you would please just get some sleep."

"Who can sleep at a time like this? Here, have some wine." Juliette poured out a second glass and raised her own before Cyd could object. *"Senegal libre! Plus d'esclavage!"*

They touched glasses.

"How are you holding up, *chèrie*?"

"May I ask you a question?"

*"Mais oui* (but yes)."

"I'm just curious. It sounds like your husband was quite a bit older than you. How did the two of you meet?"

Juliette looked away with a bittersweet smile. "I was an orphan myself, you know. I made my living any way I could."

"You were a . . .?" Cyd was shocked. A prostitute? This woman?

Juliette saw the look on Cyd's face and laughed. "No, no *chèrie*. I sang. I had a beautiful voice and could sound just like Edith Piaf whenever I wanted. You know Edith Piaf?"

"The Sparrow. France's national singer. A legend of love, loss and sorrow."

*"Exactement* (exactly)! Before I was even a teenager, I stood on the street corners and sang, and people would crowd around and give me money. Jean-Luc, he literally took me off the streets. He put me through school and when I was old enough—his wife had passed away by then—he married me."

"How old were you?"

She laughed. "Age is not the same in France as it is in America. Jean-Luc didn't just love me, he positively worshiped me. I could do no wrong. Oh, I had my lovers and so did he, but there was never a time when we were not close." She looked away sadly, smiling to herself. "It was the happiest time of my life."

\*\*\*

Fat Boy and Little Man, never doubting that their patron would win the presidential election, busied themselves designing their new RO plant, and coordinating with their company in Israel to commence construction the moment the election was over. They were so happy, so absorbed in their work, that whole days passed without a single insult passing between them.

Nelson Slade designated a full square mile of sub-Saharan land for Cyd and Alex's Cannastar plantation. The acreage was relatively close to where Fat Man and Little Boy were planning to build their RO facility. Slade's instructions were that they were to begin planting their miracle drug the moment he won the election. Cyd and Alex, thrilled and excited, rented a 4WD Land Rover, and drove out to see where they would be living and working.

It was early afternoon. They sat on a knoll under the sparse shade of a giant baobab tree enjoying the picnic lunch Juliette's cook had made for them. Below them on a flat, brown plain was a grazing herd of giant eland—a huge species of striped antelope with long, spiraled, swept-back horns and turkey-wattle necks. Beyond the herd in the distant trees a family of elephants, two adults and a baby, were blissfully eating the bark off another baobab tree. Except for the elephants, the elands and baobab trees instead of barrel cactus, the official location for their new Cannastar plantation was not that different from the Arizona desert where their first Grow still flourished.

Cyd took off her hat and mopped at her brow. "I think I'm going to melt. How hot is it?"

"You don't want to know." Alex looked off to the west where the Atlantic Ocean drew a thin blue line across the horizon. "Cyd, what are we doing here?"

"Doing here?"

"We are so in over our heads with the promises we've made to this Slade character, with thinking we can set up a Grow in one of the most hostile and remote places on earth. I know we've talked and planned and hoped for this, but neither of us are farmers. Not in the sense Otis, Annie and Abe are back home. If I had a green thumb, I'd probably treat it for gangrene."

Cyd leaned back on her elbows and looked out at the endless view. "Africa doesn't seem to have a beginning or an end. It's as if eternity came and never left. As if time never existed."

"Did you even hear a word I said?"

"Relax, my love. Slade promised he'd provide us with real farmers to do the work. Men who have been growing things in Africa their whole lives and know the land like they know their own heartbeats. Besides, what could possibly go wrong in a magical place like this?"

He pointed. "Well, for one thing, that pack of lionesses sneaking through the long grass down there are probably not here to see to it that those elands have a nice day."

\*\*\*

Amid the turmoil over the coming election, Malick Mbaye opened his *Maison d'Enfants*. The word had barely gotten out that Children's House was accepting runaways before all one hundred bunk beds were filled and the shelter echoed with the raucous sounds of homeless boys. The sudden change in their fortunes infused the orphans with hope and promise. Many could hardly believe they might actually get to eat real food and go to a real school on a regular basis without having to spend most of their time begging and being beaten if they didn't produce.

Nelson Slade was scheduled to attend the grand opening of Malick's orphanage and give a commencement speech. The day arrived and Cyd and Alex accompanied Juliette to the home to help organize the festivities.

The street outside *Maison d'Enfants* was jammed with cars and clogged with people dressed in their colorful best. A black limousine was slowly making its way through the teeming crowds and loudly honking its horn. It pulled up in front of Children's House, the rear door opened and Nelson Slade' long legs swung out. Elegantly dressed in a western business suit and wearing his trademark dark glasses, the presidential candidate stood smiling and waving to the cheering mass of well-wishers. A group of beefy bodyguards stepped in, moved him along and quickly whisked him inside.

Juliette met Slade gleefully as he entered and introduced him to the Rasta-haired Malick who was brightly dressed in varying shades of yellow and orange. Smiling humbly, he welcomed the candidate to his modest facility.

Nelson Slade was genuinely impressed with what he saw. "You are a guiding light for Senegal," he told Malick as he toured the facility, stopping to greet the children. A group of tiny black faces were smiling up at him, and he smiled back admiringly. "What is begun here today is my own hope and dream for our nation," he declared. "An end to slavery and a bright new tomorrow for the children."

Cyd and Alex watched as the candidate fawned over the boys, patting and caressing them, asking questions and listening with great interest to their answers. His brief asides to them generated spontaneous giggles and laughs. He clearly adored the youngsters and was clearly adored in return.

Cyd looked on with growing concern. "Is he petting them or fondling them?" she whispered to Alex.

"He likes kids," Alex shrugged.

Outside in the street, a great commotion had begun as another black limousine was seen forcing its way through the crowd. Inside Children's House they heard the shouts and cheers go up and everyone followed Nelson out to investigate.

Standing on a flag-draped, makeshift podium that had been hastily erected outside the gates of *Maison d'Enfants* for candidate Slade to speak, they saw Nelson's father waving to the crowd. President Léopold Slade trapped the microphone, recoiled as it shrieked back, then raised his arms for silence.

A sudden absence of sound blanketed the crowd.

"*Citoyens de Dakar* (Citizens of Dakar)!" the President began in French. "*Bienvenu!* Welcome to our newly erected home for lost boys. My administration has worked long and hard to make this day a reality and I am here to assure you that this is only the beginning. In my next term as president, I will continue to erect sanctuaries like this one with the goal of delivering Senegal forever from the tyranny of homelessness and slavery. My solemn promise to you is that our nation will soon be free from the chains of the past, and well on the road to becoming a modern, industrialized society!"

The crowd cheered respectfully, and the President graciously returned their affections with a magnanimous smile. Léopold Slade was a murky man, and a disaster as a president. Big, tall and overweight, he had the round, vacant face of a lazy bureaucrat. His success as the leader of his country could be attributed to the crafty intellect and ruthless nature that lurked behind his sleepy eyes.

"My son Nelson has decided that he would make a better president than me," *Le Président* went on. "It is a great heartache that a son of mine would betray me in this way. I had such high hopes for him. Perhaps some of you with children can understand a father's disappointment over a wayward son that did not turn out the way you hoped."

Murmurs of sympathy rippled through the crowd. Pleased that he had hit a nerve, he reminded them that his son was making a lot of empty promises. "Do not believe for a minute that Nelson will do as he says. He is a dangerous liar, my boy, and he will lead this nation down a path to destruction. This Cannastar he has promised you that he claims cures AIDS: America reports that the death toll from people overdosing on this illegal drug has risen to epidemic proportions. For every person it helps, it kills two! And as for this SWRO facility of his, this so-called Reverse Osmosis plant he says he will build so your crops will grow and you will never again run out of food or drinking water: I have it on good authority that in Israel there has been a rash of deaths from people drinking polluted sea water from their so-called osmosis plant.

"Nelson, he promises you these things to make you think your lives will be better after he's elected president. In fact, his lies will only make things worse! His lies will kill you! As your president, in the future as in the past, I will make certain that Senegal continues to flourish and prosper as a happy, healthy nation!"

Tepid applause met his remarks. His son stood to one side looking on with a frozen smile. The President finished his speech and was getting back in his limo when Nelson took the stage. Wild cheering and thunderous applause greeted his sudden appearance. Smiling and waving benevolently, he boomed out over the public address system:

"A big hand for our former president!"

\*\*\*

A week later, the general election was held and Nelson Slade won in a landslide. The son had dethroned the father and was now the new leader of the country.

Cyd had to put her fingers in her ears listening to Juliette's screams of delight. Alex, Fat Man and Little Boy joined in the celebration and they partied late into the night and in the morning they all had splitting headaches from the wine.

Nursing his hangover, Alex turned on Juliette's television. Cyd immediately reached to turn it off again when the news caught her attention: tens of thousands of fresh ballots had mysteriously shown up overnight and flipped the results. Apparently, nearly twice as many people had voted than there were eligible voters in the country. Nonetheless, it was official: Léopold Slade had defeated his son by a narrow margin and was the winner and still president. Life would go on as it always had with a president everyone knew and loved.

The recount took a week amid loud and angry accusations of irregularities and voter intimidation. Cries of voter fraud arose and rioting erupted in the streets. Nelson was everywhere at once giving brilliant impromptu speeches and claiming victory, and the vast majority of the population was squarely behind him. The highest courts in the land refused to look at the evidence or even consider the possibility that the election had been stolen. The burning and looting got worse. To quell the violence and stop the destruction, the President was forced to have his son arrested.

But then an odd thing happened.

Nelson Slade had promised the members of the military a significant raise in pay if he was elected. Other converts to his cause, government workers with little or no skill or ability, were guaranteed appointments to head the highest branches of government. Ranking police officers who never expected to make more than a living wage were promised directorships of the international businesses the new president planned to nationalize as soon as he took office. As a result, the military joined hands with the bureaucracy in backing the son. Nelson was released from prison and his father was promptly arrested and put behind bars in his place.

Supporters of the old president took to the streets in protest. Many of the new rioters were paid anarchists while others, finding joy in the chaos, just joined in for the fun. The next morning the roads were blocked with burning cars and buses, store windows were shattered, government buildings had been defaced and statues of revered national heroes lay smashed and broken on the ground. To put an end to the matter, Nelson had his father taken out, stood before a firing squad and shot. The sudden death of President Léopold Slade restored the peace, and silence like a shroud settled over the country.

## Chapter Nine

### A NEW DAY

Tens of thousands of devout Muslims crowded the vast plaza of Dakar's great mosque to celebrate the inauguration of the new president. Nelson Slade stood before them, the African sun reflecting off his dark glasses, and gave a speech. He was a gifted orator, and his inaugural address promised grand things ahead for Senegal. Everyone in attendance that day thanked Allah for the way things had turned out and went away with renewed hope in their hearts.

The international press called the Senegal election, and subsequent murder of its incumbent president, a coup. The United States and its trading partners responded by imposing strict trade sanctions and embargos. The Senegalese economy immediately slowed and began to grind to a halt.

A week after the election, President Slade telephoned Juliette. Would she be kind enough to come to the presidential palace, and bring her American and Israeli friends with her? "I want as soon as possible to start the ball rolling on their projects," he proclaimed.

With the murder of Nelson's father fresh on her mind, Cyd had serious reservations. "Alex," she argued, "how can we even trust this man? What if *we* do something he doesn't like? What happens when things don't go his way? And they will at some point, you know they will. Are we going to end up in front of a firing squad, too?"

"Unless you have political ambitions you haven't told me about," Alex smiled, "I think we're safe. Slade's father did try and steal the election, you know."

Cyd snorted in disgust. "I think his conflict resolution skills leave something to be desired."

"Senegal isn't America," he reminded her. "They have their own ways of doing things that go back thousands of years here. Let's just go and see him and find out what he has to say. Way I see it, this election could be a good thing. The chance for us to actually do some real good for a change."

\*\*\*

Dakar's presidential palace looked a lot like the White House in Washington DC—only bigger.

Cyd, Alex, Fat Man, Little Boy and Juliette went through security, were escorted across a high-domed marble entry and ushered into a wood paneled room carpeted in a Persian rug nearly the size of Persia itself. Nelson greeted them warmly and invited them to sit in gilded chairs. Little Boy climbed up into his, but his feet didn't quite reach the ground.

"And so we begin!" Nelson announced with a grand sweep of his hand to indicate his guests were included in his splendid plans. A week earlier at his inauguration, he stood before thousands in the shimmering heat wearing his trademark dark glasses and a ceremonial robe of silken blue trimmed in gold. On his head was a round white hat, and around his neck a flowing white scarf. Today, in stark contrast, he was dressed all in black with a black turtleneck, black slacks, black shoes and black gloves. Only his dark glasses remained the same. Cyd thought he looked like a porn star. He saw her expression and paused. "There is something troubling you, Ms. Seeley? Cyd?"

"Your father," she said impulsively. "Was he such a bad man?"

"He was to me, as you say in America, a sperm doner. Nothing more. As far as his execution is concerned, politics are politics. A leader must sometimes make hard choices and do difficult things for the good of his country. Now to business, unless you have further questions."

"*Certainement* (certainly)," Juliette cried quickly. "Please. Go on, Mr. President."

"I want to honor my promises to my people as soon as possible. To that end, Fat Man, Little Boy, you are hereby authorized to begin immediately the construction of your water plant. Bring me the contracts and I will sign them."

Fat Man's face turned red with happiness, but Little Boy frowned. "The RO plant we've designed, Mr. President, is going to cost upwards of five hundred million in today's dollars. Can Senegal afford to spend half a billion dollars on such a plant? I'm afraid it cannot be done for less."

Nelson smiled confidently. "Under my new economic plan, Senegal will be able to pay for its new osmosis facility and so much more. Before long we will be the most prosperous country in Africa. You wait and see!"

*I'm waiting,* Cyd thought.

Nelson turned to Alex. "As for you, my American friend, you will please begin immediately the establishment of your Cannastar plantation."

Alex smiled broadly. "We can do that, you bet."

Cyd, irritated at being ignored, looked from Alex to the President. "Starting a six-hundred-acre farm is a major undertaking," she said bluntly. "Not to mention an expensive one. If our success in the States is any indication, it will make a lot of money, but not for some time. Farming is not an overnight business. The first thing we are going to need are those farmers you promised us."

"You shall have all the Senegalese farmers you need," Nelson promised, smiling at Alex. "You just concentrate on giving Africa the gift of life, and my people will do the rest." He turned to Juliette. "As for you, my dear…"

Juliette smiled sadly. "I guess I'm out of a job. It was so much fun helping Malick open his children's home, and helping you win the election. I'm sorry it's over. I'll miss it"

"It doesn't have to be over if you don't want it to be," Nelson said.

"*Quoi* (what)?

"I want to build *more* children's homes like the school and shelter you and your friend Malick just opened. As many as possible all over Senegal! It is my plan to have every orphan off the streets by the end of my first term. Like the Cannastar though, I cannot do it alone. I need your help, Juliette. Would you, perhaps, be willing to spearhead the program for me?"

Juliette's mouth worked open and closed, but nothing more came out. They looked and saw she was crying tears of joy.

# Chapter Ten

## A FARM IN AFRICA

Nelson Slade was as good as his word. Immediately after assuming the presidency, he increased the pay of his military officers—who immediately went out and bought new cars and houses that only a short time before would have been too expensive for them to even think about. Men who had never accomplished anything in their lives were put in charge of government agencies and began exercising their newfound authority with the expertise of a pilot who has never flown an airplane before. Making good on another campaign promise, Nelson began spending massive sums of money on social programs. The money, for the most part, enriched only the people running the programs, but the economy soared and optimism in Senegal ran high.

With everything going their way, it came as somewhat of a shock to Cyd and Alex when the newly elected president started railing against international investment and calling it "foreign imperialism"—a despised phrase in a country that had lived so much of its recent past under the thumb of European domination. First it was France, then England, then America that Slade vilified. According to him, industrialized nations were all alike in their desire to exploit Senegal. His rhetoric was so vehement, so passionate, so often repeated that a portion of the population began to believe him. The seeds of xenophobia had been planted and were already sprouting unrest.

Amid great national fanfare, Fat Man and Little Boy started construction on their new SWRO plant. New roads were being built to handle the heavy loads of concrete and materials that would soon be arriving, and excavation of the site was well underway. The project was scheduled for completion in four years, and the two Israeli engineers in charge were so busy that they had to move out of Juliette's and into a pair of new mobile homes at the construction site. Little Boy had mixed feelings about the arrangement. It meant that he had to travel back and forth to Juliette's rooftop condominium most evenings for his late-night suppers with her.

"Have you noticed?" Alex asked Cyd. "I think something might be going on between Little Boy and Juliette."

Cyd rolled her eyes. "Don't you dare say anything. Let mother nature take its course."

"I think mother nature already has," he grinned.

\*\*\*

*La Maison d'Enfants* was a huge success. The runaways who were lucky enough to be living there were having the time of their lives. Juliette was so busy helping Malick open a second "Children's House" a block away from the first that she had little time to think about the wonderfully bright and witty Israeli engineer who had become infatuated with her—although being French she had to admit she adored having a lover. It was her reward like her glass of wine after a long day at the orphanages. Something to look forward to, but not abandon herself to. Her real passion, her ardor, her zeal was for taking as many abused and exploited boys off the streets and out of the *daaras* as possible. The very thought of building more shelters like the one she and Malick had just opened filled her with an excitement she had not known in years.

\*\*\*

President Nelson Slade provided Cyd and Alex with the African farmers he promised. A dozen men showed up the very first day led by a skinny old African named Oumar. Oumar had leathery skin, white hair and walked with the aid of a wooden stick that was a foot taller than he was. The stick was decorated with carvings and colorful plumage and seemed to be some kind of symbol of authority. The farmers under his command had all grown up on nearby farms and knew exactly what it took to grow a crop in Senegalese soil.

Oumar's English was peppered with French, English and mostly Arabic. It was a language of his own making, and Cyd and Alex had to guess at half his words. Proud of his trade, his traditions, his heritage, the elderly African informed the two white Americans if they wanted their strange plant grown in Africa, then Africans would be the ones to grow it. He would allow no interference from foreign devils. They were to be overseers alone with the sole responsibility of providing the farmers with whatever they needed to do their job. It was not a negotiation; Cyd and Alex were to do exactly as told. Oumar handed them a list of supplies, materials and food that was to be on hand at all times. The one thing that was not on the list was water. They questioned him on this and were informed that these men were dry farmers. "In Senegal dryland farming—pulling the weeds and controlling the runoff—that is how it is done. Anything else," Oumar insisted in Arabic, *"is mustahil* (impossible)".

Under the African overseer's casual eye, his farmers began preparing the soil. Alex thought if they worked any slower, the grassland they were plowing under would have time to grow back before they got around to planting it. Meanwhile, he and Cyd telephoned Otis in Arizona and asked him to ship them more Cannastar seed. The jolly undertaker-turned-Arizona-farmer wanted to know what happened to the seed they had with them. When they told him about the shipwreck, he was horrified. Cyd went to great lengths to explain that they were unharmed and alright. She did, however, need him to send her more Cannastar leaves for her own consumption. "My supply was lost at sea when our boat went down. It seems like my breast cancer is gone forever, so I might not even need to be drinking the tea anymore, but I don't want to take the chance."

Otis said he would send her all the Cannastar she needed via 'international priority.' "You should have it in a couple of days. Absolutely. Now about these dryland farmers of yours. I hope they know what they're doing. Personally, I think you're looking at a disaster. Cannastar needs lots of water to grow and mature properly. You could be making a big mistake."

"I don't like it any better than you do," Cyd agreed, "We're guests here. Uninvited guests. We have to try it their way first."

Otis paused. "You say you have a section of land, a square mile, six hundred and forty acres?"

"Yes."

"I'm going to send you enough seed to plant one fourth of that. Think of it as an experiment, a test. No point in wasting good seed. You'll know in six months if it worked or not. Either way, I can always send you more if you need it."

"I wish you were here to help us," Cyd lamented. "We miss you."

"Not safe, man. I could still be arrested if I tried to leave the reservation."

"I understand," Cyd said sadly.

\*\*\*

That evening Alex and Cyd lingered over a glass of wine in Juliette's aviary. Overhead, the birds were busily arranging themselves for the night with flutters and cries.

Alex toyed with his glass. "Been thinking."

Cyd waited.

"With Oumar in charge of the Grow, we've got some time on our hands."

"Apparently."

"I've always wanted to open a medical clinic in a place like this. Always wanted to treat people who have little or no access to modern medicine. How would you feel about . . . ?"

Cyd smiled at the man she loved. "Malick's *Maison d'Enfants* might be the perfect place."

"You think?"

"I bet most of those kids have never seen a doctor in their lives. The adults in the neighborhood probably haven't either."

"A clinic would be expensive. What would you think about using some of the Cannastar money in our Cayman account? We've got plenty."

"Can't think of a better use for it. Could you use an assistant?"

"I'd have to train you."

"I'm trainable . . . up to a point."

"You'd have to do everything I say."

"So long as I get to train you the rest of the time."

He came to his feet with a threatening growl. "We'll see who trains who."

She squealed and ran laughing into their bedroom with Alex close on her heels.

\*\*\*

The free clinic that Cyd and Alex opened at Malick's Children's Home was overwhelmed with patients from the first day. Long lines formed outside the gates, and the doctor and his hastily trained nurse worked long hours seeing people who were desperately in need of medical attention.

Late one night after their last patient had gone, they stood leaning wearily against an examining table that also served as their only operating table, their surgical gowns soiled and spotted with blood. Gratifying as the work was, they were both exhausted. Cyd took off the rag that was tied around her head and used it to mop her face.

"You are one great nurse, I'll say that for you," Alex smiled, marveling at how fortunate he was to be loved by such a remarkable woman. "I think you missed your calling."

"It seems to have found me whether I like it or not," she sighed. "Alex, we're seeing so many patients with HIV. I'm going to call Otis and see if he can't send us enough Cannastar to start treating these people until our first crop comes in."

"Okay by me."

Alex affectionately rubbed the head of a ten-year-old Senegalese boy who was eagerly standing by. Imbued with boundless energy, the youngster lived at the orphanage with the other *talibés* and had attached himself to Cyd and Alex as their unofficial assistant the first day they opened the clinic. "Momo, do you have an informed medical opinion on the matter?"

Momo grinned his irresistible grin. "Okay by me, Doctor Boss." The boy was small for his age with big, intelligent eyes. His light skin and relatively delicate features suggested that at least one of his parents might not have been African. Everything Cyd and Alex did seemed to fascinate him. They were amazed at how quickly he was picking up their language. "English easy," he bragged. "Momo remember words first time, every time."

Cyd smiled admiringly. "That's remarkable. I wish I could do that."

"Momo smart," the ten-year-old grinned.

When he wasn't at his Quran lessons, he was always in the clinic asking questions. Alex's cell phone was a source of endless fascination for him, and he was forever asking to borrow it. Before long he knew more about smartphones than Alex would ever know. Cyd and Alex came to rely on him as their official translator. He took his job very seriously and with the patients assumed an air of professional authority.

Tireless and enthusiastic despite the late hour, Momo picked up a broom and swept some soiled bandages off the floor, then emptied his dustpan in the trash, brushed his hands together and looked from Alex to Cyd with a big smile. "Another day, another dollar, *oui*?"

Cyd laughed and gave him a hug. "Where on earth did you pick that up?"

"From you, Nurse Boss."

"Off to bed with you," Alex ordered. "It's way past your bedtime."

The boy started to leave, stopped and looked back with a solemn expression. "Momo decide," he stated firmly. "Momo going to be doctor and help his people like Doctor Boss."

Alex went to him and dropped to his haunches so that he was eye level with the boy. "And a fine doctor you will be, my man. Want to know how I know? I was about your age when I decided to be a doctor. Never regretted it for a minute."

Momo nodded. "One less thing to worry about, *oui*?"

"*Oui*," Cyd laughed, bending and offering him her cheek. "Now where's my kiss?"

Momo brushed her cheek reverently with his lips and ran grinning out of the room.

## The Organ Grinder Factor

Cyd sighed and looked around their crude clinic—a cramped, relatively sterile room with a small attached waiting room that had been intended for storage when Malick's new school and dormitory was built. Her gaze fell on Alex. "Tell the truth. What we're doing here. This clinic. Is it what you wanted? Are you happy?"

"Never happier. I love it."

She smiled wearily. "I can't believe it, but so am I."

\*\*\*

Malick opened his second Children's Home up the street from his first, and Juliette was so busy helping him order supplies, staff it with reputable *marabouts* and counselors, and screen and admit the new residents that she was once again hardly getting any sleep. It troubled her greatly that they were able to accommodate only a small number of the boys who applied. The newspapers ran stories with quotes from the new president bragging about how his policies were removing countless child beggars from the streets, and how every day more *talibés* were finding their way to the Children's Homes he was building.

Cyd and Alex returned to Juliette's condominium late one night after a long session at the clinic to find Juliette pacing the floor in alarm, and Little Boy trying unsuccessfully to calm her. Cyd hurried to her side, made her sit and asked what was wrong?

"*Tout!*" Juliette cried, her French accent thicker than usual because of her distress. "Everything! More and more boys, they are disappearing off the streets every day."

"I heard," Cyd replied soothingly. "Isn't it wonderful?"

"You don't understand. Disappearing as in vanishing! Evaporating! Going away and not coming back! We were able to take in another hundred at our second shelter, but that doesn't account for anywhere near all he boys who have gone missing. It doesn't add up. Something is wrong."

"What makes you think the boys are gone?" Alex asked. "How can you know?"

"The boys at our shelters, they tell me things. They're afraid. One child we took in from the *daara* you visited with me said all the boys who lived there are gone, and a whole new group has replaced them. Boys who are only six or seven years old."

Cyd felt sick to her stomach. "You're sure? He wasn't just making this up?"

"I went out to see for myself. I didn't recognize a single child that was staying there."

Alex went to the window and stared out with rising anger. "We need to have a little talk, this *marabout* and me."

\*\*\*

The *daara* looked the same as the day they first visited it, and Cyd was every bit as disgusted. Ruined cinderblock walls stood with only the sky for a roof, and the ground was littered with even more garbage than before. Alex looked across the filthy rectangle and saw the buck-toothed *marabout* sitting on his gas can with a whole new group of students cross-legged on the ground before him. The boys were clearly younger than the ones he had seen earlier. Their Quranic teacher wore the same dirty blue kaftan, and above his head was the same medallion of the coiled black snake with the watchful eyes.

Alex had asked Juliette to come along as interpreter, and Cyd had insisted on coming to support Juliette. They followed Alex as he marched across the open compound.

"Hey, you!" he shouted. The *marabout* continued the rhythmic flow of his hypnotic chant. Alex stood over him looking down. "I'm talking to you, numbnuts!"

The *marabout* looked up slowly with an unctuous smile.

"Juliette, translate for me," Alex ordered. "Where the hell are the other boys? The ones we saw here last time? What have you done with them?"

Juliette spoke in rapid French and translated the response in English as the class of new *talibés* looked on in open-mouthed wonder. "He says they all have gone home."

"Home? What the hell is that supposed to mean, home?

Juliette translated his question and repeated the answer. "He says home to their destinies, to their . . . how do you say . . . proper purpose under heaven."

"Where's that, exactly? When are they coming back?"

The *marabout* shrugged indifferently.

Alex pulled him to his feet by the lapels of his kaftan. "I'm going to need you to be a little more specific there, chief."

The religious teacher laughed in his face, and Alex recoiled from his breath. Flaring, he balled his fist and hit the man in the mouth. The *marabout* went reeling backward and sat down heavily on his gas can. Looking up, he leered at Alex with huge, bloody teeth.

"Allah is watching," he grinned in perfect English.

# Chapter Eleven

## A BUMPER CROP

A few months into his presidency, Nelson Slade deemed it in the national interest to nationalize the assets of all the foreign imperialists. International companies who, in good faith, had made massive investments in Senegal lost everything, and their executives were summarily ejected from the country.

The news media erupted in anger, and the new president responded by shutting down their websites. Any journalist who dared suggest that Nelson had stolen the assets of Senegal's most valued investors was arrested. In an impassioned speech, the president announced that he had appointed trusted members of the police force to run the industrial, chemical and scientific firms that the country now owned. "The foreign usurpers have at last been stopped from exploiting our nation!" he claimed. "A seamless transition of power from corrupt management to state run prosperity is underway! Our great national companies are now poised to realize their full potential and show a profit that will benefit all of Senegal!"

The international banking community, led by the U.S., responded with sanctions against the Senegalese banks and currency. Embargos were imposed, and the country's ability to conduct international business came to a halt. Gross Domestic Product fell precipitously, and a sharp spike in inflation followed.

As the benign benefactor of all his people, President Slade increased government spending on sweeping social reforms—which in turn created hyperinflation. Price controls were immediately imposed, the value of the local currency dropped to nothing, and the dollar and the euro became the only viable means of exchange. Suddenly local producers could no longer get paid enough to cover their costs, there was a shortage of almost everything, and it was all unaffordable anyway. Black markets sprung up everywhere to fill the need and narcotics of all kinds were suddenly available on every corner.

Massive street protests followed, a nationwide curfew was imposed and civil liberties were suspended. Efforts by the national assembly to restore order were rewarded with the president taking away their power. In no time at all, a once-viable, democratic country had been reduced to ruin. Backed by a loyal and powerful military, Nelson Slade was now dictator of Senegal and ruled by decree.

\*\*\*

A boy disappeared from *Maison d'Enfants*, and Malick called Juliette, Cyd and Alex together for an emergency meeting. They arrived late that night and found Momo waiting with Malick in his kitchen. In the shadows was a man who sat silently and made no effort to acknowledge their presence when they entered. All they could tell was that he was slightly built, wore wire-rimmed glasses that reflected the dim light, a rounded skull cap and was dressed in the robes of an academic. The new arrivals sat at Malick's rickety kitchen table and were served tea which no one touched.

"What do you mean a child has disappeared?" Juliette demanded. "From this shelter? How is that possible?"

Malick shook his head. "Momo says he saw him go out with a plastic bowl to beg in the streets."

"Rules say boys who live here don't beg," Momo declared. "Boy broke rule."

Cyd was as upset as Juliette. "Are you sure? Have you looked everywhere?"

"He's gone," Malick assured her.

"Black Mamba, he take," Momo claimed. "The other boys, they are all afraid."

Alex turned the boy gently to him. "Think hard, son. How do you know it was the Black Mamba?"

Malick answered for him. "These boys of the street, they know everything that happens out there. They absorb it through their skin, feel it in their hearts. It is how they survive."

Juliette was furious. "This is supposed to be a safe haven for them and we've let them down!"

"Don't be afraid," Cyd told Momo. "You know you're safe with us."

"Momo not afraid of Black Mamba."

His reply surprised her. "And why is that?"

The boy forked two fingers and jabbed the air. "Momo poke snake's eyes out if snake get too close."

Alex rubbed his head. "Atta boy."

"There's someone I want you to meet," Malick said, nodding at the man in the shadows. "He has information you need to hear."

The man in the corner drug his chair over to the table, sat back down and settled himself comfortably.

"This is Albert Dado," Malick went on. "He returned from Oxford when he learned what was happening in his country. He is the new leader of the resistance."

"There is a slave ship," Dado began without preamble in a formal British accent with French overtones. He was not at all fearless to look at, but something in his gentle manner suggested an iron will and indomitable courage. "It comes up the coast of Africa twice a year buying boys from the slave states. 'The Ship of No Return' it is called, and it is due here in a few days."

Cyd and Juliette stared at him in disbelief.

"Slave ship?" Alex couldn't believe his ears. "What do they do with them, the boys they buy? Where do they go?"

"From Senegal, the ship makes one last stop in Mauritania just north of here to take on more *cargo*. It then continues on through Gibraltar, through the Mediterranean and down the Suez Canal. It's first port of call is Saudi Arabia where a slave auction is held onboard. If they still have boys left after that, they continue on around to the Persian Gulf where they sell the rest in Qatar. There is a huge market for child sex slaves in both places."

Juliette was red in the face. "This ship of slaves," she demanded, "how do we stop it?"

"With careful planning," Dado replied quietly, "it might be done."

"*Monsieur* Dado is raising a rebel army to take back our country," Malick explained. "When that happens, many things will change. We are hundreds strong already."

Alex was both appalled and angry. "You're going to need a lot more men than that if you're planning to take on Slade's army."

"Before long," Dado remarked softly, "Nelson Slade will be unable to pay his military. When that day comes, the soldiers will join us, and so will the people."

"A coup might succeed if you're lucky," Cyd speculated. "If it doesn't get everybody killed."

"Chaos is the ground from which revolution springs," Dado said. "We seek only peace."

"Meanwhile," Juliette insisted, "how do we get our missing boy back?"

"The Ship of No Return, it will *not* be invisible when it comes," Dado replied. "We'll know, and we'll be waiting."

\*\*\*

In an effort to unite Senegal's fractured and increasingly angry population, Nelson Slade stepped up his rhetoric of antisemitic hate. The Jews were an easy target given the endless humiliating defeats Muslims had suffered at the hands of the Israelis during the 20$^{th}$ century—and nothing united a people faster or made them easier to manipulate than a common hatred. Political Islam in the 21$^{st}$ century consumed the Arab world, and Nelson exploited it to his full advantage. "Jews have too much power in the international marketplace!" he cried in one of his fiery speeches. "Look what they have done in this country to our currency alone. Everyone knows they are responsible for most of the world's wars! See how they have crushed the Arab people in their own lands and kept them under their thumb. It is easy to see that Senegal is next to fall if we don't stop them in their tracks.

"As many of you know," he went on, "I am a water engineer, a master of hydrology. That is how I conceived of building a plant to convert sea water to fresh water for my country. I have been closely monitoring the reverse osmosis facility the Jews have under construction outside of Dakar and I have discovered some alarming information. Not only is Senegal being exploited by the staggering profits Israel is making off the project, I have it on good authority they plan on poisoning our water system with it. It is no secret that the Jews want to kill as many Muslims as they can as quickly and efficiently as they can. What better way to do it than to drug the very water we drink? As your president, you have my solemn oath: I will never let this happen—even if I have to take over construction of the new water plant myself!"

His message resonated with the people and resentment toward the Israeli crews and engineers building Senegal's revolutionary new RO plant grew daily. Meanwhile, the country was rapidly running out of money and was dangerously close to ruin. President Slade wasn't worried since he had started paying everyone, including his military, in local currency instead of euros or dollars. He may as well have been paying them in Monopoly money for all the local Franc was worth. His next plan was to impose sweeping new tax reforms that would provide a constant income stream for the government and raise millions. Any hardships the new taxes might impose on the population as a whole were not his concern. In times of crisis everyone needed to pull together and share the sacrifice.

\*\*\*

It took what seemed like forever for Oumar's farmers to get the Cannastar planted. The crop had been in the ground six months now, and it wasn't anywhere near ready to harvest. Given the economic turmoil that was going on under Nelson Slade's leadership, Cyd and Alex had little faith that the distribution of the Cannastar could be handled without corruption, or that the healing drug would even end up in the right hands. They passionately wanted to provide Africa with a cure for HIV and other viruses, but not if the Cannastar was going to end up on the black market. They drove out to the Grow for one of their regular inspections with the feeling that something was terribly wrong, but not knowing what it was or what to do about it.

When they arrived, they found the farmers all sitting with Oumar under the shade of the towering baobab tree on the hill. The old man got up out of a dirty upholstered arm chair that apparently served as his throne, and with great dignity limped over to where they were getting out of their rented Land Rover.

"*Voilà!*" he announced with a majestic sweep of his stick to indicate the Cannastar field. "The first crop, as you can see, she is ready for harvest."

Cyd looked out over the field of Cannastar plants thinking she had misunderstood his garbled stream of words. The hundred acres of Cannastar wasn't anywhere near ready for harvest. In fact, it didn't even look like Cannastar.

They walked down the nearest row of plants in dismay with Oumar following resentfully behind. Alex broke off leaves and crumbled them to dust in his hands as he went. Cyd stopped and ran her hand over the tops of plants that should have been above her head by now and only came up to her chest. "This is a total ruin," she moaned. "Not only are the leaves shriveled and half dead, their size and shape are all wrong."

"It sure isn't what Otis and Annie grow back home," Alex agreed. "Not even close."

"I mean, look at these seed pods!" she despaired. "They should be all the colors of the rainbow, and they're pale and faded as lima beans. Whatever we do, we can't do this again."

Alex pulled up one of the plants by the roots. It came up with no effort at all and he dropped it on the ground in disgust. "Burn it!" he declared. "Even if we wanted to take the chance of distributing this . . . this dehydrated disaster, it wouldn't have the strength or potency to cure the common cold, let alone the flu. Burn the lot."

The fury on Oumar's ancient face as he looked on was a sight to behold.

"I knew from the beginning it was a mistake to plant this way," Cyd lamented, furious with herself for ignoring her intuition.

"It's not the end of the world," Alex sighed. "What we need to do is get rid of this bunch of farmers and grow it hydroponically ourselves the way Otis does."

"We're not Otis," Cyd protested. "We need help."

Alex turned to confront the old man. "Oumar, tell your men to get kerosine from the shed and light this field on fire."

Oumar stood seething with anger and refused to move.

"*Allumettes*. Matches!" Alex made a combustible motion with his hands and an explosive sound with his mouth. "Fire! Burn! You understand?"

Oumar shook his stick in Alex's face and began shouting what sounded suspiciously like French and Arabic expletives.

The garlic on the old man's breath made Alex gag. "Burn the damn plants, Oumar, or so help me I'll do it myself." He watched the wrinkled face turn to stone and saw he was getting nowhere. "Fine," he said, walking away. "I was a boy scout once. I know how to make a fire."

Cyd followed him to a big metal shed they had erected on the property to store tools and supplies. The interior was dim and hot. Alex rummaged around angrily until he found a can of gasoline. Cyd grabbed a box of marches off a shelf and together they started back outside just as an ominous sound rose up.

They came out into the daylight to find the farmers arrayed in a semi-circle shaking their farm implements at them and repeating a chorus of what sounded way too much like a war chant. The Africans began advancing toward them, beating their tools together while stamping their feet and chanting louder.

Cyd and Alex were about to turn and run when they heard a loud honking of horns. Looking around, they saw three black SUVs headed toward them in a cloud of dust with state flags waving from the fenders.

The vehicles came to a halt and the chanting abruptly stopped. Security guards with automatic weapons jumped out of the cars and stood rigidly at attention. The driver of the middle limo exited, opened the limo's rear door with courtly formality and Nelson Slade's tall, lanky form emerged.

The president approached surveying the scene and smiling as if he had just arrived at a cocktail party in his honor. He was dressed all in black as usual including the black gloves but had substituted a black muscle shirt for his black turtleneck. The sun reflected off his sunglasses.

Cyd stared at his exposed forearms with a racing heart. She hadn't been imagining things in his office after all when she thought she saw the tattoo of a snake on his arm. Big and black, the image etched into his skin was in fact a coiled and smiling snake. *It's him,* she thought, and a chill went through her. *It has to be! Nelson Slade is the Black Mamba!*

The president acknowledged Oumar with a formal nod, then turned to Cyd and Alex. "I received word that the Cannastar was ready for harvest and came out to commemorate the occasion." He saw Cyd's horrified look and his smile froze on his face. "I hope you don't mind."

She looked quickly at Alex to see if he had noticed the tattoo.

"Not at all," Alex answered. "You're just in time to see us burn the field."

Nelson showed no surprise. "I'm afraid I can't allow that," he replied. "The crop is already sold."

Cyd tried to speak and her throat went dry.

"There is no crop," Alex flared. "Thanks to these farmers of yours, the Grow is a total bust."

Nelson's smile broadened. "Did you know that our Oumar here is himself a *marabout?* A shaman of unimpeachable integrity? He tells me his men have done a marvelous job producing a robust, healthy harvest. I can see for myself that Allah has rewarded their hard work." He sobered. "Kindly prepare the plants for shipment."

"Shipment?" Alex was aghast. "What shipment?"

The President drew himself up to his full height, a man in complete control of himself and the situation. "To South Africa, of course."

"South Africa?" Cyd repeated. "What in God's name are you talking about?"

"Nearly twenty-five percent of people living with HIV in Africa live in South Africa," Nelson explained patiently. "They know about your Cannastar from what they see on social media and are willing to pay Senegal a small fortune for its first crop."

"You might as well sell them oregano for all the good these plants will do them," Cyd raged. "If it *was* a viable crop, it would go to the people of Senegal who paid for it in the first place, and it would be free for the asking! This is *not* a for-profit farm."

The president looked down at her from his towering height. "This is a commercial enterprise and you work for me, Ms. Seeley! I am ordering you to prepare and package this crop for transport immediately. And the next crop you plant, see to it that you use all of the land I provided you, not just a portion of it. This is a cash crop and a cash business, and we must maximize its potential."

Alex smiled without humor. "Maximize this. We're done. We quit."

"Guards!" Nelson shouted. "Escort the doctor and his woman back to their car. See that they return safely to their clinic where they can at least do some good for the people they are here to serve." He turned on his heel to walk away. "My farmers will take it from here."

"If you want these guys to grow something you can sell," Alex said angrily as the guards came for them, "try peanuts. Nice tattoo, by the way."

The president glanced down proudly at his arm. "Being foreigners, you wouldn't know. This is the symbol of a great and ancient Senegalese warrior."

"I bet the kids are wild about it," Cyd said.

Slade lowered his sunglasses and looked at her over the top of the frames.

Cyd saw the cold and deadly expression in his eyes and gasped.

## Chapter Twelve

### THE BIG BURN

"You saw it too!" Cyd cried the moment they were back in their Land Rover and driving away. "That tattoo! He's the Black Mamba, I knew it!"

He glanced in his rear-view mirror and saw that one of the black SUVs from Slade's entourage was following them. "There's nothing we can do about it at the moment. Not without proof."

"I have all the proof I need," she cried. "The feeling is too strong. The man is evil, Alex! Did you see his eyes?"

"Right now what we need to do is stop him from selling worthless Cannastar plants to South Africa, and giving millions of people false hope that their pain and suffering will go away."

"How?"

"We started out to burn the field. Let's finish the job."

"We can't do that," she began, then stopped. "Can we do that?"

"You bet we can. We'll go back tonight after we're done at the clinic and torch the whole damn thing."

She hesitated. "We told Nelson we wanted to destroy the field. We'll be the prime suspects."

"We can get Malick and Lynette to vouch for us. Say we were at the clinic all night seeing patients and never left."

"That might not be enough."

"You may be right. Let me think about it. If he gets away with this, nobody in Africa will trust that Cannastar can help them ever again."

\*\*\*

The line of men, women and children with medical problems outside their clinic that day was especially long by the time they got back. The black SUV that had followed them from the Grow lingered in the street until they were safely inside, then drove away.

"Where's Momo?" Cyd asked as they began seeing their first patients. "It's not like him to be late for work."

"He'll show up. Bandage this for me, will you, while I tend to that woman who needs her boil lanced?"

Alex worked quickly and efficiently, all the while mulling over their dilemma and trying to formulate a plan. Cyd was so upset over what had happened that afternoon she kept dropping things. Alex finally closed the door to the packed waiting room and took her aside. "I've given this a lot of thought. We burn the Cannastar tonight and by tomorrow we'll be wanted fugitives."

"That's your plan?"

"They'll come to arrest us and question us, and no matter how good our alibi is, chances are they won't release us."

"No, they won't."

"I want you to go find Malick and Juliette. Tell them what we're planning to do and why. Tell them after we burn the field, we're going to need somewhere to hide until we can figure out how to get out of the country without getting killed or caught. See if they know a safe place."

"I need to talk to Juliette anyway. Tell her what we learned about Nelson Slade today."

"I wish you wouldn't."

"Why?"

"We can't prove it, and I'm not sure she would want to hear it even if we could. She's so invested in these kids of hers, if she really gets that Slade is the Black Mamba, there's no telling what she might do."

"I see your point."

"When we leave Senegal, she needs to come with us."

"She'll refuse, I know she will."

"If she won't go, we'll have to make her go. This country is coming apart at the seams. There's going to be a civil war and she can't get caught up in that."

"What about Fat Man and Little Boy?"

"They'll have to come too. With Slade whipping up all this antisemitic hate, they're in real danger."

"So much is happening. Maybe we should wait to burn the Grow."

"Soon as they harvest, they're going to want to ship, Cyd. That wilted, worthless crop of Cannastar could be on its way to South Africa by tomorrow."

"Little old arsonist, that's me," Cyd sighed, and glanced at the door. "Momo hasn't shown up yet. I think something has happened to him."

"He's tough and he's smart, that kid. I wouldn't worry."

"I *am* worried."

\*\*\*

Cyd spoke with Malick and Juliette and returned to the clinic just before midnight. Alex was seeing his last patient. They closed up shop, turned out the lights and left. Dakar experienced frequent power outages, and Malick kept several five-gallon cans of gasoline outside the building to run an old generator incase the electricity went out. Before heading for the Grow, Alex loaded two of the heavy cans in the back of the Land Rover.

The Cannastar plantation was just ahead. Alex switched off the Rover's headlights and gave the planted field a wide berth, circling the darkened area on a rutted wagon track. Cyd sat perched on the edge of her seat helping him watch for potholes and getting bounced around every time he hit one. "Malick, when I talked to him, said if they came to question him, he would say we left two days ago on a tour of villages to see patients and that we wouldn't be back for a week."

"Excellent."

The Rover hit a deep hole and both of their heads grazed the headliner.

"Juliette was great," she went on. "Apparently, she owns a second furnished condo in her building that she rents out and that just came vacant. She says as long as we stay away from the windows no one will ever know we're there."

"She's the best, bless her heart."

It was some time before they managed to reach the tree line on the far side of the open savannah. They parked, got out and Alex went around the back and opened the tailgate. He took out the two five-gallon cans of gasoline he'd brought from the clinic and carried them to where Cyd stood looking out at their ruined Cannastar farm. He set the cans down, looked up and saw tears in her eyes. He put his arm around her and together they gazed out across the grassy expanse of land. Behind them the jungle howled and roared and growled and cried, and the sounds carried far in the still night air.

She wiped at her cheeks. "It's all just so sad. We had such high hopes."

He hugged her to him. "I know."

A mile away on the small hill their storage shed was silhouetted in the moonlight. Next to it was the great tubular trunk of the baobab tree where they had first sat looking out over their land, and where Oumar sat during the day in his overstuffed throne. Between there and the jungle's edge where they were parked lay their field of Cannastar—which had already been harvested! The entire crop of water-starved plants had been pulled up by the roots and sacked in a pile twenty feet high that sat in the center of the hundred acres of cultivated dirt.

"You were right," Cyd whispered. "By this time tomorrow the whole lot will be bagged up and on its way to South Africa."

"Take your gas can," Alex whispered back. "At least with no wind and the plants being in the middle of a plowed field, there's no danger of the fire spreading."

Cyd tried to lift the metal container and set it back down with a heavy thud. "No way can I carry this thing across that field," she objected. "It weighs a ton."

"Leave it. They've made it easy for us by stacking it all in a pile. One can of gas should be more than enough."

Cyd helped him lift the remaining can and together they carried it across the open ground. "Nothing to it doing it this way," she whispered happily.

He put a finger to his lips for silence.

They had nearly reached the towering stack of Cannastar plants when they heard a loud snoring, looked up and saw the outline of someone sleeping in Oumar's chair.

"Looks like the guard might have drunk himself into a stupor," Cyd grinned.

"Let's hope."

Quickly, quietly, they circled the perimeter of the pile pouring gasoline from the can. When they got back to where they started, Alex took a box of matches out his pocket and offered them to Cyd. "Care to do the honors?"

"With pleasure."

She opened the box, struck a match and dropped it in the moat of gas they had made. Flames ran in a rapid circle, there was a great 'whoosh,' and the entire mountain of dried leaves, branches and roots went up in a giant inferno.

Cyd stood gaping at the colorful conflagration. "Now *that's* what I call a bonfire."

Alex took her by the arm, motioned urgently that they had to go and they started back across the field in a crouch. Behind them shouts of alarm went up. They turned and saw armed guards in various stages of undress bursting out of the storage shed yelling and running in circles.

"Maybe we should hurry a bit," Alex suggested.

"I think maybe you're right."

They ran for the car, and by the time they got there they were laughing so hard they could hardly stand. They got in, Alex started the engine and they looked back out through the windshield. A volcano of fire rose into the nighttime sky with tiny figures running around helplessly in the dark trying to put it out.

Cyd smiled. "Wouldn't you love to see Nelson Slade's face when he finds out his little money-making scam just went up in flames?"

Alex was about to say *Let's hope we never have to see his ugly face again* when the Land Rover's engine sputtered and died. He turned the key, the motor ground over but nothing happened. "Come...*on!*" he cried, trying it again with no luck.

"Have you checked the gas gauge?" Cyd asked innocently.

He looked down. "Shit, shit, shit!"

"Good thing that other can of gas was too heavy for me to carry."

"What?" He was so distracted with the predicament they were in he hadn't heard her.

"Five gallons should get us back to Malick's, no problem."

His face turned red with embarrassment.

"Just sayin'."

\*\*\*

Cyd and Alex returned to Malick's Children's Home at dawn tired and excited after their successful burning of the Cannastar field. They walked into the kitchen and were startled to find Momo sitting at the rickety table with Malick, Albert Dado and Juliette. The boy ran into Cyd's arms and she embraced him, laughing with relief. "Where have you been?" she cried. "We were worried sick."

"Momo came back an hour after you closed the clinic and left," Malick explained, his long face flushed with anger. "I called Juliette and Dado as soon as I heard what he had to say. We've been waiting for you."

Alex saw that the boy was filthy dirty and scratched up. "You'll live," he concluded after giving him a quick once-over. "Now let's have it. Where did you run off to?"

Momo looked at Malick who nodded encouragingly. "Go on, boy. Tell him what you saw."

"Momo was sweeping front courtyard," he began eagerly. "Gate was open and two men drive by slow . . ."

\*\*\*

Earlier that afternoon, a friend of Momo who lived at *Maison d'Enfants* as well was helping him clean the stone patio behind the gate. The other boy opened the gate so Momo could sweep the dirt he had collected into the street. A small, mud-splattered car was driving by. It slowed, came to a halt, a man jumped out and grabbed the boy holding the gate. Momo looked up in time to see his friend being thrown kicking and screaming into the back seat. He dropped his broom and ran shouting after the car, then stopped and stared helplessly as it sped away.

A small, battered bus painted in a frenzy of colors was just passing by. Momo grabbed the rear ladder, swung aboard, scrambled up the rungs to the luggage rack and flung himself on top of a swaying load of bags and boxes. Clinging tightly to the tie-down ropes, he watched the kidnapper's car weaving in and out of traffic just ahead. The load shifted, threw him to one side and he had to grab quickly at the ropes to keep from getting thrown off.

The car he was following was having only slightly better luck than the bus in making its way through the congestion of cars and trucks that snarled the road. The slow-motion chase went on until the car with the kidnapped boy inside went one way and the bus another.

Momo scampered down the ladder, jumped off and saw the muddy vehicle disappearing up a narrow street. Looking around in desperation, he saw a jumble of motor scooters parked at the curb, jumped on the first one he came to with a key, started it and wobbled off in frantic pursuit. The car kept disappearing and reappearing again in heavy traffic that continually got in his way. Momo jumped his scooter over a curb and took to the sidewalks, scaring pedestrians and knocking over vendor's stalls as he went.

The chase led him to a warehouse district crowded with trucks that were loading and unloading crates of produce and live, protesting animals. The truck traffic gradually thinned out, the road narrowed to one lane and the warehouses became seedier and shabbier. Ruined hulks of forlorn structures that were old and falling down rose above him on either side.

Up ahead, the kidnapper's car stopped at an abandoned warehouse with rusted metal sides and half the roof caved in. Momo skidded to a halt in the deserted street, got off and hid himself and his motor scooter behind a crumbling brick wall. Peering out, he saw his friend being taken out of the car still struggling and carried inside the building.

It was nearly midnight by the time Momo came out of hiding. He snuck up on the warehouse, hid beneath a wall lined with small, broken windows, rose up and looked through one of the jagged frames. Inside he saw two dozen boys sitting and laying on sleeping pallets in a barred cage that looked like a drunk tank in a jail. Food wrappers and garbage littered the floor and water dripped in puddles from the rusted rafters. His friend sat on a dirty pile of blankets with a tear-stained face staring at the cell's padlocked door.

Momo hurried along the outside wall until he found an unlocked door and eased it open. It creaked and he shrunk back. A group of five men were guarding the boys. They sat in a circle around a fire that crackled and popped in a metal drum. A cigarette that smelled like marijuana was being passed around. Momo snuck closer listening to their crude laughter. A pile of twisted, abandoned machinery was right ahead of him and he hid behind it. Pressing his ear to one of the small holes in the carelessly stacked equipment, he tried to make out what they were saying.

***

Momo paused in his story to cast a sheepish look in Alex's direction. "Momo had to *borrow* motor scooter. Sorry, Doctor Boss."

"Never mind that," Alex urged. "What did you hear?"

"Ride fast back here to tell," he answered emphatically. "Kidnapped boys being held for shipment. The Ship of No Return, it comes any day now."

Juliette had come to her feet and was anxiously pacing the floor. "This is too horrible for words. Those boys, they can't get on that ship. We have to stop them!"

Dado took off his wire-rimmed glasses and cleaned them on his handkerchief. "I can have a raiding party together by tonight." He carefully refitted his glasses back on the bridge of his nose. "Momo, son, you need to give me directions."

"Momo go with you!" the boy cried. "Show Dado everything."

"Momo is not going anywhere," Cyd ordered. "Momo is staying put until this thing is over and we have those other kids back. *D'accord* (all right)?"

The boy's shoulders slumped and he turned away to sulk.

"I'm in," Alex declared. "I can help."

Dado studied him a moment. "To have a doctor along would be good for the men and good for the boys. Be back here at Malick's right after dark."

"Somebody should be watching that warehouse," Alex warned.

Momo looked up quickly at the suggestion.

"A slave ship wouldn't dare show up in the daytime," Dado argued. "It will come at night and they won't dare to move the boys until then."

"Hope you're right." Alex clearly disagreed, but he wasn't in charge.

Juliette turned to Cyd and with great effort managed to bring herself under control. "Meanwhile, let's get the two of you back to the apartment and safely hidden. I assume you had a successful night?"

"They won't be looking for us yet," Cyd said with a grim smile, "but it won't be long."

\*\*\*

Later that same day, an angry mob formed outside the gates of the construction site where Fat Man and Little Boy were working on their osmosis plant. The two engineers were inside one of the construction trailers going over calculations for stress loads on the massive concrete foundations for the facility when they heard muffled chants coming from outside. They exchanged a worried glance just as a rock came flying through the window. The explosion of glass nearly gave them a heart attack.

"Jews go home!" came the shouts as a hail of rocks began hitting the trailer. "Jews go home! Jews go home!"

Peeking out the broken window, they watched in terror as the mob started pushing against the wire security fence that surrounded the property. More protesters waving homemade signs joined in and the fence buckled inward. Armed security guards hired to protect the site appeared but were badly outnumbered and had to fall back.

"Don't they know we're here to help them?" Fat Man cried.

Little Boy pulled his big friend away from the window. "Mindless mobs know nothing. Keep down!"

"Easy for you to say, keep down! They're going to kill us!"

"They're not going to kill anybody," Little Boy replied with little conviction. A heavy brick hit the trailer and they grabbed each other in fear.

"Damn that Slade!" Fat Man cried. "What did he think was going to happen with all that hate he's been spewing?"

A great roar went up as the fencing gave way and the mob surged through. Behind them a truck full of military personnel pulled up and the soldiers poured out.

Fat Man and Little Boy huddled in a corner clinging to one another as the door burst open and a SWAT team rushed in. "Avi Ben-Haim and Ashraf Shaviv!" the officer in charge announced as his men hauled the pair to their feet. "You are under arrest for crimes against the state!"

"Crimes against *what*?" Little boy screamed, struggling as he was handcuffed. "Are you out of your mind?"

The officer in charge referred to a piece of paper that he awkwardly pulled out of his pocket. "Genocidal conspiracy," he read aloud. "Attempted mass murder."

"You're hurting me!" Fat Man howled, lunging in a hopeless attempt to get free.

## Chapter Thirteen

### MOMO

The condominium where Juliette took Cyd and Alex to hide was several floors below her own. It was considerably smaller than her penthouse but well-furnished and perfectly nice. It too faced the Atlantic Ocean with an excellent view of the bay and the ferry boats making their daily trips from Dakar's waterfront to Gorée Island so the tourists could experience the infamous slave island and see the 'Door of No Return.'

Juliette let them into her rental unit and handed them the pile of Arab clothing she was carrying. They were resistant at first, then put on their new disguises and stood laughing in front of a full-length mirror.

"Lawrence of Arabia!" Cyd cried in admiration of Alex's costume. "All you need is a camel!"

"Alex of Africa, please." He made a dramatic flourish with the hem of his robes, covered his face with the cloth from his turban and addressed her in a slightly effeminate British voice. "As for you, Cydney Seeley, I'm afraid you look a bit like Bertha the Burka Dancer in that outfit."

Cyd peered out through the holes in her black hood and quoted from the movie, " 'I can't make out whether you're bloody bad-mannered or just half-witted, Major Lawrence.' "

He smiled arrogantly at himself in the mirror. "'I have the same problem, sir,'" he quoted back.

Juliette smiled at their foolishness. "Get some rest, you two. I'll check in on you later."

\*\*\*

When Nelson Slade learned that the Cannastar field had "accidentally" caught fire during the night and burned to the ground, he sat staring in silence. ". . . Find them," he said at last, blind with fury.

The messenger was frightened. "Find who, Mr. President?"

Slade looked up slowly. A vein pulsed in his forehead and his eyes burned red. "The Americans, you fool. We wouldn't want them to miss their own execution."

\*\*\*

The sun was just going down when Juliette reentered the condominium where Cyd and Alex were hiding. She went into the bedroom and found Alex adjusting the Arab *thobe* and refitting the *keffiyeh* on his head. Cyd was sound asleep under the covers. Juliette started to speak, but he put his finger to his lips and motioned her out of the room.

"Leave her be," he whispered, closing the door gently behind them. "She's exhausted."

"Did you get any rest?"

"Some."

"She's going to be very angry if she wakes up and she finds out you left without her."

"Better angry than dead. It's too dangerous for her to come."

"I know that, but she doesn't. Just find those boys and get them back before it's too late."

He started for the front door with a flourish, got his robes stuck on a chair and had to disentangle himself before he could go out. "Please make sure you're here when she wakes up. I don't want her to be alone."

"Worry about yourself, we'll be fine. I have to run back upstairs for a few minutes, but I'll be right back to stay with her.

The Organ Grinder Factor

\*\*\*

It was dark by the time Alex returned to Malick's orphanage. He got out of his Land Rover and saw five canvas-covered military transports lined up on the street in front of the gate. Two men were in the cab of each truck and the benches in back were all empty. Dado came out, got in the rear seat of a small car that was parked in front of the lead truck and motioned for Alex to join him.

"Where did all the trucks come from?" Alex asked as he got in with Dado. "And who are these men, they look professional?"

"*Aller* (go)!" the rebel leader ordered. His driver accelerated away from the curb and the line of covered trucks followed.

"The trucks are Senegalese army," Dado answered grimly. "As are the men."

"Senegalese army?"

"Slade has been paying his military in worthless script. He never had their loyalty to begin with, and now he can no longer buy it. The men with us tonight, they are still in the army, but they fight now for us, for a free Senegal."

"There's others?" Alex asked. "How many?"

"More all the time. We are the future. The only hope."

They rode on in silence for a while. The streets narrowed as they entered the dingy warehouse district that Momo had described. The truck caravan slowed, switched off its lights and traveled the remaining blocks in the dark. Rolling quietly to a stop, ten men with rifles got out of the five trucks and rallied around Dado, Alex and their driver. The scurrying, scratching sound of rats could be heard in the ruined structures around them.

Dado pointed to the most dilapidated of the warehouses, a rusted building with a partially-collapsed roof that leaned in on itself at precarious angles. His men nodded that they understood this was their target.

Alex shifted his rifle to his other shoulder. "It's too quiet," he cautioned. "Something's wrong."

Dado motioned for four of his men to go around the back of the warehouse, motioned four others to take the two sides and indicated the remaining three were to stay with him and Alex. "Wait on my signal," he ordered. "And don't let any of the children get caught in the crossfire."

Alex, Dado and three of his men ran in a silent crouch beneath the line of broken windows, then regrouped at the side door where Momo had entered. The safeties on all five of their rifles clicked off.

"Now!" Dado shouted, and they exploded through the door. The sound of three other doors being kicked echoed through the warehouse at the same time. Thirteen men rushed inside . . . and stopped, staring in silence at the waste and ruin of an empty warehouse. In the middle of the crumbling floor was a barred cage with the door hanging open. Filthy sleeping blankets, torn clothing and trash littered the cell's floor. All that could be heard was the water dripping from the rafters. Everyone looked at Dado.

"Boy's have been moved," he remarked dismally.

Angry and heartsick, Alex entered the empty cage. The stench was so bad he had to cover his face with the cloth from his headdress. A cell phone rang, breaking the silence. Alex realized it was his phone, dug it out of his pocket and answered. "Text me your location," he ordered. "And don't do anything until we get there. Stay put, do you understand me?"

***

## The Organ Grinder Factor

Earlier that morning, after not being allowed to join the raiding party that was going to rescue the kidnapped boys that night, Momo obediently joined his schoolmates for breakfast and pocketed the food. Afterward, he attended his morning Quran lesson where he was uncharacteristically silent. When class let out, he said he was tired from being up all night and went back to his bunk in the deserted dormitory. From there he slipped out a window, found his "borrowed" motor scooter where he had hidden it, pushed it away before starting it and jumped on.

Nobody paid attention to the boy carefully riding his motor scooter through the crush of trucks and commerce that crowded the busy warehouse district. Leaving the congestion behind, Momo entered the narrow street lined with abandoned buildings and quietly reclaimed his hiding place behind the brick wall. From here he had a perfect view of the old warehouse where the kidnapped boys were being held prisoner.

The day was hot and humid and as the hours passed, he dozed off and on, shaking himself awake each time. The sun finally began to go down and he pulled the sausage rolled in bread from his pocket that he had stuffed there earlier and sat listlessly eating it. Glancing around the corner of his brick wall in the failing light, he saw a truck pull up to the warehouse and stop. He scrambled to his feet and stared anxiously as twenty-four boys were quickly marshalled out of the building and loaded into the truck. The rear door rattled down and was padlocked, quickly grabbed his motor scooter and fumbled to start it. The motor caught and died. He frantically checked the gas and saw the tank was still partially full. His next try was more successful as a great cloud of black smoke backfired from the exhaust. He jumped on and shot away.

The truck was moving fast. Momo leaned forward over the handlebars to try and break the wind, but he was losing ground. They entered a popular, well lighted section of town where a profusion of colorful, outdoor cafes lined the street, and the traffic mercifully slowed. He caught up with the truck, then fell in behind. Desperate for help, he had no idea how he was going to contact anyone.

A man who was having dinner with his wife and three children at one of the sidewalk eateries had stepped away from his table and moved around the corner to telephone his girlfriend and tell her he would be a little late meeting her tonight. Momo saw him standing alone talking on his phone and bounced his scooter up onto the sidewalk. Hurling past, he grabbed the phone out of the man's hand and kept on going. The man howled in protest, but it was too late; the thief on the scooter was gone.

The kidnapper's truck approached the waterfront and slowed. Momo fell back, stopped in the shadows and got off to watch. The truck drove out onto one of the loading piers, and came to a halt next to a small, decrepit freighter with rust streaks down the sides. The cargo ship looked like it should have been sold for scrap long ago. It was flying a Somali flag, and a bunker barge was alongside pumping thick, heavy bunker fuel into its tanks in preparation for a quick departure.

Momo left his scooter and crept closer. A pile of metal shipping containers was stacked on the dock waiting to be loaded on another ship. He ducked behind them and watched as the rear door of the truck was unlocked and thrown open. The boys inside were prodded out by the men who had been holding them in the warehouse and herded up the gangway onto the ship.

Momo took his stolen cellphone out of his pocket and dialed a number.

Alex answered and listened to a breathless explanation of what the boy was witnessing.

"Hurry, Doctor Boss," Momo whispered. "The ship, I think, it is leaving soon."

"Text me your location," Alex instructed. "And don't do anything until we get there. Stay put, do you understand me?"

***

After Alex left the apartment to join Dado, Juliette slipped out quietly so as not to wake Cyd and took the elevator back upstairs to her penthouse to keep a scheduled phone appointment with one of her attorneys in Paris. When she entered, she saw that her avian caretaker was still in the aviary feeding her birds and cleaning their big wire cage. She smiled and waved and went into her office where she closed the door and sat at her desk. The desk phone rang immediately. She let it ring twice before picking it up.

Her Paris attorney asked if she had made a decision yet, and she said she was still thinking about it. The attorney repeated his earlier advice: instead of taking the money from the development group that wanted to buy one of her older buildings—money she didn't need and had no use for anyway—she should subordinate the land, and become a participating partner in the multi-use, high-rise complex the buyers intended to build. "Your return on investment will be much higher than any other investment we can find for you at the present time given the current interest rates."

"I just now made up my mind," Juliette announced brightly. "I am going to invest the proceeds on a big new orphanage and school right here in Senegal. One that will accommodate a thousand children and perhaps make a real difference."

The attorney was in the middle of advising her to set her emotions aside and be reasonable for once when her cell phone chirped that she had a text message. She looked down, saw it was from Malick and opened it. It read, "Emergency! Call immediately!"

"I'll have to call you back," she told her attorney, hanging up and hitting the speed dial for Malick's number.

He answered on the first ring. "You need to get Cyd out of there *now*!" he warned urgently. "My informant tells me you're being watched! They're coming for her!"

She cried out in alarm and started to hang up.

"Wait!" Malick said quickly. "One more thing. Fat Man and Little Boy have been arrested and taken to Rebeuss prison. They're being charged with attempted mass murder."

Juliette gasped. "Impossible. Positively ridiculous. You must be mistaken . . ."

"There is talk of a public execution."

"I don't understand. How . . .?"

"Slade," Malick said in digust. "That's how."

***

The elevator door opened with a *ding* on the floor where Cyd was staying and Juliette burst out in a state of near hysteria. A loud noise spun her around, and she saw men in military uniforms breaking down the door to her rental condo. Stifling a shriek of terror, she shrunk back into the elevator and started frantically pushing buttons.

***

Cyd was torn from a peaceful sleep as a nightmare of sound exploded around her. A blur of men all shouting at once were suddenly all over her with rough hands, pulling and tugging her out of bed.

"Alex?" she screamed. "Alex!" Her head hit the floor, and her arms were wrenched behind her. "What are you doing!" she cried. "Get out!"

"Cydney Seeley," a heavily accented voice commanded. "You are under arrest for arson. Burning public property is a capital offense."

"Are you crazy? Who are you?"

"Where is Alex Farmer?"

Her heart froze in her chest. "Who?"

"Alex Farmer!"

"Never heard of him."

Then something, a fist maybe, hit her in the face, and everything went black.

## Chapter Fourteen

### RETURN NO MORE

Dado and his men huddled with Alex and Momo behind the shipping containers where the boy was hiding when he telephoned Alex. Looking out, they saw the deck hands from the bunker barge finish fueling the rusted freighter, disconnect their hose from the fill pipe on deck, coil it back aboard their barge and motor away with a slow thudding of its motor. The engine faded into the night and was replaced by the heavy throb of the slave ship's engines starting up. Light from the ship's main cabin glowed yellow in the dark, reflecting off the mist, and a fog horn moaned from somewhere out in the harbor.

Dado pointed to the pair of armed slavers patrolling the deck of the ship and motioned to four of his men to go and deal with them. The four rose and started to sneak away.

"Hold up," Alex whispered harshly. "They should be preparing to cast off, and the ship is just sitting there. They're waiting for something."

Just then a sleek, modern, black-hulled motor yacht glided up to the dock, and its motor fell silent. Three men got out and climbed the ladder to the pier. One was considerably taller than the other two and dressed all in black. It was impossible to identify him other than by the grace and poise of authority with which he moved. Bow and stern lines from the yacht were secured to dock cleats by the two shorter men who hurried to catch up with the taller one, flanking him as he marched up the gangway and disappeared into the main cabin.

"Your men can secure the deck now," Alex told Dado, "but do it silently."

Minutes passed . . . and two soft thuds were heard aboard the ship. One of Dado's soldiers waved from the deck that all was clear. Dado and the rest of his squad crept out of hiding and hurried toward the gangway.

Alex turned to Momo. "You move from this spot and you're fired from the clinic, you got that?"

"Momo had to *borrow* cellphone. Sorry, Doctor Boss."

"You did good. Now stay put and don't move."

The boarding party joined the four men who had subdued the deck guards. Dado and Alex bent low and led the way along the deck toward the main cabin. The cabin windows were open to try and get some ventilation in the hot, sticky air, and harsh words could be heard coming from inside.

"It's a negotiation," Dado whispered.

Alex listened. "One of those voices I think I recognize."

Dado sent six of his soldiers below to try and locate the kidnapped boys. They disappeared through a heavy iron door to the interior of the ship, and his remaining men closed ranks behind him. Dado and Alex rose up cautiously to look through one of the open ports. Lowering themselves quickly back down, they exchanged a look of shock.

"Slade?" Dado asked. "The Black Mamba?"

Alex nodded bitterly. "Counterfeit, lying bastard! What kind of soulless devil. . .?"

Dado was no less appalled. "From that pile of cash on the table," he whispered, "it looks like our devil got a good price for the kids he sold them."

The tone of the voices coming from inside the cabin changed and became more conciliatory. Dado and Alex rose back up to see Slade stuffing the cash into a briefcase. He shook hands with the two Somali slavers in charge—ugly, skinny men with sunken, skeleton faces and protruding eyes—then turned abruptly and headed for the door. His two bodyguards followed on his heels.

Dado tensed and started to give the order to attack. Alex grabbed him and stopped him. "Let them go," he hissed. "You attack now, and you'll alert the whole ship."

Dado nodded reluctantly and they ducked behind a bulkhead as Slade and his men came out of the cabin and descended the gangway. The President, briefcase in hand, reached the motor launch first, and climbed down the ladder while bodyguards were untying the dock lines.

Dado looked for a moment like he was going to jump up and fire down on them, and Alex again had to restrain him. "Remember why we came," he rasped. "There could be a hundred kids in the hold of this ship. Above all else, our job is to get them out."

Slade's launch roared loudly to life and motored away . . . as muffled shots and shouts came from below deck. The noise of fighting grew louder as more shots were fired, and the rest of Dado's men stormed below. The two Somali slavers who had bought the boys from Slade came bursting out of the cabin with their guns drawn. Dado emptied a clip at them and nearly cut them in half. Alex gave him an approving nod, they scrambled to their feet, stepped gingerly over the bloody remains of the slavers and hurried below to join the others.

Below deck it was chaos. Smoke clouded the air, and gunfire echoed down the metal hallways. Alex had a clear shot at one of the other slavers but was forced to pull up to keep from hitting one of Dado's crew who had darted in front of him. His eyes burned from the smoke, and he rubbed to clear them as another Somali appeared not ten feet away. Vile and surly, he pointed his weapon. Alex dropped him with a single shot, vaulted his body, and was running when he saw Dado just ahead grab his leg and go down. Alex shot the man that shot him, and the shooting suddenly stopped. The last of the slavers lay dead at his feet.

Bending over Dado, he quickly examined his bleeding leg and determined that his gunshot wound was a through-and-through and hadn't nicked the artery. Tearing the hem off his robe, he pressed the wad of cloth to the seeping hole and told Dado to keep pressure on it. Then jumping up, he ran after the raiding party and caught them at the door to the cargo hold.

The lock was shot off, and Alex followed the others inside with a racing heart. A deafening chorus of frightened, high-pitched voices rose up in semi-darkness, and the stench of the prisoners crowded together without a toilet made him gag. Squinting in the dim light while covering his mouth he was able to make out rows of barred cages filled with ragged, underfed African boys staring out with huge, horrified eyes.

The locks were quickly pried off the cages and the doors flung open. The boys shrank back at first, then at the gentle urging of their rescuers realized they were free and rushed out in a shouting, screaming mob.

***

The horde of panicked youngsters swarmed out onto the main deck babbling at the top of their lungs in half a dozen different languages. Their cries of freedom filled the night as Dado's soldiers tried desperately to calm them. Momo ran up the gangway, spied the friend he had seen kidnapped from Malick's Children's Home, and the two of them fell together in joyful reunion. Alex was the last one up from below. He had Dado propped up under his shoulder, half carrying, half dragging the rebel leader along. Blood oozed from the wound in his leg leaving a thin dark trail along the deck.

The scholar-turned-revolutionary grimaced through clenched teeth as Alex lowered him down and knelt beside him. Dado glanced over at the two Somali slavers he had cut to pieces laying sprawled at awkward angles a short distance away.

"Could be worse," he observed wryly. His bloody hand was still holding the rag against his thigh. Alex pulled it away and reexamined the wound. Dado watched him anxiously. "My other men . . .?"

"They weren't stupid enough to get shot," Alex said. "Lucky for you, bullet wounds are my specialty." Fishing in his backpack, he dug out the emergency medical supplies he had brought with him, dressed Dado's wound and gave him a shot for the pain. Two of his men were standing by, and Alex handed their leader up to them with instructions to take him back to his medical clinic at Malick's where he could clean and care for the wound properly.

Dado started to say thanks, and Alex stopped him. "It's us who should be thanking you. Without you and your men, these kids would be on their way to a life of slavery right now."

Dado smiled peacefully. "Whatever was in that shot you gave me, doctor, is all the thanks I need."

Alex joined in helping to evacuate the last of the boys down the gangway and off the ship. The last of Dado's men was leaving when Alex stopped him. "Borrow a couple of those grenades there on your belt?" he inquired.

The man looked at him with a blank expression. Momo, who had been hovering nearby, stepped up and translated. The man smiled broadly, handed over the grenades and hurried off the ship.

Alex pocketed the small bombs and rubbed Momo's head. "You're a fine brave soldier, son. Can you do one more thing for me?" Momo nodded eagerly. "I want you to make sure every last one of these boys gets to the street, and into one of our trucks, as quickly as possible. Can you do that?"

Momo hesitated. "What Doctor Boss want with exploding eggs?"

"Doctor Boss going to make egg salad, now hurry."

Momo ran down to the crowd of men and boys milling about the dock shouting, "Hurry, hurry. Doctor Boss's orders! Into the trucks now!"

Alex crossed over to the other side of the deserted ship through a darkened passageway. Hurrying along the deck, he found the fill pipe that was used to fill the fuel tanks. A wrench was hanging from a chain next to the pipe. He picked it up, removed the bolts that secured the cap and threw it aside. Fishing the two grenades out his pockets, he gripped them in both hands, pulled the pins with his teeth and held them carefully over the open pipe. "Abandon ship," he muttered with a nervous grin and let go.

He managed to make it all the way down the gangway to the dock before the explosion rocked the waterfront and knocked him flat. Scrambling to his feet in a daze, he kept running and didn't stop until he reached the trucks. The boys lining the benches inside the military transports stared in open-mouthed amazement as a giant fireball rose to the heavens, then cheered loudly as it engulfed the ship and sent it slowly sinking to the bottom.

Momo ran up to Alex as he arrived. The two embraced and together turned to watch the fireworks. The heat from the fire was hot on their faces.

"Ship of No Return, it return no more," the boy grinned.

\*\*\*

Rebeuss prison was five miles from Dakar's waterfront, but the exploding slave ship sent dust sifting down from the mortar joints in the stone walls and onto the prisoners. Small windows high up near the ceiling provided the cells with the only light during the day, and no light whatsoever at night—except at the moment with the sky lit up from the burning ship. The fireball woke the entire prison. A great roar went up from the startled inmates who began bellowing and howling like frightened animals. Inside one of the cramped cells, Fat Man and Little Boy sat holding each other in fear.

"We're going to die!" Fat Man wailed, shaking uncontrollably. "I know it. We're going to die!"

Little Boy tried with little success to comfort him. "Something blew up is all, Avi. It was a long way off. We're fine."

"Fine?" the other moaned. "How can you say fine? I should never have let you talk me into this."

"Into what?"

"Coming to Africa in the first place!"

"We've had this conversation. Coming to Africa was your idea, remember? You talked *me* into it."

His enormous companion blinked rapidly. "What did we do, Ashraf? How did we come to this?"

"No good deed . . ." Little Boy quoted.

"We had a good life, didn't we?" Tears ran down his face. "Tell me we had a good life!"

"We did. We do."

"Don't lie to me, tell the truth."

"About what?"

"Will it hurt, do you think?"

"Will what hurt?"

"When they kill us? When they execute us?"

"You won't feel a thing, believe me."
Fat Man wailed like an air raid siren.
"You'll wake the dead! Be still."
"We *are* the dead. Dead men walking!"
Little boy smiled gently. "Not yet we're not. A lot can still happen."
"Like what, for instance? Do you love her?"
"What?" He was confused. "Who?"
"Juliette."
"I think so. I suppose. Why ask a thing like that now?"
Fat Man wailed again, louder than before.

\*\*\*

Nelson Slade was almost back to the presidential palace with his overstuffed briefcase of cash when he heard the explosion, turned and saw it was the slave ship that had blown up. He shrugged indifferently. He'd been paid and paid well for the boys he sold—and in Euros, not in the worthless currency of his country. What happened now was not his concern. The only inconvenience, he realized, was going to be finding new slavers to buy his next group of captives. *Shouldn't be a problem*, he told himself. *Plenty more slave traders where they came from*. Maybe he'd branch out this next time, expand his product line as it were, and start dealing in girls—although he couldn't imagine why anyone would be interested in a girl when they could have a boy.

The next morning when he heard the news that a hundred kidnapped boys had been rescued from the slave ship before it blew up, he saw it as an unexpected opportunity, as one more achievement that he could lay claim to in the speech he was writing. Not that he needed anything more to help unite his fractured nation. He had the American female arsonist in custody who had burned his Cannastar field. He had the two Israeli engineers in prison who were plotting to poison the nation's water supply. More than enough kindling to ignite another firestorm of hate. *Let them eat hate,* he thought. *The executions today will be glorious.*

## Chapter Fifteen

### VIVE LA SENEGAL

It was pandemonium inside Malick's *Maison d'Enfants* when the boys from the slave ship arrived at dawn in the trucks. Malick was everywhere at once trying to get the newcomers settled, washed and fed. He was so excited and thrilled with the success of the raid, he was practically in tears. The high-pitched voices of the youngsters all swarming about and talking at once in their native languages was deafening. Dado's men tried everything they could to calm them but with little success.

Not knowing where else to turn, Juliette had hurried to Malick after Cyd was arrested. She was there when the kidnapped boys arrived and tried to help, but her distraction over the arrest of first Fat Man and Little Boy, and now Cyd, was so great that she would stop in the middle of what she was doing and just stare. She turned to Malick, and in a vague and distant voice asked what was to become of all these refugee children.

"We are looking for people right now who speak their languages," he replied, his arms full of extra bedding he was carrying to the dormitory. "Those who wish to go home will be returned to their native countries. Those who wish to stay, we will arrange asylum for them."

Juliette was seized with sudden panic. "Alex, is he back? Where is he? He doesn't know about Cyd!"

Malick pointed to the infirmary with his chin and hurried off with his armload of bedding. "In his clinic. Fixing Dado's leg."

The Oxford scholar turned rebel leader lay writhing in pain on Alex's examining table now that the pain shot was wearing off.

"Hold still," Alex ordered, probing gently at the wound in his thigh. "I have to see if the bullet left any pieces in here." Digging deeper he added absently, "A bullet can pull outside material and debris into a wound and cause an infection, and you definitely don't want that." He glanced over at Momo who was watching in fascination. "Get me a sterile hypodermic from that tray over there and find the antibiotics. Look in the drawer on your left, there's a good lad."

"You got it, Doctor Boss!"

"There's no telling if there's any nerve or muscle damage," Alex told his patient. "You're just lucky the bullet didn't hit your femoral artery or you'd be . . ."

"With Allah right now telling him my job on earth isn't finished. Can you hurry it up?"

"I should start you on an IV." He raised his voice and looked around. "Anybody seen Cyd? I need her to help me start checking the health of all these new kids!"

"Cyd's been arrested," Juliette sobbed, bursting through the door. "The military, they came and took her. It's all my fault! I had no idea I was being watched."

"When?" Alex demanded, his heart in his throat. "How long ago?"

"Last evening after you left. I went back down to . . ."

His face turned red with fury. "Where have they taken her?"

"I don't know," Juliette wept. "Rebeuss prison, I assume. Same place they took Fat Man and Little Boy."

"Fat Man and Little Boy?" He was incredulous.

"The rumor is they were plotting to poison the water system. They're going to be executed."

"What do you mean, executed?"

Dado struggled painfully to sit up. "Slade will want to make an example of all three of them, you can bet on it."

"What are we going to do?" Juliette cried.

"Do?" Alex said coldly. "Get them back, that's what we're going to do!"

Dado tried to get off the table and fell back. "We need a military coup. If only Senegal was ready for one."

"Then make it ready!"

"How?" Dado groaned.

"You're the goddamn revolutionary, how should I know? Figure it out. All I know is, the woman I love, and two of the dearest men I ever met, are *not* going to die!"

Dado struggled again and this time managed to swing his legs off the table. "I'll start rounding up my men."

"You need to stay off that leg. Tell your men from now on they're taking orders from me."

"If your people are in Rebeuss prison, it's going to take an army to get them out, and you don't even speak the language. Shoot me up with painkiller, Doctor. We have to move!"

"Lay back," Alex ordered in frustration. "I still have to suture your wound."

"I'll help," Juliette offered tearfully.

Dado watched as she nervously washed her hands. "Has anyone told her yet who the Black Mamba is?"

"Black Mamba is Nelson Slade!" Momo announced eagerly. "We catch President selling boys to slavers!"

The color went out of Juliette's face, and she started to hyperventilate. "Oh no . . . Oh no . . . Oh no . . ."

Alex was injecting around Dado's entrance and exit wounds so he could stitch them up, his eyes on his work. "It was Slade alright. We had eyes on him. Unfortunately, we had to let him go."

"Let him go?" she shrieked. "You didn't kill him?"

"It would have endangered the mission," Dado informed her, relaxing a bit as the injections took effect. "Alex was right. Rescuing the boys had to come first."

She staggered and caught herself, then backed away in horror. "What have I done? How could I have been so naïve? The clues were everywhere . . ."

Alex was intent bandaging Dado's leg as quickly as he could. "You did it for the children, Juliette. You wanted with all your heart to get those boys off the street. It's not on you."

"I lied," she sobbed. "I knew what he was and I lied. To myself, to everyone! I helped get him elected for God's sake!"

Alex was no longer listening. His fear for Cyd was so great he could think of nothing else. He finished with Dado's leg and told him to keep it elevated.

Dado sat abruptly, swung both legs off the table and ordered Momo to hand him a pair of crutches that were leaning in a corner. The boy did as he was asked and handed them the sticks. Dado tried putting weight on his leg, and almost collapsed from the pain. Gritting his teeth, he tried again, and hobbled out of the infirmary shouting to his men that they were leaving. "We need to find a place to hide you until we can make a plan," he told Alex who was following him out. "They'll be looking for you, too."

"Let them look," Alex had grown frantic with rage. "I'm not hiding anywhere until I get Cyd back." He realized in his distraction he'd forgotten about Juliette. Malick was rushing by on his way to the kitchen, and he caught his arm. "Have you seen Juliette? She shouldn't be alone. Someone needs to stay with her."

"Juliette run away crying," Malik informed him as he hurried on. "I see her go out the door a minute ago. She gone."

# The Organ Grinder Factor

\*\*\*

A scattering of spectators lined the streets as a two-wheeled cart drawn by a scrawny horse rumbled past carrying the three condemned prisoners to their execution. A few shouted curses from the curb, and others seemed curious, but most remained silent as the tumbrel rolled by.

Standing in the cart with their hands bound behind them, Fat Man cowered behind Little Boy, and Cyd stared straight ahead in horror. A kangaroo court had convicted the three of them early that morning of the worst kinds of crimes. Their sentence was death by hanging.

Casting about desperately with her eyes, Cyd was only vaguely aware of the onlookers. She would have expected them to be jeering and cheering, frantic with hate. Instead, it was almost as if they had come to pay their respects. Bouncing along in anguish, she ducked as a rotten tomato hit the riot shield of one of the armed soldiers escorting the cart. She was too frightened to notice that their military escort was protecting them rather than allowing them to be harassed and attacked.

Under the previous administration, corrupt as it was, being a member of the military was a good job, a respected profession. It didn't pay much, but it paid enough for a man to house and feed his family. Under Slade's administration all of that had changed. Inflation had devalued the currency until a soldier's pay would hardly buy a loaf of bread. Many had already defected to find work, any kind of work, that didn't pay in Senegalese currency. Others were afraid to quit for fear of reprisal. Most of these had already lost their homes and moved in with relatives or were working two and three jobs just to keep a roof over their heads. Tensions were high, and anger and resentment were growing. Things couldn't go on as they were. It was a revolt waiting to happen.

President Nelson Slade stood waiting patiently beside a hastily erected gallows at the entrance to *Mosquée Massalikoul Djinâne* (The Paths to Paradise), Dakar's great mosque.

The imams who ran the mosque had been vehemently opposed to a heinous event like an execution desecrating their sacred grounds. In the end they had little choice but to allow it when confronted by Slade's soldiers.

Resplendent in his ceremonial robes, Slade repressed a smile at the thought of a tumbrel lumbering through the streets of Dakar. A wooden cart to haul the condemned had been a last-minute idea. If tumbrels were good enough for the French Revolution, they were good enough for him. He wished he had a guillotine instead of a gallows though, and sighed. A good hanging would just have to do.

Looking out over the sunny plaza while waiting to mount the platform, Slade watched thousands of onlookers slowly filling the open square. He was surprised there weren't more of them. A public execution of this magnitude had never been held in Senegal before, and by now he expected the square to be filled with spectators screaming in hate. There was still time, he told himself. Who in their right mind would want to miss a spectacle like this?

Slade had done all he could with his endless rhetoric to convince the masses that foreigners were the cause of most, if not all, of Senegal's recent problems, and the three foreign devils being jostled along in the cart just now were the very personification of that evil. The newspapers and media dutifully echoed his sentiments claiming Slade was loved and worshiped by all, stating that the country was solidly behind him. The truth was just the opposite. The Senegalese people feared and despised their president. They knew how bad things were, and they knew who was responsible. He had proven himself to be just another despot, a corrupt and tyrannical dictator whose sole goal was lining his own pockets at the nation's expense.

The closer the horse-drawn cart got to the mosque the louder the crowd noise became, but it was more of a murmur than a howl for blood. Cyd heard the muted sounds as they approached and thought it must be coming from worshipers assembling for prayer. She envied them their faith.

The tumbrel reached the outer fringes of the rapidly-filling plaza and started making its way slowly through the crowd toward the gallows where Slade stood waiting. The soldiers escorting the cart thought they were going to have to keep the crowd from tearing the prisoners to pieces. Instead, the spectators parted solemnly to make way for the condemned. Cyd looked down at them in passing. What she saw puzzled her. Some had their heads bowed in actual prayer.

The convicts reached the makeshift gallows, were handed down from the cart, marshalled up the wooden steps and made to stand in a line for all to see. Beneath their feet were three trap doors, and above their heads hung three ropes tied in hangman knots. While most in the audience seemed to be in dread of what they were seeing, others looked on in rabid anticipation, eager for the sight of falling bodies and breaking necks.

*Enjoy yourselves,* Cyd thought, searching desperately for any sign of Alex. *It's not your funeral.* Fat man was quivering in fear on one side of her and on the other side she could hear Little Boy repeating over and over, with little conviction, that everything was going to be alright. *Where is he?* she grieved. *Why hasn't he come? I can't go through this alone!*

Slade's long legs took him up the gallows' steps two at a time, and he emerged onto the platform to scattered applause. Behind him rose the five towering minarets and gold dome of the lavish mosque. Stepping up to the microphone, the President raised his arms for quiet, and a sullen silence fell over the square. Looking out in satisfaction, he noted that his heavily armed soldiers were positioned everywhere. So long as he had the military behind him, it mattered little what the people thought or wanted. He was a god and would rule as he pleased.

"Citizens of Senegal!" the President began in stentorian tones.

Alex, disguised in his Arab garb with a head scarf across his face and an automatic rifle hidden under his robe, was elbowing his way toward the platform from the back of the plaza. His fists were clenched in fury and his knuckles were white with rage as he pushed and shoved. Some resisted but most seemed to sense his urgency and moved aside to let him through. Over the tops of their bobbing heads he could see Cyd, Fat Man and Little Boy on the gallows looking small and unreal in the distance. Each time he caught a glimpse of them a bolt of fear went through him, and he redoubled his efforts to get there in time.

A squad of Dado's men surrounded Alex and were helping him clear the way. Dado struggled along hobbling at his side. Between them, they carried enough weapons to start a small war, but no one had the slightest idea how they were going to do them. Dado tried to force his way through, someone pushed back, and Alex caught him just as he was about to fall.

"Leg feels better," the rebel leader claimed, pushing on. "I think the antibiotics are working."

Alex, absorbed in watching the gallows through the crowd, knew how badly his leg must be swollen, and how much it must be hurting him. "You're a terrible liar, Dado."

Slade's voice boomed out over the loudspeakers. "Today we send a message! Foreign imperialists beware if you think you can come to Senegal, exploit our nation and plot to do us harm as these three have done! Behold your fate! This is what happens to foreign invaders!"

## The Organ Grinder Factor

Weak applause met his remarks, and the speaker forced a smile. "We come together today to make a new beginning!" More half-hearted clapping. "Together, we march forward into the future, united as one against our common enemies!"

The President paused to cast a confident glance at the hangman who was placing his nooses round the necks of the felons. Alex saw the heavy knot press Cyd's head to one side and grew frantic in his efforts to reach her.

"And there's more good news," the President went on as if bestowing yet another gift on the audience. "After much investigation and hard work, your government has located and destroyed the slave ship that has been stealing our children! The explosion you heard last night was your tax dollars at work! I am happy to report that every last child from that foul vessel was safely rescued and is being well cared for as we speak!"

The cheers and applause were more genuine this time.

Slade raised his arms again for silence. "We mark this day with the execution of the woman and the two Jews who came to our country to destroy the very freedoms and prosperity that Senegal so deeply cherishes. Their deaths mark a turning point in our history. One that will be remembered as the catapult that launched Senegal into the twenty-first century and beyond! *Allahu Akbar* (God is Most Great)!" he cried as a long drumroll began to rise and a thrill of anticipation went through the crowd.

Fat Man whimpered loudly. Little Boy closed his eyes in prayer. Cyd's eyes went wide with terror, and she screamed out Alex's name as the drumroll reached a crescendo. Slade raised his arm to signal the release of the trap doors, and the crowd held its breath.

From out in the audience Alex heard Cyd's scream and lunged forward yelling, "No-o-o-o-o-o-o-o . . .!" His cry reached her ears. She saw him rush the steps of the gallows . . . as a single shot from a high-powered rifle rang out.

The drumroll dwindled and died, and a ghastly silence fell over the square. The soldiers looked at one another in confusion, then turned to see what everyone was staring at. Up on the gallows President Slade had grabbed his chest and was looking down as blood poured out between his fingers. His eyes rolled back, a gasp went up from the crowd, and he fell dead to the floor. A pool of dark blood spread out around him.

Panic gripped the stunned audience as everyone searched for the shooter. Alex charged the platform, grabbed Cyd around the waist and flung the noose off her neck. The hangmen, confused but seemingly indifferent to the turn of events, dutifully removed the nooses from Fat Man's and Little Boy's necks. Fat Man began touching himself all over, afraid to believe he was still alive. Cyd fell shaking uncontrollably into Alex's arms, and he held her as she wept.

A hundred yards or so out in the crowded plaza a tiny woman had thrown off her burka and was standing motionless in her street clothes staring stoically up at the dead man on the gallows. In her hand was a smoking elephant gun.

Cyd looked out through tear-filled eyes and gasped. "Juliette!" she cried in sudden recognition.

An angry crowd was closing in on the assassin. Little Boy recognized Juliette at the same time as Cyd and rushed off the platform in a desperate attempt to reach her before the group of soldiers who were closing in on the petite French woman. One of soldiers got there first, and gently pried the rifle out of her hand. Another leaned in close and put his mouth to her ear.

"*Bon travail* (good work)!" he whispered.

Dado was waiting at the bottom of the steps as Alex brought Cyd down. "This is your chance," Alex told him in passing. *"Carpe diem!"*

"What?"

"Seize the day, you fool. Take the microphone. Tell them what they want to hear!"

Despite his wounded leg, Dado managed to bound up the stairs. Stepping over Slade's blood-soaked body and taking the microphone in hand, he cried out to the confused and frightened throng.

*"Vive la Senegal!"*

Dead silence.

"Long live Senegal!" he cried again, and the crowd took up the chant. Softly at first, growing louder as they went along.

*"Vive la Senegal! Vive la Senegal!"*

And the cry was heard throughout the land.

# Chapter Sixteen

## SO LONG SENEGAL

A Gulfstream GV (G-Five) sat on the tarmac of Dakar's *Aeroport International Blaise Diagne* with its engines whining loudly and its pilots going through their preflight checklist. The long-range, thirteen-seat jet had been sent by Fat Man's and Little Boy's engineering company to pick up a party of six—"and get them the hell out of there."

Albert Dado, scholar, rebel leader and current candidate for President of Senegal, stood at the base of the aircraft's boarding steps saying goodbye to his friends. The passengers clustered about him had to shout to be heard over the noise of the plane.

Alex was shaking Dado's hand. "Best of luck, Mr. President."

"Not 'Mr. President' yet," Dado replied dryly. "I still have to win the election."

"Oh, you will," Juliette assured him in a happy rush. "I know you will. And I'll be back for your inauguration."

"You will do no such thing," Dado ordered. "Right now, you're a national hero for ridding the country of an evil man, a real monster. And for your role in stopping the child slave trade in Senegal. Let's try and keep it that way, shall we?"

"There is so much work left to be done," she protested. "I . . ."

"I will see to it that Malick has all he needs to carry on his work."

"He needs me, the children need me . . ."

"You killed a man, Juliette."

Her face flushed red with anger. "And I'd do it again in a second."

"I'm sure you would," Dado assured her. "The problem is that people have a short memory. If you were to come back and things were to change, you could still be arrested and tried for murder."

She sighed and hugged Momo to her. "I suppose you're right. If I can save one boy, it will have to be enough."

"I'm going to go live with *Madame* Juliette in Israel!" Momo proclaimed proudly. "*Madame* says I can go to any school I want. When I'm old enough, I'm going to come back home and be Doctor Boss of my own clinic."

"And a fine 'Doctor Boss' you will be," Alex told him, rubbing his head. "I don't doubt it for a minute."

"This is what you want?" Dado asked of the boy, watching as he nodded enthusiastically. "In that case, I will arrange for a passport to be sent to you." He adjusted his glasses and turned to Fat Man and Little Boy. "Should I win the election, I'd like the two of you to return and finish your RO plant. Can I count on you for that?"

Fat Man shook his head vehemently. From the expression on his face, you would have thought Dado had suggested he throw himself under a bus.

"We'll make sure our company sends you some first rate engineers," Little Boy promised.

Dado repressed a smile and turned his attention to Cyd. "From Tel Aviv, you should be able to catch a plane to anywhere the two of you want to go."

"The question is where," Cyd lamented. "We still have to find a place that's safe enough and fertile enough to grow our Cannastar."

"We might be able to help with that," Little Boy offered.

"He's right," Fat Man added. "Let us do some checking when we get back to Tel Aviv."

Their goodbyes said, the passengers boarded the plane. Dado waved as the aircraft door was closed and the plane taxied away.

\*\*\*

The Gulfstream's twin BMW-Rolls Royce engines hummed softly in flight. Momo was up in the cockpit with the two pilots, his eyes big as saucers and asking a million questions. The others sat back in the main cabin. The spacious compartment was appointed with plush leather cream colored recliners and looked more like the presidential suite atop an expensive hotel than the interior of an airplane.

Juliette and Little Boy sat side-by-side holding hands, and Fat Man facing them on the other side of a burl wood coffee table making no secret of his jealousy. Juliette saw his consternation and smiled. "Avi, I'm not taking him away from you," she assured him. "Momo and I are just joining your little family is all."

Fat Man forced a smile.

Cyd turned in her leather chair to stare pensively out the window at the bone-dry savannah some twenty-five thousand feet below. Dotted here and there among patches of green were sparce stands of baobab trees.

"So long, Senegal," she said under her breath.

"What?" Alex asked, sitting beside her peeling a jumbo shrimp and sipping his first beer in a very long time.

She turned abruptly. "Been thinking. Since coming to Africa, I've been shipwrecked, jailed, chased, arrested, jailed a second time and almost hung for arson. You really know how to show a girl a good time."

"I try," he smiled, adoring her with all his heart.

She shook her head at the irony. "I absolutely love you, Alex Farmer."

"Why would you say a thing like that?"

"When I figure it out, I'll let you know."

His smile faded. "Cyd, if you wanted to go home right now, and forget this whole crazy business of trying to start a Cannastar farm at the ends of the earth, I wouldn't blame you."

She looked away. The thought of going back to her ranch and a daily routine of meaningless, endless chores, the thought of sitting on the sidelines and watching her life slip away before her eyes, sent shivers up her spine. So much had happened, and there was so much more to do. A restlessness burned inside her. A hunger for the new and different, for something of value to contribute to the world. An ordinary life was no longer an option; she wanted more! She wanted to discover all the wonders that were out there just waiting to be found. What those wonders were, she hadn't a clue. All she knew was a life of silent desperation wasn't for her. *I'd rather die having fun than die of boredom,* she thought, and looked bravely into the distance.

"Let's finish what we started, Alex. After that, we'll see."

## Chapter Seventeen

### HELMUT STEIN

The Sorek Saltwater Reverse Osmosis desalination plant was located on Israel's Mediterranean coast ten miles south of Tel Aviv. Fat Man and Little boy stood at the plant's observation rail enthusiastically pointing out the innovations they helped engineer to Cyd and Alex. They're guests, trying to appear interested, looked on in total confusion. To them, the vast complex of pipes and ponds and metal buildings made no sense at all.

"You must be very proud," Cyd smiled politely, shielding her eyes from the bright sun glaring off the acres of industrial infrastructure, and wishing she could get in out of the heat.

"We are, we are," Fat Man said. "The heart of the system uses sixteen-inch membranes in ten thousand modules with eight membranes per vessel to . . ."

"This place got a cafeteria?" Alex interrupted. "I'm starving."

"First, you have to see the remineralization process," Little Boy insisted. "It's so important to reintroduce calcium and other elements back into the water . . ."

"And the ingenious way we return the brine to the sea without harming the sea life," Fat Man added. "You definitely will want to see that."

"Where are you hiding Juliette?" Cyd asked quickly. "I haven't seen her since we got here."

Little Boy beamed at the thought of his new ladylove. "She's out shopping for a new condominium for us as we speak. She's also busy looking for a good school for Momo that teaches the sciences."

"I'm told I can have my own bedroom in their new place," Fat Man pouted.

"I envy you," Alex said. "Israel is a wonderful country. I just wish we could stay."

"Maybe you can," Little Boy suggested. "There's someone I want you to meet. A German scientist named Helmut Stein. His laboratory is in Jerusalem."

Cyd frowned. "German scientist?"

"He's a little eccentric," Little Boy advised. "A lot eccentric, actually. He's developing something that could change the face of modern medicine forever."

"How does that help us?" Alex asked.

"It doesn't," Little Boy replied. "But the man providing the research and development money for Stein's project, Ambrose Kilgore, he just might help you. If you can convince Stein of the importance of your Cannastar, if he gets the significance of what you are trying to accomplish and sees how much he has in common with you, he might be willing to refer you to his investor."

"Investor?" Cyd asked. "What kind of investor?"

"Ambrose Kilgore is allegedly one of the richest men in the world. Without Kilgore, Dr. Stein's project would never have been possible."

Alex was intrigued. "And you say we have something in common with this Dr. Stein?"

"You've been fighting a long time to get the medical community to accept your breakthrough," Little Boy replied. "Before long, Helmut is going to be fighting the same uphill battle to get his breakthrough accepted."

"What kind of breakthrough are we talking about?" Alex asked.

"Better I should let him explain it," Little Boy replied. "Unless you see for yourselves, you're not going to believe it. He's quite the genius, Herr Stein."

***

The directors of Fat Man and Little Boy's engineering company felt deeply indebted to Cyd and Alex for twice playing a role in saving the lives of their two valued engineers. To show their appreciation, they offered them a new Toyota SUV for their drive to Jerusalem and arranged for them to stay at the suite the company kept at the King David Hotel.

It was an hour's drive down Rt. 1 from Tel Aviv to Jerusalem. On the way, Cyd looked out the passenger window of the Toyota admiring the low rolling hills and rich, fertile land they were passing through. Farms and fields and green-growing orchards stretched as far as she could see. "Wouldn't it be grand to have a Cannastar farm in a place like this?" she mused.

"Not if they were always trying to lob rockets at us from behind those hills," Alex said.

"Doesn't look like a war zone to me."

"The whole region is a war zone, and Israel is ground zero."

"Hard to believe, looking at all this peace and abundance."

Entering Jerusalem, Alex used the Toyota's navigation system to negotiate the crowded streets, and arrived without getting lost at the 5-star King David Hotel. Cyd bought a guidebook at the gift shop as Alex was checking in, and they went up to their suite. Walking in, they were stunned and amazed at their luxurious surroundings. From their balcony, they looked out at the old walled City of Jerusalem. A mile or so away, the gold topped Dome of the Rock sat atop Temple Mount.

Cyd had been studying her guidebook. "Says here the Old City of Jerusalem is one of the most intense places on earth, and the heart of the Jewish, Islamic and Christian religions. Oh, let's go, Alex. I want to see it. There's so much history here!"

He put his arm around her and together they admired the view. "After we meet with this Stein character tomorrow morning, we don't have anything else to do. Might be nice to be tourists for once without somebody trying to kill us."

Just then a distant explosion lit the sky.

"What on earth was that?" Cyd cried.

He hugged her to him. "Nothing to worry about. Israel's Iron Dome protecting the city is all. Their mobile air defense systems shoot down four hundred or more rockets and artillery shells a year that are fired from Gaza and the West Bank. They say its ninety percent effective."

"Ninety percent?" She was appalled. "What about the other ten percent?"

"They don't mention that."

That night they made slow, lazy love in a king size bed with wonderfully soft sheets, slept better than they had in months, had a leisurely breakfast out on their balcony the next morning and watched as the teaming city came alive below them. At 9:00 a.m. they arrived for their appointment with Dr. Helmut Stein.

Stein's research facility was a modern structure of angular steel and glass attached to Kilgore Health, Jerusalem's newest and most modern hospital. The sprawling complex was a wonder of state-of-the-art medicine, and the envy of the Middle East.

They went in through big glass entry doors, passed through security, and were escorted down a long, sterile hallway to the laboratory where Stein was working. Their armed guard opened the door for them and let them in. They entered and stood staring at what looked like a cross between an operating room staffed by gowned and masked personnel, and a vast computer lab with rows of operators sitting at their terminals. Racks of servers bristling with colored wires lined the walls.

A short, stout, bandy-legged man in surgical scrubs looked up briefly from a group surrounding an operating table, put down what he was doing and approached the newcomers.

"Helmut Stein," he said, pulling down his mask to reveal a bristling walrus mustache. "You vould be the Cannastar people I vas told about. *Goot.* You are in time." He turned abruptly, and marched back to the crowded operating table. Cyd and Alex, assuming they were to follow, were stopped by a pair of nurses who gowned and masked them.

Stein pointed with a gloved hand. "You see here Antionette, a young chimpanzee vith congenital heart disease. Ve give her a new heart today, ya?"

Alex, greatly intrigued, looked over the scientist's shoulder. Laying on its back on the operating table was an anesthetized chimp. The hairy female was about five feet long and weighed about eighty pounds. Above the chimp's chest, rotating slowly in midair, was a computer-generated hologram of the animal's heart that he later learned had been created from three-dimensional x-rays.

"Open heart surgery?" Alex asked.

"You know nothing," the German declared. "Surgery, it is finished. *Kaput*! A thing of the past. Pay now attention and learn."

Cyd and Alex exchanged a look of disbelief. Is this guy for real?

"Start!" Stein ordered, and the surgical staff commenced a flurry of activity. "First ve insert a series of probes arthroscopically around the organ that is to be replaced." He glanced over at his guests, his blue eyes crinkling with intensely. "Long, skinny needles they look like, ya?"

Cyd nodded in bewilderment as a dozen or more probes were inserted into the chimp's chest in an elliptical pattern. Alex, with all his medical knowledge, was as confused as Cyd.

"Next," Stein proclaimed as if addressing a class of first-year medical students, "leads, they are attached to the ends of the probes. Through these leads pass massive amounts of data from the computers. Through these leads also pass the basic building blocks of the human body, the components from which all cells are made. These materials you see here in the reservoirs." He gestured behind him.

Cyd and Alex turned. Vats of liquid and semiliquid substances were lined up in a long row like barrels of bulk goods at a grocery story.

"Included, of course, are the four major classes of biomolecules," Stein explained impatiently. "Carbohydrates, lipids, nucleic acids including DNA and RNA, and proteins, ya?"

"Proteins," Cyd echoed.

"You know chemistry?"

"A little," Cyd replied. "In school I studied . . ."

"Then you should know that protein makes up eighty percent of all organs."

"Eighty percent," Alex repeated.

If Stein heard the sarcasm in his voice, he ignored it. "Available for infusion also are sulfur, phosphorus, oxygen, nitrogen, carbon—very important, carbon—hydrogen, potassium, sodium, chlorine, magnesium, fat and water, plus a few others."

"So how does it all work?" Cyd persisted.

Stein frowned up at her from under his bushy eyebrows. "You know, I assume, how a desktop printer vorks?"

"Reservoirs of ink?" Cyd ventured.

"Reservoirs of four basic colors, ya. Cyan, magenta, yellow and black. From these alone a computer prints all the colors of the rainbow, and all the colors that aren't in the rainbow."

"I guess," Cyd said.

"In the same way, from the reservoirs of the basic human components you see here, ve make every cell in the human body!"

"How do the components get to the organ?" Alex asked, genuinely intrigued by now.

Stein looked down at the comatose chimp, and fondly stroked her head. "The probes in Antoinette's chest generate a beam of light in the form of a broad, thin membrane. The membrane carries all the data from the computers and all the materials from the reservoirs. Starting at the top and looking something like the wide tail of a fiery comet, the beam moves down ever so slowly over the organ. As it goes, it grinds up and removes one microscopic layer after the other of damaged or diseased tissue and replaces it simultaneously with healthy cells that are exact duplicates of the ones it just eliminated."

Alex was stunned. "What about nerves?"

"Anything that is no longer functioning properly, it replaces. Healthy cells it does not touch. Only cells that no longer serve the host are replicated. The organ itself continues to function normally during the entire process."

Cyd remained skeptical. "How long does all of this take?"

"Mice and rabbit organs, we find, can be replaced in as little as one or two hours. To replace a fully functioning heart like Antoinette's, it vill take the Organ Grinder three or four hours."

"Organ Grinder," Cyd repeated doubtfully.

"You vould, perhaps, call it a garbage disposal *fräulein*?"

"I'll wait and see how Antionette does before I call it anything," she replied.

"The ultimate 3-D printer!" Alex exclaimed. "You replicate organs in place without having to surgically remove them first."

"*Wunderbar!* An American with a brain!"

Alex's eyes were full of humor and curiosity. "We Americans have our moments."

Three and a half hours later, Antionette's heart had been replaced and the procedure was complete. Stein stripped off his gloves, and his assistants began removing the probes from her torso. The chimp's chest was still going up and down, and according to the monitor, her heart was still beating.

Stein turned on his heel and headed for the exit.

"Ve have lunch now. You come. Ve talk."

The cafeteria served both the research facility and the hospital. It was after the lunch hour, so most employees and visitors had already eaten. The hard surfaces of the big, impersonal dining hall echoed with every sound.

Cyd and Alex sat across from the German scientist at a long, empty table. The food they were eating had been sitting in warming trays for hours and was dried out.

Stein pushed his plate away nearly untouched and wiped the bristles of his mustache with his napkin. "My friends Avi Ben-Haim and Ashraf Shaviv, they tell me about you. Fat Man and Little Boy, they are brilliant engineers."

"They are," Alex agreed. "You've heard of Cannastar then?"

"I vould not be speaking with you had I not. American politicians, they are so stupid to make it illegal. Your discovery and mine, they go hand in hand. Cannastar is almost as important to medical science as the Organ Grinder."

"Almost," Cyd repeated.

"We're looking for a way to grow it and distribute it to the rest of the world," Alex explained. "Some way that won't get us killed or arrested."

Cyd tried to sound sociable. "Little Boy said that the man who made your project possible might be able to do the same for us."

"Ambrose Kilgore," Stein scowled. "You know of him?"

Cyd and Alex shook their heads.

The German inventor steepled his hands and let out a long breath. "Much has been said and written about this man. How much is true, I do not know. Vhat I do know is that he is not to be taken lightly. You ask vhy. First," he went on as if talking to himself, "it is true. Without Ambrose Kilgore's money and support, the Organ Grinder would not exist. His name, you should know, is not Kilgore. It is Ishmail Marlovic. He changed it to Ambrose Kilgore to avoid being swept up in the ethnic cleansing during the Bosnian war. Masquerading as a Jew, he participated in the murder of over 100,000 of his fellow Bosnian Muslims. Following the end of the Bosnian war in 1995, he emigrated to Israel with the wealth he helped confiscate from the Muslims he helped kill. Once here, he became an Israeli citizen, and an international investor of legend."

"Legend?" Cyd asked.

A medical worker passing their table mumbled a greeting which Stein ignored. "Based on inside information, Kilgore made a billion dollars shorting the stock market ahead of the 911 attack in 2001. Being a Muslim himself despite his conversion to Judaism, he knew ahead of time that the Saudis were planning to attack the World Trade Center in New York. Then in 2008 in the midst of the financial crisis he is said to have made more billions with advance knowledge that the U.S. Congress was going to turn down the bank bailout bill. The stock market crashed, the housing bubble burst, and Ambrose Kilgore became one of the richest men in the world. Despite continued efforts to bury information and rewrite history about himself, his reputation as an investor with uncanny market skills is based solely on his ability to know the right people to bribe at the right time."

"This is true?" Cyd asked.

"Stories," Stein shrugged. "Who can say? His legitimate investments are public knowledge. In association with the Chinese government, he founded Yangtze.com, and became Amazon's chief competitor in the online retail market. His marketing plan for Yangtze was simple. With China as his partner, he was able to make the same goods, in the same Chinese sweatshops and slave factories, that the brand name companies made and sold on Amazon. By bypassing the companies everyone had heard of, he was able to sell the same products with Yangtze's name on them for half the price. His business grew to the point that just last year he was able to buy Amazon and absorb the entire company into his own organization. He is now the largest online retailer in the world."

Alex whistled softly.

"Kilgore is ninety years old," Stein went on. "He has the energy of a man half his age. His charm is as legendary as his investing. Many find him irresistible; I know I did at first. His wife, Jia Li, is a Chinese beauty queen half his age. The perfect porcelain doll, this woman. Hard and cold and elegant."

Cyd was stunned. "So many secrets."

"Ambrose Kilgore has attained the wealth of kings, and the woman of a thousand and one delights," Stein claimed. "And his only pleasure in life is ruining the lives of others."

"Your life included?" Alex asked.

"Not as yet. He has too much invested in my research to sabotage it. His only goal at this point is to live forever. He vill tell you. He considers his investment in the Organ Grinder his ticket to immortality."

"Immortality?" Cyd asked in confusion.

"You don't know? The Organ Grinder, in replacing organs that vear out or become damaged in some way, it has the potential to double the human lifespan."

"Cannastar should be right up this guy's alley then," Alex ventured.

"Perhaps," Stein nodded.

"What's your arrangement with him?" Cyd asked. "What did you have to promise him to get him to invest in your Organ Grinder?"

Stein sighed. "Ambrose Kilgore is a venture capitalist. If he invests in something, he wants to control it."

"Kilgore has controlling interest in the Organ Grinder?" Alex was shocked.

"Seventy percent. A deal with the devil, I'm afraid. He keeps pressuring me to test it on human beings. *Pfui!* The Organ Grinder, it is still in the experimental stage I tell him. Not until I am one hundred percent certain it is safe would I even consider testing it on a person. Too risky. Absolutely irresponsible. If he keeps pressuring me though, if he threatens to terminate my research, I do not know what I will do."

"Set up a meeting," Alex said abruptly.

Cyd touch his arm. "Alex!"

"Thanks to Kilgore, Dr. Stein here has been able to create something of monumental importance. No harm has come of it. I would at least like to meet with the man and hear what he has to say."

Stein let out a long breath. "As you vish then. Leave your number. Kilgore vill be most anxious to see vith his own eyes the results of Antoinette's heart replacement. I vill ask, vhen he comes, if he vill speak vith you. Perhaps he vill do for you what he has done for me, you never know."

## Chapter Eighteen

### HOLY WAR

With nothing to do but wait until they heard from Stein about their meeting with Kilgore, Cyd was anxious to explore Jerusalem and begged Alex to come with her to see the Old City.

Guidebook in hand, she led him into the ancient walled district through the Damascus Gate. The clash of Middle Eastern music, voices and noise rising from the Muslim Quarter enveloped them immediately. A profusion of vendor's stalls and throngs of visitors crowded narrow, cobbled streets and stair-stepped alleyways that had seen over three thousand years of human history. Overwhelmed by the sights and sounds, they strolled along under colorful arrays of clothing and fabric hung over walkways that shaded the busy, crowded bazaar below.

At an intersection, they stopped to let a funeral procession pass. A furious mob of mourners went rushing by carrying a small wooden coffin above their heads while wailing and shouting for revenge. The angry wave of sorrow and misery rose and fell, and in its wake hung silence as the tide moved on and the noisy business of the living rushed back in to fill the void.

The press of smelly bodies and the cacophony of different languages all being spoken at once were beginning to give Cyd a headache. She grew tired of merchandise being shoved in her face by frenzied merchants and told Alex she wanted to see one of the holy sites.

They entered the Christian quarter and were relieved to see fewer vendor stalls cluttering the streets. The convoluted thoroughfares were a little wider here and the crowds a little less intense. Above and around them on all sides rose age-stained, sun-washed buildings that looked older than Christianity itself. Up ahead they could see the Church of the Holy Sepulchre and minutes later found themselves in its outdoor courtyard.

The church's open-air plaza was about twice the size of a basketball court and enclosed on three sides by a confusion of ancient stone walls with blocked-up windows, doors and archways from abandoned remodeling projects. The rough rock walls and foot-worn paving stones reminded Alex of the oppressive fortifications of a prison, cold and hard and depressing.

"See that?" Cyd said, pointing excitedly to an eight-foot wooden ladder on an upper ledge at the far end of the courtyard. The ladder leaned casually against a wall beneath one of two arched windows. Under the two windows were twin arched entrances to the church. One of the entrances had been sealed off with blocks of stone. Visitors were passing in and out through the other one.

"It's called the Unmovable Ladder," Cyd read from her guidebook. "It's been in exactly that same place since the early eighteen-hundreds."

"Must be a union job," Alex mused, eyeing the silent monks that stood guard around the plaza wearing slightly different styles of robes. Their task was apparently to watch the tourists and make sure they behaved themselves. In reality, they seemed more interested in keeping an eye on each other than on the sightseers.

"Half a dozen orders of Christian clerics run this place under something called the Status Quo," Cyd went on happily, her nose in her book. "For anything to get fixed, repaired or changed around here, they all have to agree on it. The monks can never agree on anything, so nothing ever gets fixed. Parts of the church are falling down, but if any one religious order were to touch anything without the consent of the others, a war would break out. Every few years the Status Quo falls apart, a riot erupts among the clerics and the police have to be called in."

Alex was amused. "Cooped up like they are, the boys probably need to let off a little steam now and then."

"Be nice," Cyd chided, leading the way toward the entrance while referring again to her guidebook. "Couple of hundred years ago, the church had a fire and dozens of people were trampled to death trying to get out this very door."

Inside, candles flickered in the soft light and a reverent hush hung over the cool stone interior. A crowd of worshipers were worshipfully touching and taking selfies around a large, raised slab.

"Stone of Anointing," Cyd read as they passed. "Christians believe it's where Jesus' body was prepared for burial. The Crusaders apparently had it or found it in the twelfth century, but the stone wasn't actually installed here until the early nineteenth century."

They walked on past a busy staircase that led to the top of the hill that the church was built on. "That leads to Golgotha," Cyd read. "Traditional site of the crucifixion. We absolutely have to see that before we go."

Alex noticed other monks guarding the beautiful, gilded altars. Once again, he thought they seemed more focused on guarding one another than the treasures they were assigned to watch.

The further Cyd went, the more enthralled she became in the shrine. Passing out of the church they entered a large rotunda with sunlight streaming down from a dome in the ceiling. A smokey beam of celestial light fell on a tall crypt in the center of the floor. The rectangular monument was adorned with columns, ornaments, cornices, inscriptions and paintings. A crowd of worshipers were patiently waiting to enter, some with their heads bowed in prayer.

"That's the Edicule where the tomb is," Cyd whispered. "I want to..."

Alex's phone rang. He answered and leaned aside in an effort to hear. "What? Can't hear you. Have to call you back!" He hung up and turned to Cyd. "That was Stein."

She nodded absently. "All this history makes me think how arbitrary and fleeting life is. I've never prayed. I'd like to try."

Alex gave her a quick kiss. "Follow your heart. I'll be outside in the courtyard where there's better cell reception. Let's hope our German friend has some good news for us."

Cyd nodded and solemnly joined the others waiting in line.

The warm sun was a welcome relief on Alex's face after the cold interior of the stone church. He leaned against a wall in a distant corner of the courtyard, checked his phone for bars and dialed Stein back. While waiting for him to answer, he glanced around the plaza. The monks guarding the area were filing out at the end of their shift leaving the place deserted for the moment.

Stein answered with a triumphant shout. "Antoinette, she is recovered!" he cried. "The chimp is eating and drinking and walking. I called Kilgore and told him the good news. He vill be here tomorrow morning at ten to see for himself the results."

"Did you get a chance to tell him about our Cannastar?" Alex asked.

"I did indeed. He can't vait to meet you."

"We'll be there," Alex promised. "Thanks." While he was talking, he watched a lone black man, thin as a spear and nearly seven feet tall, come out of the church and glance around for prying eyes. His head glistened with corded scars, but his skin was so dark his features were almost indistinguishable.

Failing to see anyone, the African scaled the church's stone façade like a long-legged spider going up a wall. In an instant, he was on the stone ledge above the entrance to the church that had been sealed in stone. Reaching out, he laid the Immovable Ladder over on its side and was down the wall again in a flash. Turning to go back in, he saw that he was being watched.

The two men stared.

Alex wasn't about to get involved in something that didn't concern him, but he didn't like what he'd seen, either. The next shift of monks began filing silently out of a side door. The African saw them and ducked back inside the church. None of the clerics spoke as they took up their assigned positions.

And then it happened.

An Eastern Orthodox monk noticed that the Unmovable Ladder had been moved. Outraged, he ran across the courtyard shouting and pointing up at the ledge above the entrance, angrily accusing the Armenian Apostolic monk who stood beneath the ledge of moving the ladder. The Armenian looked up to see what the Greek was so upset about. Before he could look back, the Greek sucker-punched him in the head. A Roman Catholic monk saw what happened and attacked the Greek thinking he was the one who had moved the ladder. Coptic, Ethiopian and Syriac monks came pouring out of the side door blaming Greeks, Armenians and Franciscans for the crime, and within minutes the plaza was a writhing sea of black-and-brown-robed men pummeling each other with their fists.

Word of the brawl spread like a church fire and reinforcements from the various orders rushed to join the fray. A crush of tourists poured out, jamming the entrance in a frantic effort to witness the brawl. Then, a monk took a swing and missed and punched a retired cop from Chicago in the mouth. The cop instinctively swung back and inadvertently blindsided a dentist from Lebanon. A woman screamed, and before long the stones in the courtyard ran red with the blood of nations.

Alex inched his way along the rock wall trying to reach the entrance in time to protect Cyd when she came out. Arriving at the entry, he had to press himself against the stones to keep from getting trampled by the tourists who were still pouring out. Sirens wailed in the distance growing louder by the minute. The monks swarming the plaza were too busy beating each other to a pulp to notice.

The doorway finally cleared and Cyd still had not appeared. Frightened that something had happened to her, Alex was about to dart inside when she emerged laughing happily with another couple. Following close behind them was the black man who had moved the ladder.

Alex gathered Cyd in his arms in relief.

"I just met the two most wonderful people," she exclaimed, casting a concerned glance in the direction of the melee. "Alex, this is Sam, Nikki and their first mate Tashtego. They have a boat. A salvage ship that's anchored in Haifa. They're treasure hunters, isn't that exciting?"

"Church thieves is more like it," Alex said, taking her arm. "We need to get out of here, Cyd."

"We're not here to steal anything," the man Cyd had introduced as Sam stated flatly. Thirty-five years old, blond haired and fair complected, Sam Sorini had the broad shoulders and long, whippy arms of a natural swimmer. His narrow face and chiseled features were deeply tanned. Behind the subtle humor in his ice blue eyes was something cold and dangerous.

"This fellow, what's his name, Tashtego?" Alex said, locking eyes with the African. There was an air of violence about the silent black man, savage and dangerous. "He's the one that moved the ladder and started this whole mess. I'm guessing it was to create a diversion for you."

"It was," the girl admitted freely, laughing in delight. "A diversion so we could find what we were looking for without the monks bothering us." Anna Nicole 'Nikki' Perez was a beautiful young woman from the island of Dominica in the Caribbean. She had straight black hair that hung to her waist, skin the color of coffee with cream, amber eyes that looked like they could see in the dark and a small gap between her two front teeth—which on her looked cute. At the age of twenty-five she still wore horn-rimmed glasses that were too big for her lovely face and walked with the awkward gait of a schoolgirl carrying her books and clarinet to class.

"Supposedly," Nikki went on enthusiastically, "it was hidden in the walls when the church was built in the fourth century. The man who hid it there had nothing to do with the church, by the way. He was a stone mason."

"I assume you found it," Alex said, moving Cyd along without taking his eyes off the African.

"Tashtego, stand down," Sam ordered. "The gentleman has gotten the wrong impression of us."

"What did you take?" Alex insisted.

The treasure hunters didn't answer.

"That's what I thought. Cyd, we need to go. Now."

The police arrived and began wading in among the hordes of bloody combatants, many of whom had begun milling about in dazed confusion. Those with fight still left in them were handcuffed, and they all were given a stern warning. While this was going on, a pair of monks, too old to fight, appeared with an aluminum extension ladder. They set it up against the wall at the back of the plaza and the younger of the two, a man of about eighty, painfully climbed the rungs and set the wooden ladder back up in the exact position it had been before the atrocity occurred. Several monks looked up from the courtyard and fell to their knees in prayer.

Cyd and Alex had gotten well away from the church by this time, but he still was gripping her arm.

"Alex, you're hurting me!"

He quickly let go, checking over his shoulder to make sure they hadn't been followed. "Sorry. Don't know if Israel has an extradition agreement with the U.S. or not, but I sure don't want to find out. We can't afford to get arrested and have them run a background check on us."

"You were rude to my friends back there."

"Your friends rob churches."

"You don't know that."

"Okay. They just enjoy creating riots and digging in church walls."

She made a mocking face. "What did Stein have to say?"

"We have an appointment with Kilgore tomorrow morning at the lab."

"That's terrific. How's Antoinette?"

"Stein says she's up and doing fine."

"How wonderful! I'm so happy for her."

## Chapter Nineteen

### AMBROSE KILGORE

The next morning, Cyd and Alex arrived at Stein's laboratory for their appointment with their potential investor. They parked in the highrise garage that served both the lab and the hospital and walked to the research facility's big glass entrance next door. Going in, they couldn't help noticing the long black limousine parked illegally in front of the entrance. A liveried driver leaning casually against the fender smoking a cigarette.

Once inside, they went through security and were escorted down the long hallway to the laboratory where they had observed the Organ Grinder procedure two days earlier. They entered and were met with the loud, insistent screeches of a chimpanzee. Following the sound, they saw Antoinette in her cage gripping the bars, jumping up and down and crying out with a big-lipped grin. The operating table, where her heart had been replaced, sat starkly vacant in the middle of the room now surrounded by a cold confusion of wires, tubes and electronics.

Helmut Stein and Ambrose Kilgore stood to one side trying to talk over the noise that the chimp was making. They looked up when Cyd and Alex entered, Stein motioned them over and curtly introduced them to his guest.

Kilgore's tiny mouth formed a thin, humorless smile. "I have been looking forward to meeting you," he intoned in a slight Bosnian accent. "Doctor Stein here tells me you are the Cannastar fugitives from America." He looked like a badly preserved mummy in the last stages of whatever killed him. His gray hair was pulled back in a stingy ponytail, his round face and puffy hands were covered in liver spots and his eyes were red and watery. Heavy bags of wrinkled skin hung under his eyes.

"And you would be the investor he's told us about," Alex replied, gripping the man's icy hand in a friendly handshake.

"It is a tremendous responsibility having so much money," Kilgore sighed. "I have dedicated my life to doing what I can to help end pain and suffering around the world. I would like to think there is still more I can do."

"There is," Alex said. "That's why we're here."

"Then let us talk," Kilgore agreed. "Doctor Stein's success with the Organ Grinder gives me hope that his is not the only miracle out there."

Antoinette screeched loudly. Cyd glanced over her shoulder and gave the chimp a compassionate smile. She did not have a good feeling about Kilgore and wanted to get as far away from him as possible. While he and Alex began their conversation, she wandered over to the primate's cage. The moment she arrived the chimp began happily grunting, hooting and jumping up and down.

Cyd turned to one of the white-coated lab assistants. "Can she be let out?"

"She's very tame," the lab assistant assured her, unlatching the barred door.

Antoinette bounded into Cyd's arms and threw her hairy arms around her neck with a cry of delight. Cyd laughed, bouncing her on her hip like a small child. "Look at you!" she exclaimed. "You look like you've never been sick a day in your life!"

The chimp squealed, jumped out of Cyd's arms and began doing backflips in the middle of the floor. Cyd clapped in delight. Antoinette did another flip, took Cyd's hand, and led her on a somber tour of the lab.

Listening to Kilgore, Alex was encouraged by how much the billionaire seemed to know about Cannastar and its ability to cure viral diseases. "Our primary goal," he told his potential sponsor, "is to establish a plantation in a safe and friendly place, a farm where we can grow enough Cannastar to supply the rest of the world. Our Grow back home can barely keep America supplied as it is."

"I am very interested," Kilgore admitted. "Before we can go further, however, I must speak with my contacts in the Israeli government. If they chose to serve the pharmaceutical companies as your government did by making it illegal, then my hands are tied and I can't get involved. If, however, the Israeli government chooses to serve humanity rather than Big Pharma, then I believe we can make a fortune together."

Alex hesitated. "We're not in it for the money."

"Let's cut the bullshit, shall we? Everyone is in it for the money." Kilgore saw Alex's offended expression and laughed. "You look surprised, Doctor. Charity is a myth; altruism is a lie. Nobody does anything if there isn't something in it for them."

"Whatever you say. All Cyd and I want is for sick people to get well without having to go bankrupt with medical bills in the process."

"And all I want is for my Yangtze.com customers to live happier, healthier lives, and have more money to spend on our cradle-to-grave goods and services. It's a win-win, wouldn't you agree?"

Alex was distracted by the chimp who had resumed her backflips and was doing them faster and faster.

"Two miracles in one day!" Kilgore declared. "The Organ Grinder that's ready to be tested on human beings, and the Cannastar that we already know saves lives. Text me your number, Doctor Farmer. I'll check with my people and get back to you in a few days."

Alex watched with growing concern as Cyd tried to slow the frantic chimp down. Kilgore gave him a number and he entered it in his phone.

Just as he hit 'send', Antoinette let out a terrible scream, had a seizure in midair and fell dead on the floor.

Cyd cried out and fell to her knees in horror, stroking the head of the lifeless primate. Kilgore looked on indifferently as anxious lab attendants rushed to investigate. Cyd was pried away and forced to stand. Alex took her in his arms where she began to weep, staring over his shoulder at the tragedy.

"Antoinette had only a very short time to live in any event," Stein told Cyd consolingly. "Her heart disease was extremely advanced even before the procedure. She gave her life for science. This is not a failure. We will do a thorough autopsy, find out exactly what caused the problem and correct it."

"See that you do," Kilgore ordered in disgust, heading for the door. "And be quick about it."

Stein called after his retreating back. "This is exactly vhy ve experiment on animals, Ambrose, and not on human beings!"

"I'll be in touch," Kilgore told Alex as he went out.

## Chapter Twenty

### LETTING GO

Cyd and Alex slept late the next morning and lingered over a leisurely breakfast of coffee and pastries they had sent up to their room. During the night, Cyd had dried her tears, put her sorrow over Antoinette's death aside and managed to get a good night's rest. She took a last sip of coffee, stood and told Alex she was going to take a shower. "Then, I want to continue on with our tour of the city."

He didn't respond.

"Please? We've got nothing else to do until we hear from Kilgore."

"Sure," he shrugged. "Why not?"

Next on her list was Temple Mount. "Site of more religious conflict and bloodshed than any other thirty-five acres on earth," she read from her guidebook while vigorously drying her hair. "Only Muslims can actually go inside the dome, but we can still visit the mosque and the Wailing Wall. Won't that be fun?"

"Can't wait."

His lack of interest frustrated her. "You don't have to be religious, you know, to appreciate the history and culture in this place."

They approached the Old City and were about to enter through the Mughrabi Gate when they heard loud shouting and crowd noises coming from inside. An Israeli officer denied them entry, telling them to turn back. "A dangerous riot is going on at Temple Mount," he warned sadly. "Jews and Muslims, Muslims and Jews. Palestinians and Israelis always hating each other. Already today we have two reported dead."

Disappointed, they turned away and for the rest of the day visited places of interest in and around the ancient city. By evening, they were both exhausted.

"I feel like I just walked the full length and breadth of Israel," Alex complained over dinner at their hotel. "My feet are killing me."

"A good night's sleep will fix you right up," Cyd promised. "Tomorrow I want to go to Bethlehem and see the Church of the Nativity." She saw his dismay and laughed. "If you don't want to go, I'll go by myself."

"Can we at least take a tour bus?"

"I don't like being crowded in with a bunch of yokels. Don't forget your passport though. Guidebooks say we have to go through a checkpoint to get into the West Bank."

The next morning, they again slept in. The sun was high in the sky by the time they got on the road and were headed south to Bethlehem on Route 60 in their borrowed Toyota. According to Cyd's guidebook, the curving mountainous road to Bethlehem had the grim nickname of 'Blood Highway' because of its reputation for frequent shootings, stabbings, car-rammings and clashes between Israelis and Palestinians. A high, protective concrete wall ran along one side of the highway most of the way to shield it from Palestinian gunmen.

The ominous wall overhanging the freeway made Alex nervous. "Maybe we should turn around," he said. "We can go back and spend the day at the hotel swimming pool eating and drinking our way to spiritual nirvana."

"Don't be silly," Cyd argued. "Millions of people use this highway all the time. If Kilgore comes through and we end up starting a big commercial Grow, we'll be too busy for sightseeing." She put her hand on his collar and smiled at him. "This means a lot to me, Alex. You don't really mind, do you?"

Her touch warmed his heart. He glanced her way to smile back, and that's when the shoulder-fired missile, launched from somewhere in the West Bank, got through Israel's Iron dome and landed in the road in front of them. The blast blew a crater in the highway and launched their Toyota in the air. The SUV flipped, rolled and landed in a tangled wreck among a pile of other cars and trucks that had gotten caught in the blast.

Alex's ears were ringing. He shook his head to try and clear it, and realized they'd been in some kind of explosion. He was cut and bleeding but was able to move his arms and legs, so he assumed he wasn't that badly hurt.

Looking over, he saw Cyd hanging limp in her seatbelt. Her airbag hadn't deployed! Horrified, he reached to check her pulse.

"Cyd, it's alright! You're going to be okay. Open your eyes . . . oh, God!"

Her eyes fluttered and she gasped. "Alex, I can't breathe! Feels like an elephant on my chest . . . Stomach hurts . . ." Her voice was thin. There was panic in her eyes.

*Liver or spleen,* the doctor side of him thought objectively. The rest was screaming in terror. She coughed and winced painfully as sirens began to wail in the distance. *Collapsed lung. Need a needle or a chest tube.* Her eyes fluttered closed, and blood trickled from the corner of her mouth. *Internal bleeding!* He quickly checked her chest for punctures and saw only purple bruises. *Blunt trauma. Organs crushed or punctured . . . Blood tests . . . CAT scan!*

\*\*\*

Alex ran alongside Cyd's gurney as EMTs rushed her from an ambulance into the ER at Kilgore Health.

"Transfusion!" he shouted. "Start an IV! X-rays stat!"

Nurses struggled to restrain him.

"Sir, we've got this. You'll have to wait in the waiting room . . ."

"I'm an ER doc! I know trauma!"

"So do we, doctor."

The doctor on call took charge, checking Cyd's eyes with a penlight while ordering a battery of tests. "Please," he told Alex. "Have a seat. We'll let you know as soon as we know anything."

Alex sat in a room full of hurt and distraught-looking people staring desperately into space and jumping up every five minutes to demand an update from the nurse's station. Time stood still. At some point, he looked up and saw Helmut Stein standing before him.

"I came as soon as I heard," the German scientist said. "I am so sorry, Doctor Farmer. If there is anything . . .?

Alex shook his head.

"Vhat vord?"

He again shook his head in desolation, then looked up quickly as a door opened and the ER doctor came out stripping off his gloves. Alex saw to his horror that his scrubs were spattered in blood.

"I'm afraid there is nothing we can do," he told Alex gently. "There is too much trauma."

Alex came to his feet. "Nothing?" he raged. "What do you mean, nothing? What do the films say?"

"Extensive damage to the lungs and liver. Kidney damage. Her injuries are massive."

"Then do something! Anything! Transplants!"

The doctor shook his head sadly. "Even if there were organs available, she's too weak. She wouldn't survive the surgery."

"How . . . how long?"

"Hours. A couple of days at the most."

"I want to see her! Is she awake?"

"She's conscious," the doctor allowed. "The nurse will take you back."

Stein followed behind as the nurse led Alex to a curtained cubical and held back the drape. Cyd looked up from her hospital bed, her dark hair plastered to her forehead, and smiled weakly. An oxygen tube ran to her nose, another tube ran from a bag on a pole to her arm, and wires connected her to a bank of monitors that beeped softly.

Alex took her hand and smiled down.

She searched his battered face. "You should get those cuts looked at." Her voice was barely a whisper. "You could get an infection."

"I wanted to check on you first. Make sure you were alright."

She smiled thinly. "I'm fine. Dying is easier than I thought."

"Don't you give up," he sobbed, "you hear me?"

"It's not about giving up," she coughed. "More like letting go. Like finally seeing the only thing that matters."

"Thing? What thing?"

Her lips moved . . . but nothing came out.

He put his ear down close to her mouth. "Say again?"

"Love." It was more a breath than a word. A small cry escaped him, and she tried to sit up. "The Cannastar, Alex. Promise me you'll . . ."

"We'll start our plantation together, Cyd. You and me. Just like we planned."

Her eyelids closed.

"Cyd!"

They opened again slowly. "I'm still here . . . Thirsty . . ."

He reached for a cup of water on a tray, held the straw to her lips and watched as she took a tiny sip. It was as if a hand was reaching down his throat trying to rip out his heart.

She fell back on her pillow with a sigh.

Alex had no idea how long he had been sitting there. It had grown dark outside. He checked and Cyd was still breathing. A nurse came in, cleaned and dressed his wounds, and left in silence. The doctor appeared. Asked Cyd if she wanted something more for the pain.

"No drugs," she murmured. "Want to be around for the grand finale." What she really wanted was for Alex to go away and leave her in peace. Her energy was fading, and it was too hard to keep him in focus. She could tell she was retreating into herself, and knew that when her emotions were gone, he would feel abandoned. She hated the thought and wished he would go but didn't know how to tell him.

Stein stood to leave. "I vill give the two of you some privacy . . . "

Alex looked up. "The Organ Grinder!" he cried in sudden desperation. "Is it working? Did you fix it?"

"Antoinette, she did not have to die," Stein admitted. "The program read the protein requirements for her heart wrong. She received only a small amount of the protein she needed for a healthy heart. It weakened her heart walls, and that is what killed her. The membranes, they vere too thin to withstand the pressure of the blood. The fix vas simple. The problem has been corrected and it vill not happen again."

"That's it then!" Alex cried. "That's the answer! Quick, get a gurney! We have to get Cyd over to your lab."

Stein threw up his hands. "Ridiculous!" he sputtered. "Impossible. I can't allow it."

"It worked before!" Alex insisted. "It would have worked on Antoinette if your machine had been calibrated properly."

"I . . . I cannot be responsible. It's unethical."

"Unethical?" He wanted to strangle the German. "Cyd is dying, Doctor Stein! Do it! Now! Before it's too late!"

"There is the liability to consider . . ."

"I'll sign a release! Cyd will sign a release. Nobody's suing anybody, okay?"

Stein sighed. "Ve first must ask the patient's permission."

"Cyd?"

She tried but couldn't keep her eyes open.

"Cyd!" Alex yelled.

Her eyes sprung wide.

"The Organ Grinder! Doctor Stein needs your permission to use it on you!"

Her eyelids fluttered and she laughed, feeble with pain. "What do I have to lose?"

\*\*\*

A group of doctors and nurses from Kilgore Health volunteered to help, some out of compassion, others merely out of curiosity. Alex didn't care, he was glad for the support. The head of anesthesiology from the hospital agreed to monitor Cyd's bodily functions, manager her breathing and do his best to keep her alive during the experimental procedure—provided his name be kept out of it should anything go wrong.

Stein's lab was cold as a meat locker despite being crowded with members of his research staff and personnel from the hospital. Banks of computers blinked rapidly, their operators sitting ready at their terminals. Cyd lay mildly sedated on the operating table staring up at holograms of her lungs, liver and kidneys that were rotating slowly above her. Alex and Stein stood at her side.

The German referred to the revolving images. "You can see here clearly the darkened areas. They show the damage to the organs. This is what ve vill be attempting to replace with healthy tissue."

"How long?" Alex asked.

"The entire procedure? Between fourteen and sixteen hours, I estimate."

Alex took Cyd's limp hand.

She smiled up at him bravely. "Do I look as sexy as Antoinette laying here?"

"Not quite," he replied.

"What if I were to grow a hairy chest?"

"Grow a new set of lungs. That will make me happy."

"Don't hold your breath."

"How can you joke at a time like this?"

"Who's joking?" She paused to gather her strength. "Alex, I want you to do something for me."

"Anything."

"I want you to go on to the Church of the Nativity where we were headed when the bomb hit."

"What? Why?"

"I want you to go there and pray for me."

"I need to be here with you."

"I don't want . . . I want you to go to Bethlehem and pray in the place that Jesus was born."

"Cyd, no. I can't leave. Not with you . . . "

"Alex, please. For me. Go . . ." Her strength was fading and so was her voice. *I don't want you to watch me die,* she thought. *It's humiliating.*

He looked at her feeling absolutely helplessness. "I didn't think you were all that religious."

"Death can change your mind about a lot of things."

"Cyd . . ." he pleaded.

"Just go and pray for me, okay? Pray that I make it. Nothing for you to do here." A dry cough. "You'll be back before I wake up. You can worry over me then . . ."

He started to say that their Toyota had been wrecked in the explosion.

"Take my Mercedes," Stein offered as if he had read Alex's mind, handing him the keys and telling him where it was parked. "I vill call the minute ve know anything."

Alex looked down hoping she would change her mind. Her expression told him her mind was set. He turned to Stein who nodded encouragingly. *Thinks I'm a distraction,* Alex realized. *Probably he's right.* The reason Cyd didn't want him there, he couldn't imagine.

"One thing before I go," he told her.

"Hmmm?"

"Will you marry me?"

She looked up with a weak smile. "If you think I'm not going to hold you to that when this is over, you're crazy."

Leaving her there on that table was like tearing his own arm off and leaving it behind.

"Count backwards from one hundred for me," the anesthesiologist said softly, injecting her IV.

She turned her head to watch him go. "One hundred . . . ninety-nine . . ." *Goodbye, my darling.*

"Start!" Stein command as he went out the door.

The sidewalk outside the lab was deserted. Alex pulled his collar up against the cold, hunched his shoulders and walked slowly toward the parking garage. It was early dawn and the sky was overcast and the streets were wet with rain.

# Chapter Twenty-One

## WEST BANK

The parking garage was cold and damp and echoed with his footsteps. Alex found Stein's Mercedes, got in, started the engine and just sat there staring out. He'd been up for over twenty-four hours, but sleep was impossible. Imagining Cyd at the mercy of an experimental machine that could save her life or end it with a single miscalculation left his mind in turmoil. He looked down and for the first time saw that his shirt and pants had blood on them. Cyd's blood! Horrified, he slammed the car in gear and hurtled out the garage with the tires making tortured screams on the concrete.

Back at their hotel he stood under a scalding hot shower scrubbing vigorously. Looking down, he saw the water running red down the drain. The soap slipped from his hands and he slid down the tile on his back until he was sitting on the floor hugging his knees. The shower cascaded over him, muffling the sounds of his heart-wrenching sobs.

Up until now, the reality of what had happened was too awful, too terrible, too unthinkable to imagine. The bomb that had exploded in front of their car exploded again and again before his eyes, and he kept falling into the crater that it made.

He didn't know how long the water had been pounding down on him when a thought floated up. *If it's prayers in Bethlehem that Cyd wants, then its prayers she'll have.* Having a job, a mission, an assignment . . . this was meaning . . . this was purpose. Something to do besides obsess over all the horrors that could go wrong. He dried his tears, stood and quickly dried himself on one of the hotel's luxurious towels. It reminded him of how much Cyd loved the hotel's soft linen, and he fought back tears.

Driving Stein's old Mercedes south down the high-walled highway to Bethlehem was like steering a heavy tank along a winding road. Numb with exhaustion, his mind was empty when he came to the wide patch of fresh asphalt on the road where Israeli road crews had repaired the bomb crater from the day before. He stared out the windshield, and then in his rear view mirror as he passed the black burn streaks and skid marks that spread out from the repair in every direction. A blinding rage swept over him. He could have killed every Palestinian in the West Bank in that moment and not given it a second thought.

A few miles further on, he came to the checkpoint that marked the entrance to the West Bank and stopped in a line of cars waiting to get in. It hadn't occurred to him that the crossing might be closed after yesterday's violence, but to his relief saw the car in front of him crawl forward. He rolled ahead with it. When it came time to show his passport and enter Palestinian controlled territory, his anger flared again.

"Purpose of your visit, sir?" the Israeli military officer asked politely, glancing at Alex's passport and smiling when he saw he was American.

"Pray," Alex said, staring straight ahead. His knuckles were white from gripping the steering wheel.

The officer nodded, and mutely waved him through.

Arab squalor greeted Alex on both sides of a modern expressway as he drove into Bethlehem. Above and around on all sides he saw colorless, hastily built Israeli housing projects crowding the low-lying hills. He drove to Manger Square, parked the big Mercedes, crossed the street to a stark, fortress-like structure and entered a stone courtyard enclosed by forbidding stone walls. Not being of a religious nature himself, he thought the church was one of the ugliest piles of stones he had ever seen.

At the far end of the walled enclosure was what appeared to be the only way in—a small, rectangular opening less than four feet high. He walked toward it and was about to follow the other tourists inside when behind him he heard a young woman's excited voice reading aloud.

"The Door of Humility was built to keep marauding hordes from riding their horses and camels inside."

Thinking it was Cyd voice he'd heard, he spun around with a pounding heart only to discover an attractive blond in her twenties reading her guidebook to her bored husband or boyfriend. He realized at that moment he hadn't heard from Stein, quickly checked his cellphone and saw he had no messages. Relieved that he had reception at least, he bent low and went through the opening. Behind him he heard the girl still reading.

"Built in 330 AD, the Church of the Nativity is run by Roman Catholic, Greek Orthodox and Armenian Apostolic authorities all competing with one another for jurisdiction over it."

*What else is new,* Alex thought, straightening up inside. His eyes slowly adjusted to the gloom. Two rows of tall, polished columns ran down either side of a long, narrow, empty chapel. Hushed visitors were wandering in and out between the columns admiring the faded paintings of saints on their smooth sides. The three different orders of monks stood around in isolated packs jealously guarding their exclusive area of the church. In the middle of the vacant flagstone floor was a trap door that was thrown open so tourists could admire the intricate design of the original mosaic tile floor some three feet below the floor joists. Water was dripping from rotted roof timbers onto the ancient tiles.

Alex noticed that some of the monks were clutching rocks in their fists. They looked like the hateful clerics he had seen beating each other to a pulp five days earlier in Jerusalem, and he shuddered. Behind him he heard the girl still breathlessly reading her the guidebook to her indifferent companion in Cyd's voice.

"The purpose in confirming Bethlehem as the birthplace of Jesus was to conform to the Old Testament prophesy that foretold of the Messiah coming from here. The church has been a flashpoint for endless conflict and violence ever since." She looked up from her book and pointed in awe to the far end of the church where a shaft of dusty sunlight was streaming down through high windows and striking the floor in front of an altar. "Under that very spot where the sun is hitting is the Grotto of the Manger where Mary gave birth to Christ!" She took her man's hand and led him toward it. "Book says a staircase leads down on either side."

It occurred to Alex that Cyd would think the Grotto was the perfect place to pray. He followed the couple up the center of the long nave. The twin staircases were right where the guidebook said they were, and he followed them down the stone steps to an underground cave.

"Altar of the Nativity," the girl ahead of him read, pointing reverently to a niche in the eastern end of the crypt. Set in the marble floor beneath the altar was a sixteen-point silver star surrounded by fifteen silver lamps. Another girl with khaki skin and coal-black hair was kneeling on the marble before the star praying softly under her breath. As Alex watched, she reached her hand down inside a hole in the center of the star.

"She's touching the stone that Mary laid on when she gave birth to Jesus," guidebook girl whispered to her partner, who looked like he was wishing he was anywhere but here.

Alex stepped forward and knelt beside the praying woman. Looking down at the star, he steepled his hands and tried to think of a prayer. His mind went blank. He hadn't a clue what to say.

"Just tell God what's in your heart," the girl beside him urged softly.

He closed his eyes and was surprised at the words that flowed. He didn't ask for anything for himself, only for Cyd, and only in the words he imagined she would use. When he opened his eyes again, he was disappointed to find that he felt nothing at all. No sensation, nothing. *I tried,* he told Cyd miserably. *I'm sorry. I don't know what else . . .*

"I recognize you," the girl beside him on her knees said brightly. "We met a few days ago at the riot that our man Tashtego started for us."

Alex looked over, and for a moment he didn't recognize her. Then to his astonishment he saw the horn-rimmed glasses that were too big for her beautiful face, the small gap between her two front teeth, and it all came back.

"Find what you were looking for in that hole in the star, did you?"

She gave him a curious look. "Did you find what you were after?"

"No magic here, if that's what you mean."

"God has had so many names over the centuries. Energy is energy no matter what you call it. Intuitive energy is everywhere; you just have to know how to look with your heart."

His empirical, scientific mind could make no sense of what she was saying. "Whatever you stole, put it back," he said impatiently.

Nikki laughed lightly. "In the Dominican Republic where I'm from, everyone is Catholic. I was trying to remember what it was like is all." She smiled in delight. "Sam will be so happy that I ran into you. He liked you the minute he met you, and it normally takes him forever to warm up to people."

"He's upstairs casing the joint, I assume?"

She bounded to her feet and held out her hand. "Alex, isn't it? Will you come with me, Alex? I'd like to explain something to you, but I need Sam's help. Where's Cyd, by the way? I just adore her."

He ignored her hand and stood on his own. "Cyd couldn't make it today. I came instead."

Just then a loud explosion reverberated through the church that shook the grotto. The dull, staccato sound of automatic weapon fire could be heard coming from somewhere outside.

Alex grabbed Nikki by the arm. "Now what the hell have you done?"

She broke loose and ran up the stairs.

"I haven't done anything!"

# Chapter Twenty-Two

### WORDS ON THE WIND

Alex followed close behind as Nikki bounded up the steps. On the main level, he saw her running down between one of the two long rows of columns that flanked the church, calling Sam's name. Movement at the far end of the chapel caught his eye and he stopped, staring in disbelief.

Monks were running in every direction at once as a mob of armed Palestinian militants broke into the church through the Door of Humility. Black masks hid their faces and cartridge belts crossed their chests. Under the cartridge belts, they wore sweatshirts with athletic logos on them. Firing their rifles in the air, they began hurriedly barricading the Hobbit-size hole they had just come through with tables and benches.

The monks were rounded up and herded behind the columns on one side of the church where a pair of hyper invaders held them at gunpoint. The International media would be quick to report that the masked fighters were a mix of Fatah, Hamas, Palestinian Islamic Jihadists and Palestinian Security Forces fighting for a Palestinian state, free of Israeli control. To the frightened tourists who were being herded behind the columns on the other side of the nave, they looked like terrorists. As far as the Israeli authorities were concerned, they were common criminals.

A small Palestinian boy, about ten or eleven years old, appeared and stuck a large rifle in Alex's ribs, motioning for him to join the others. Prodded along, he found himself crowded behind a pillar with a small group of tourists that included Nikki, Sam and their African mate Tashtego. Sam nodded a greeting that Alex ignored.

Nikki felt badly for the boy who was guarding them. He looked so frightened, so lost and alone. She gave him a sympathetic smile and the boy smiled back shyly. *Handsome lad*, she thought and asked him his name. The boy remembered himself, lost his smile and assumed the fierce expression of his companions as the explosions and gunfire fell silent outside.

Orders were shouted over bullhorns in Arabic telling the militants inside the church to surrender. The cornered insurgents yelled back with arrogant threats and shouts of defiance that echoed through the cathedral. A smoke grenade was tossed in through one of the beautiful stained-glass windows, shattering the glass. Palestinian guns poked out through the broken window firing blindly. The Israelis fired back, and a bullet pinged off the pillar where Alex was hiding.

"What do we do now?" Nikki whispered in desperation.

"Nothing," Sam whispered back. "We sit tight and wait until one side blinks. I'm guessing it won't be the Israelis."

Nikki saw that Alex was watching them suspiciously. "We had nothing to do with this," she declared.

"I imagine you'll still find a way to use it to your advantage," Alex said.

"Let's hope you're right," Sam agreed.

The Palestinians released their demands. In addition to a free and independent Palestinian state, they insisted on the immediate release of the thirteen Palestinians the Israelis had recently arrested and charged with terrorism. Within hours, the whole world knew of the Siege of Bethlehem, and the press had a field day blaming the Israelis.

Not knowing if Cyd was alive or dead was torture like Alex had never known. He could think of nothing else. No matter how many times he checked his cellphone, it still showed no reception. He felt like he was buried alive, and the loneliness of death overcame him.

Days passed, and the siege drug on with no relief. The moment it started the IDF (Israel Defense Forces) shut down all the nearby cell towers so the barricaded fighters couldn't communicate with the outside world. Army snipers set up positions on the rooftops of the surrounding buildings, and at night searched out targets with night vision goggles and lasers. Every shot was answered with a blaze of gunfire from the church. Three Palestinians were killed, and an Armenian monk was wounded.

Nikki cringed every time she heard shots. Sam held her to him trying to comfort and protect her while Tashtego stood guard, an ebony statue that never seemed to sleep. Groups of hostages huddled behind each of the other pillars on their side of the church. Without baths, they grew dirty and ragged.

Monks and tourists alike were caught in a no-man's-land between incomprehensible politics and ancient religious hatreds. Neither side was going to give up. Not now, not ever. The death of a few hostages would be of little consequence to anyone. A week after it happened nobody would remember, or even care, that a few church visitors had been killed. They were pawns, as disposable as the cartridges the Palestinians were firing from their Russian-made guns.

Nikki tried to go to the bathroom and came back gagging. The toilets were broken and backed up from overuse. The stench of human waste was overwhelming. Food was in short supply. Insurgents and hostages alike lived on dwindling supplies of the monk's rice, beans and olives. Fortunately, the church had a good well, so at least there was drinking water. There were candles as well, but the militants would not allow them to be lit at night for fear of the snipers. Explosions set off in the buildings that surrounded the church ignited fires, and smoke filled the chapel day and night.

Alex overheard hushed discussions between the broad-shouldered treasure hunter with the sun-bleached hair and the tall, razor-thin African. Apparently, there were areas of the church they had already searched, and areas they couldn't access without alerting their captors. Their frustrations over not finding whatever it was they were looking for seemed to be eroding their confidence in ever finding it.

"What kind of name is Tashtego anyway?" Alex asked Nikki one night while listening to yet another murmured discussion between the two men.

Nikki smiled admiringly at their black friend. "He won't tell anyone his Maasai name. First time they met, Sam saw him trying to wrestle a huge fish he had harpooned into his skiff and called him that."

"Because?"

"Because Tashtego was the harpooner aboard Ahab's Pequod in *Moby Dick*."

The African smiled at Nikki with the biggest, whitest teeth Alex had ever seen.

"He likes it when I explain his name," she smiled back. Turning to Alex, she gave him a searching look. "Is Cyd your wife?"

"Girlfriend, best friend, partner. Whatever."

"Do you love her?"

The question surprised him. "More than my own life. She *is* my life."

Nikki smiled happily. "That's why I don't mind being Sam's *whatever*." Her attention drifted, and she tilted her head to one side as if trying to make something out that she couldn't quite hear. Reaching out with both hands, she placed them carefully on the stone column they were hiding behind and brought her ear in close to it. After listening a moment, she removed her hands, placed them palms down on the flagstone floor and brought her ear down to the stones.

"What is she doing?" Alex whispered to Sam.

"You wouldn't believe me if I told you."

Nikki looked up with a bright smile. "Found it, Sam! I know where it is!"

"Of course, you do."

Alex thought he heard a note of exasperation in his voice.

"It's under the floorboards." She listened again, nodded that she understood and grinned. "A section of the original tile flooring comes up."

"You sure?"

Nikki lowered herself down until she was lying flat on the floor. "Knowing is not the same as being sure, you know that." Glancing up, her pupils were huge, her yellowish-tan eyes glowing in the dark almost as if they had their own light behind them. And then she was gone, slithering across the flagstones on her belly.

Alex turned to Sam in alarm.

"She does this," the treasure hunter shrugged, straining to keep sight of her. "Just watch."

Nikki's darkened figure reached the open trap door in the floor. She stopped and looked around to make sure she hadn't been spotted. A drop of water from the leaking rafters fell on her head and she impatiently wiped it away, then slid over the edge and disappeared into the hole.

Tashtego saw what she had done and quickly followed, crossing the floor on his stomach like a giant boa constrictor and curling himself protectively around the opening. It was impossible to tell in the dark that he was even there. Restless noises came from the militants on the other side of the church. Alex held his breath. The noises faded, and silence returned.

Minutes passed . . . then Nikki's head popped back up again. Tashtego plucked her straight out of the hole in one silent movement like he was ice fishing, and a moment later they had snaked their way back behind the pillar.

Nikki handed Sam something. "Right where I thought it would be," she whispered, breathing hard.

Tashtego beamed proudly at her as Sam gave her a quick kiss. "You are a wonder."

"I know," she smiled excitedly. "Is it what we were hoping for?"

Sam took a small, round magnifying glass from his pocket, put it to his eye and began examining a thin piece of badly oxidized bronze about a foot square. Taking the jeweler's loupe from his eye, he looked up with a spreading grin. "This is it," he declared. "The last piece. We've got it!"

Nikki stifled a squeal of delight, and silently clapped her hands

Alex was not liking what he was seeing. "You want to tell me what's going on here?"

Sam looked at Nikki.

"Go ahead," she said. "We can trust him."

"I wouldn't count on it," Alex remarked.

Nikki gave Sam an encouraging nod.

"Here it is," the treasure hunter began. "This is the last piece of a map we've been searching for. The map itself is a kind of triptych. Three pieces that fit together and, in this case, tell a story."

"Story?"

"The man who made the map was an escaped Jewish slave named Avraham. He was part of a rowing crew on a Roman ship that was caught in the tsunami that destroyed Alexandria in the fourth century. The ship was carrying gold, silver, amulets and jewels that they had looted from an Egyptian tomb. They were bound for Rome with their treasure when the tsunami struck. The wall of water leveled Alexandria and hurled their ship inland for miles. Avraham was apparently the only survivor. He buried the loot somewhere in the desert and made his way back to Judea where he was living before his arrest. The man was a stone and tile mason by trade. His *hobby,* apparently, was counterfeiting the gold coins the Roman Empire used for money.

"Gold coins," Alex repeated.

"Once he was back in Judea, Avraham assumed a new name and resumed his old occupations of mason by day and forger by night. His plan was to stay invisible as a common laborer while forging enough fake wealth to mount an expedition back to Egypt and retrieve the plunder he'd hidden.

"It didn't work out for him. Best laid plans, and all that. He grew old and was never able to get rich enough with his phony coin scheme to realize his dream. I'm guessing he was not a very good counterfeiter. At any rate, that's when he made his map that shows where he buried the treasure the Romans stole from the pyramid they raided."

Nikki broke in enthusiastically. "By this time, churches like this one that had been built as monuments to Christianity were burned, damaged or destroyed in one religious conflict after another. As a master mason, Avraham got the job of helping to rebuild them. He cut his map into thirds and hid the three pieces in the walls and floors of three of the churches he worked on. So the pieces wouldn't be lost forever, he cast three gold coins, really big ones, from Roman coins he'd melted down to gold plate his counterfeit ones. His coins told where the three different map pieces were hidden."

Sam dug into his pocket. "We found the coins. Avraham had sealed them in an iron box that was part of the cargo a ship was carrying that went down in a hurricane. A ship we were diving on in the Bahamas." He withdrew his hand and opened it. A gold coin covered his entire palm. "This is the coin that led us here."

"Beautiful, isn't it?" Nikki exclaimed. "Let him hold it, Sam."

## The Organ Grinder Factor

The coin had been cleaned and polished and gleamed even in the dull light. Alex took the heavy disk, marveling at its antiquity, weighing it his hand. The story was too fantastical to believe, too real not to believe.

"How could you possibly know all this about him?"

"Part of it is written in Hebrew on the coins themselves." Sam pointed to the illegible symbols stamped in the gold. "See here? The rest, most of the story, was written on the first two map pieces we found. One we found in a church up north in Nazareth, the other was in the church in Jerusalem where we first met. I take pictures of the map and coins, text them to a friend in the States, a Jewish scholar, and he translates them for me."

Alex handed back the coin. "That still doesn't explain how Nikki knew where to find the piece of bronze she just dug up."

She hesitated. What if he laughed in her face?

"Show him, Nikki."

She adjusted her oversized glasses and held out her palms. "Hands, please."

Alex placed his hands cautiously in hers.

Nikki closed her eyes, then flinched as if something had hurt her. "Cyd is injured," she said slowly. "An explosion."

Alex felt his mouth go dry.

"There's this amazing invention." She inclined her head, listening carefully. "A wonderful new machine that replaces body parts without having to remove the old ones first. Does that make sense?"

Alex could barely speak. "Organ Grinder," he croaked.

Nikki nodded, concentrating hard. "It's not perfected yet, is it? An animal died. A monkey of some sort." She fell silent, and a look of distress came over her. "There's another death. A tragedy that brings on madness."

Alex tried to pull away, but she wouldn't let go.

"It's not true!" he cried. "Don't say that!"

"It's not a woman," she went on. "A man . . . Old . . . He will not be mourned."

"What . . . what are you saying?"

"Cyd has a message for you. Would you like to hear?"

He moaned in despair.

Nikki's voice changed and became more like Cyd's. "Don't cry for me, Alex. This is not goodbye."

Nikki let go of his hands, opened her eyes and saw that he was crying. "Cyd is going to live, Alex. She's going to be fine. Don't worry."

He wiped fiercely at his eyes. "I . . . I don't understand. How . . .?"

"Nikki's grandmother was from Africa," Sam said. "A shaman, or so I'm told. The real deal."

"They say it skips a generation," Nikki smiled modestly.

"That still doesn't explain . . ."

Nikki took a deep breath. "I have guides," she admitted. "Soft voices. They whisper things to me. It sounds like the wind. Words on the wind. It took me a long time to learn to listen and hear."

"It's a gift," Sam added. "*Nikki* is a gift."

She gave him a pointed look. "He doesn't always see it that way, do you Sam?"

"And you say Cyd is going to be okay?" Alex asked anxiously. "She's going to make it?"

"Better than new," Nikki promised. "Like getting a new generator for your . . . boat? Did the two of you have a boat?"

## Chapter Twenty-Three

### REVOLT

Alex wanted with all his heart to believe what Nikki had told him—that Cyd was going to live, that she was going to survive—but his practical, rational, scientific mind wasn't going for it. The argument went on ceaselessly in his head with no resolution in sight. Every time he ruled that one side had won, that Cyd was going to be "better than new", the other side made its case all over again. His jury was hopelessly deadlocked.

A voice broadcast over loudspeakers from outside the church was blaring a message in Arabic to the militants barricaded inside. Alex, Sam, Nikki and Tashtego watched from behind their pillar as the Palestinians, clustered together under the broken window on the other side of the church, began arguing loudly among themselves. A thick-lipped, white-bearded man with drooping eyes and a face spotted in black moles was clearly their leader. His hoarse, ill-tempered voice overruled the objections of the others as quickly as they were voiced.

One of the fighters shouted something out the window, and quickly ducked back inside. Two others ran over and began unbarricading the Door of Humility. Minutes later a tall, distinguished, middle-aged man entered. Straightening up inside, the hostages saw that he was wearing a turned-around collar and a St. Louis Cardinal's baseball cap with a red bird embroidered on it.

"Mediator," Sam speculated. "Man of the church. Cardinal from the looks of his hat."

As they watched, they saw the ill-tempered Palestinian leader and the dignified mediator sit down cross-legged on the floor and begin an intense discussion. From what they could see, the cardinal appeared to be a gracious man who smiled politely every time the Palestinian shouted in his face.

The negotiation had gone on for some time without an apparent resolution when the white-bearded Arab stood abruptly and nodded to one of his men. The man pulled out a pistol and shot the cardinal in the back of the head.

A note was hastily scribbled and pinned to the clergyman's chest. His body was then hoisted in the air and dumped out the window. Horrified gasps and cries of fear came from behind the pillars that echoed through the church.

"What do you suppose was in the note?" Nikki asked dispassionately.

"You can bet it wasn't a takeout order for pizza," Alex ventured.

"The Israelis are going to let every one of us die before they give an inch to these Palestinians," Sam concluded.

The moment the cardinal's body hit the ground outside, a hail of bullets began riddling the interior of the church. Any windows that had not already been broken were blown out. After thirty minutes, presumably in response to whatever was in the note pinned to the cardinal, the shooting stopped. A middle-aged woman hiding behind one of the other pillars was herded out at gunpoint screaming in what sounded like Dutch or German. Her husband tried to stop the men who were manhandling his wife and was clubbed senseless.

The militants stood the terrified woman up near the open trap door where Nikki had disappeared in search for the map piece and opened fire. Her body was riddled with so many bullets that she didn't fall until the shooting stopped. The assassins picked her up, and unceremoniously tossed her out the window.

Smoke canisters came flying back in response, and the barrage of bullets began again. The church filled with smoke. Nikki was gagging so badly she couldn't breathe. Sam yanked off his shirt and gave it to her to cover her mouth.

Another half hour passed. The shooting stopped again, and an eerie silence fell over the chapel.

Nikki was laying on the floor with her head still buried in Sam's shirt. The toe of a Nike tennis shoe prodded her in the ribs. She looked up to see the small Palestinian boy she had tried to befriend when they were taken captive standing over her gesturing with his rifle for her to stand.

Her face turned to horror with the realization that she was next.

The boy prodded her with the muzzle of his gun. "*Fawq!* Up!"

Nikki struggled to her feet, and both Sam and Alex stepped in front of her.

"*Adhhab!*" the boy cried, trying to shove her guardians aside with his rifle. "Go!"

Alex lunged at him with a loud shout.

He swung his gun in Alex's direction, and Sam snatched it out of his hands.

The boy stood stunned not knowing what to do.

Nikki slapped him hard across the face.

The youngster stared. His cheek turned bright red as tears welled in his eyes. Panic swept over him. Tension, noise, the dead all around was finally too much. He lost his grip on his fanatical zeal and ran screaming for the door. Throwing himself at the barricade, he began tearing at the hastily re-erected tables and benches with bleeding fingers.

A militant on the other side of the church leveled his gun at him. Sam pointed the rifle he had just confiscated, took aim and fired. A small hole appeared in the front of the militant's head, and a rather large one appeared in the back. The terrified youngster, meanwhile, had managed to wiggle out through a hole and make his escape.

The Israelis, assuming another hostage had been executed, opened fire. A barrage of bullets peppered the flagstones and whistled past the pillars as teargas came flying through the windows. The canisters rolled across the floor and exploded, filling the church with blinding, burning smoke. Visibility was zero. Screams from the hostages mingled with the rattle of gunfire from both sides.

Alex shielded Nikki in his arms as Sam fired blindly across at the Palestinians. Then a form appeared slowly. Tashtego, emerging like a ghost out of the smoke and confusion. Someone was with him—a hostage—a Palestinian with a grizzled white beard. One black hand was around his throat, the other held a gun to his head.

Alex rubbed hard at his eyes and recognized the Palestinian leader they had seen negotiating with the cardinal. Tashtego and Sam exchanged the smallest of smiles as the church fell silent and the smoke slowly cleared.

Sam and Alex stepped out from behind their pillar on either side of Tashtego who held their hostage out in front of them as a shield.

"Tell your men to drop their weapons," Sam ordered.

The militant leader stared defiantly.

Alex spoke in his other ear. "I saw you speaking English to the cardinal, you insolent asshole. Do as he says or the next body out that window is going to be yours."

The Palestinian smiled indifferently. "They take our homes, the Jews. They take our land and slaughter our people. They do to us what the Nazis did to them. Can you not see why we hate them?"

"Tell that to the priest and the woman you just murdered," Alex said.

Smug and casual in defeat, the rebel leader smiled again and called across to his men.

## Chapter Twenty-Four

### RETURN

The militants boobytrapped their weapons before laying them down, then filed contritely out through the Door of Humility where they were immediately taken into custody. The hostages followed, crowding out through the small opening like they were abandoning a sinking ship. Outside in the courtyard, they were mobbed by spectators and the press so that the military had a hard time separating the hostages from the mob. Medical tents had been set up for mandatory physical exams, and the former prisoners were ushered toward them.

Amid the chaos and confusion, Alex melded into the crowd. He didn't want to endure what was sure to be hours of questioning by the Israeli authorities, and he sure as hell didn't want to take the chance of them running his name and likeness through their data base and finding out he was on America's most wanted list.

A hand grabbed his arm.

"Leaving so soon?" Sam asked.

"Cyd . . . he started to explain. "Gotta go . . ."

Nikki smiled up at him. "Tell her hello for me."

"How can you be so sure . . .?"

"Knowing is not the same as being sure."

"You keep saying that."

"Knowing is a feeling in your heart. Like love. It's either there or it isn't. Being sure is in your head. Something you thought up. Big difference."

Alex smiled and gave the bespectacled girl a grateful kiss, then turned to Sam. "Be sure and tell the Israelis about those boobytrapped weapons."

"Already have."

"Where's the map piece?"

Sam grinned and patted his waistband in the small of his back.

Alex extended his hand. "Don't steal anything I wouldn't steal."

"Where's the fun in that?"

They shook hands warmly. Brothers parting in a hurry.

Across the street in Manger Square, Alex found Stein's Mercedes covered in dirt and debris from the conflict. He got in and desperately checked his phone. The battery was deader than the cardinal who had left the church by way of the window. He fished around under the seat where he had stashed the keys. His hand closed on a metal ring. He straightened and fumbled to get the key into the ignition. The car fired right up, and he exhaled in relief.

Security was tight getting back into Israel. There was a long line of vehicles and signs telling drivers to stay in their cars. Alex pounded the steering wheel in frustration.

***

The filthy Mercedes skidded to a halt in front of Stein's laboratory. Alex jumped out with the engine still running and ran frantically toward the entrance. Stein was just coming out of the big glass doors, and Alex accosted him.

"Is she . . . Is she . . .?"

"Alive?" Stein exclaimed. "You have never seen a young woman more alive in your life! It vas all ve could do to keep her under observation until now. She is just being released from the hospital. If ve hurry, ve can still catch her."

Alex burst into the hospital lobby and saw Cyd being pushed out of an elevator in a wheelchair. His heart sank before remembering that all patients are required to leave the hospital in a wheelchair.

Cyd saw Alex at the same moment he saw her and cried out. Bounding out of her chair, she ran toward him, threw herself into his arms and covered him in kisses.

"You . . . you look great," he managed.

She recoiled. "And you stink!"

He hadn't stopped to think what he might look and smell like after living on a church floor for three weeks. "I'm sure I do," he laughed. "Isn't it wonderful?"

"Yes, yes, yes!" she cried, throwing her arms back around his neck. "Everything is wonderful now!"

Opening the door and entering their suite at the King David Hotel was like coming home. She helped him strip off with his dirty clothes, they got in the shower and stayed under the hot water for an hour. He couldn't stop touching her to reassure himself he wasn't dreaming. His fingers found the tiny wounds in her chest and torso where Stein's probes had been inserted.

She looked down self-consciously. "They might leave scars. Are they ugly?"

He began kissing them one by one, working his way down. "I love them all, each . . . and every . . . one."

Fresh and clean, they stood in the steamy bathroom toweling each other off with the hotel's big towels. The soft fabric seemed somehow grand and luxurious to him now and he inhaled it deeply.

"What did Stein say about the procedure itself?" Alex asked. "Anything we should be concerned about or on our guard against?"

"Herr Doctor says I'm good for another two hundred thousand miles, at least. Says I'll probably outlive everyone I know."

"As long as I go first," Alex said. "I couldn't stand the thought of losing you again."

At the little table out on their balcony, they sat swathed in fluffy white hotel robes eating the enormous meal room service had delivered. Cyd watched in fascination as Alex devoured a giant steak, his first decent meal in three weeks. Even as he ate, he couldn't stop looking up at her. It was almost as if he was afraid she would disappear again.

She asked about the siege, and he told her about Sam and Nikki and Tashtego, about the map piece the treasure hunters found, about how they had bonded as friends in their efforts to survive.

"Nikki says to say hello, by the way."

"I'd love to see her again. Where are they now?"

"On their way to Egypt, I imagine. They're good people."

"Told you."

He nodded and kept eating.

"Kilgore phoned while I was in the hospital. He's anxious to meet with us again."

"Did he say what for?"

"Don't know, but he sounded pleased. He was certainly thrilled that I'd had better luck with the Organ Grinder than poor Antoinette."

"He'll keep."

She smiled. "He'll keep."

After all this time, he thought her smile was the most beautiful smile he had ever seen. Food no longer interested him. They stood as if by unspoken agreement, joined hands, and walked silently into the bedroom.

## Chapter Twenty-Five

### WORKING PARTNERS

The next afternoon Cyd and Alex arrived at Stein's laboratory for their meeting with Kilgore. A security guard led them down the long hall to the lab. As they approached, they heard a terrible argument going on inside. They entered and saw Stein and Kilgore standing nose to nose, their faces red with anger.

The two men realized they had company and fell silent.

Stein threw up his arms and stormed past them on his way out. "He's all yours," the scientist said bitterly. "I've had about all I can take of this man for one day."

Kilgore smiled graciously. "Cydney, let me look at you!" he said, holding out both hands in greeting. "Alive and well! A miracle is what you are! I am so proud."

"The credit goes to Doctor Stein," Cyd smiled self-consciously. "I'm just glad to be alive."

"And indeed, you are! A great beginning for all of us!" He glanced at Alex. "I'm told you had a little trouble down in Bethlehem."

"A little."

"Bastards didn't get away with it though, did they? Were you afraid?"

"Terrified."

"Can't imagine. Let's go into Stein's office where we can talk."

Kilgore seated himself behind Stein's cluttered desk like he owned it, picked up a colorful plaster replica of the human heart that Stein used for a paperweight, and began turning it over in his hand.

Cyd and Alex took seats on the opposite side of the desk.

"I have secured the full support of the Israeli government for our Cannastar farm," Kilgore began without preamble. "They couldn't be more excited about it. I will provide the funding and the land. My friends at MASHAV, Israel's agency for international development cooperation, will provide any scientific assistance you need, and all the physical labor. I will set up a separate company to handle international distribution. Yangtze.com customers worldwide are about to become healthier buyers and stay healthier buyers longer. Cannastar is going to become as commonplace as aspirin!"

Cyd and Alex were too stunned to speak.

"I thought you would be happy."

Alex found his voice. "What's your end of the deal? What are you asking from us in return?"

"My usual percentage. Seventy percent."

"Seventy percent," Cyd repeated incredulously.

Alex smiled cynically. "Why not eighty percent? Why not ninety or a hundred?"

Kilgore seemed to freeze in place. A sudden tremor ran through his whole body. The plaster heart he was toying with nearly slipped from his hands. "That's how venture capital works," he said with great effort. The tremor passed and he regained his composure. "Nine out of ten ventures of this kind fail. The one that doesn't pays for the rest. Investments like this one are high risk, and the reward has to be commensurate."

"We control production," Cyd insisted. "That's not negotiable."

"Agreed. No problem. Anything else?"

Cyd and Alex looked at one another. Their wildest dream had just come true, and neither of them could think of another thing to say.

The corners of Kilgore's tiny mouth flirted with a smile. "It's a deal then?"

Alex and Cyd exchanged another look. "Draw up the papers," he said.

"Excellent! Working partners. The best kind." Kilgore rose to shake hands and lost his balance. He reached to catch himself, the plaster heart slipped from his hands and shattered on the floor. He sat back down heavily and grabbed at his head as if it was being crushed in a vice.

Alex rushed around the desk, the doctor in him deeply concerned.

The billionaire waved him away, grimacing in pain. "It's nothing... nothing. Headache is all. They come and go."

## Chapter Twenty-Six

### A FARM IN ISRAEL

Six months later, Cannastar plants stretched up and down the fertile Jezreel Valley as far as the eye could see. The giant, leafy bushes, not yet ready for harvest, were already seven feet high with flowering seedpods bursting from the stems in a kaleidoscope of colors. Tiny figures in broad-brimmed hats toiled under a blazing Middle Eastern sun, hoeing and tending their way up and down the long rows between the dense and burgeoning shrubs.

Fat Man, Little Boy, Cyd and Alex sat side by side on the bed of a flatbed truck dangling their feet over the side and looking out over the vast Grow. Behind them was a luxurious motor home, paid for out of Kilgore's generous funding for their project, that Cyd and Alex were currently living in. They had discussed buying or building a house for themselves on a few occasions, but somehow the conversation had never gone any further.

"A healthier looking field of plants I have never seen," Little Boy exclaimed.

Cyd took off her straw hat and wiped her brow with her arm. "Thanks to the irrigation system you two invented. Its effect is truly amazing."

Little boy smiled up at his oversized friend. "The remote sensors under the roots of the plants were Fat Man's idea."

Sweating like an overheated boiler, Fat Man swelled with pride. "Simple, really," he explained. "Microsensors tell the computers in that trailer out there in the field the exact moisture and nutrient content of the soil in and around each bush at any given time. Drip lines connected to the sensors feed water and supplements to the plants as needed to keep their individual growing environments in perfect balance."

Alex listened with a wry smile. "Now why didn't I think of that?"

Cyd had telephoned Otis back in Arizona and told him about the marvelous new system for growing bigger, healthier Cannastar plants that Fat Man had invented. Otis immediately called the Israeli engineer and grilled him relentlessly on the remote root sensor system until he understood every detail. By the time he hung up, he was ready to try it himself.

"Did you get our wedding invitation?" Little Boy inquired.

Cyd smiled happily. "Juliette has asked me to be one of her bridesmaids,"

"I'm supposed to be the best man," Fat Man remarked. "Don't know if I can stand the excitement."

"Weddings are a great place to meet ladies," Little Boy prompted.

Fat Man sniffed indignantly. "Bachelorhood suits me just fine, thank you very much. If I had a woman bossing me around the way Juliette bosses you, I would kill myself."

"A little bossing wouldn't hurt you one bit," Little Boy suggested.

Cyd laughed. "Stop it, you two. You know you love each other."

"It's always something with him," Fat Man complained.

"I heard from Kilgore," Alex said quietly.

Cyd turned expectantly.

"According to our *partner*, countries around the world are lining up to buy Cannastar."

"What about America?" Cyd asked. "Any shift in making it legal back home?"

"The U.S. hasn't legalized it yet, but even they have stopped criminalizing it."

"Does that mean we can go home?"

Alex was silent a moment. "Is that what you want?"

She looked out at the flourishing field and said nothing.

***

Cyd had a standing appointment at Kilgore Health for a follow-up physical every six weeks. It had been a while since they had seen Helmut Stein, and when they were done at the hospital they wanted to stop over and invite him to supper. Their fondness for the scientist had grown to the point that they regarded him now as a beloved grandparent whose bark was worse than his bite.

They approached the big glass entry doors to his lab and saw Kilgore's chauffeured limousine parked out front. *Good*, Alex thought. *As long as he's here we can give him an update on how the Grow is progressing.*

The security guards knew Cyd and Alex by this time and waved them through, telling them Stein was in his lab. They walked down the long, clinical corridor, and again heard shouting. The closer they got, the worse it got. At the door to the laboratory, they stopped and listened. Inside, they could hear Stein and Kilgore engaged in another heated argument.

"It cannot be done!" the German implored. "The machine, it vas not built for that! I can't, and it can't! I von't, and that's final!"

"In that case, you leave me no choice," Kilgore replied in a chilling voice. "A dozen women will come forward with sworn affidavits saying you sexually molested them. Such women," he snorted, "are easy to buy. Additionally, every scientific paper you ever published will be found to have been plagiarized. I am, as you may know, a major contributor to a number of universities including the ones you graduated from. Your degrees will be revoked for cheating on your exams, and you will be exposed for the charlatan you are. I will withdraw my funding for your Organ Grinder. Your laboratory will be shuttered, and your invention will never again see the light of day. As for your assets, you will be labeled a traitor for funneling funds to the Palestinians, and any money you have in the bank will be frozen. Am I getting through to you, Doctor Stein? Is your refusal worth all of this?"

"You can't threaten me!"

"I don't make threats."

"No?"

"I only make promises."

"Are we interrupting?" Cyd asked cheerfully as she and Alex entered.

The two men stood glaring at one another.

"The human brain is the most complicated computer ever created," Stein cried. "It contains more circuitry than a billion processors in a billion motherboards. The programming alone is unimaginable. There aren't enough servers in the vorld to store the data in a single person's head."

"I have scheduled my own staff from the hospital to assist in the procedure," Kilgore went on indifferently. "My personal physician will supervise to make certain you don't kill me while I am unconscious."

"I . . . I *vould* never!" Stein sputtered.

"Never say never, Doctor. Not when never has you around the throat in a death grip."

"Vhy vould you vant to risk everything on something that is sure to fail?"

"How do you know it will fail if you haven't even tried it?" Kilgore pointed to Cyd without looking at her. "Did it fail with her? You claimed her organs could not be successfully replaced. Is she not the picture of health? Let's not be foolish, shall we? Together we can make medical history, what do you say?"

Stein hung his head in defeat. "A disaster, this vill be. A calamity. To try and replicate a human brain, especially one with a fast-growing tumor the size and malignancy of yours, is like trying to replicate the stars. They are too many to count, let alone clone. The Organ Grinder, it vill fail and the vorld vill never again vant to have anything to do with it."

"The Organ Grinder was never meant for the world to begin with, Doctor Stein."

"Vhat . . . vhat are you saying?"

Kilgore clutched at his head in sudden pain. "It has never been intended for anyone but me and my immediate family. Nobody else."

"In God's name vhy?"

"Why? Because people are not supposed to live beyond their normal span of years. I want them as healthy as possible while they are viable members of society so they can buy more and spend more on Yangtze.com. As seniors age, they spend less and less. After sixty their buying decreases until they are nothing but a drain and a burden on society. A bunch of hundred-year-olds walking around is of no use to anyone. I want customers, not walking cadavers."

Stein was nearly as disgusted as he was outraged. "A humanitarian and a philanthropist you call yourself in the press? You say you vant vorld peace, that you vant to end pain and suffering? The only pain and suffering you vant to end is your own! The world and everybody in it can drop dead as far as you are concerned, so long as you get yours. How many years do you vant to live? Two hundred? Three hundred? Does destroying everything make you feel superior so you don't have to feel like the nothing you are? How are you going to hide from yourself when there is nothing left to destroy?"

The smile on Kilgore's tiny lips spread into a thin straight line that looked reptilian. "As any good politician knows, personal power comes not from allowing things to happen but from denying them, from stopping them in their tracks. Whoever controls the Organ Grinder wields the power of life and death. Not since helping to confiscate the wealth of my fellow Muslims before leaving Bosnia, have I felt such power." The agony in his head subsided and his smile softened. "As for you, Cydney, I would be most grateful if you would attend my procedure."

"Your . . ." She was shocked. "What on earth for?"

His voice took on the supplicating tone of a patient father. "Call me superstitious, but it worked for you, did it not? You survived, and clearly you have thrived. Maybe your luck will rub off on me."

"I don't see what possible difference my being here . . ."

"In case you have forgotten, my money makes your garden grow. I can just as easily stop watering it if that's what you want. Please, my dear. Indulge an old man. Tell me you'll come."

Cyd was incredulous.

"Wouldn't miss it for the world," Alex smiled in amusement.

# Chapter Twenty-Seven

## COMMON SIDE EFFECTS

Ambrose Kilgore's Organ Grinder operation was scheduled for nine o'clock the next morning.

Alex and Cyd arrived half an hour early to find the laboratory already crowded with gowned medical staff from the hospital and Stein's own white-coated personnel.

Cyd was ambivalent about being here. On the one hand, she was curious about the procedure that had save her life and wanted to see it in action when it didn't involve her. On the other hand, who wants to relive their own surgery?

Kilgore sat on the operating table smoking a cigar and chatting amiably with one and all. A benevolent Buddha with an air of intimidation about him. Doctor Stein snatched the cigar out of his mouth and dunked it disdainfully in a glass of water.

Kilgore laughed, started to light another and saw that Cyd had arrived. He held out his arms. "A kiss for luck for the old man?"

Cyd forced herself to do as he asked.

"You're not scared at all?" she said. "I was terrified."

"You're here, what's there to be afraid of? I can't thank you enough for coming."

"Best of luck, sir."

Cyd and Alex backed away to let the doctors and technicians do their jobs.

Stein told Kilgore to lay back on the table so the machine could be calibrated. "I ask you one last time," he pleaded. "Give up this foolishness."

"Get on with it," the patient ordered. "I have an important meeting in China I have to attend next week."

An anesthesiologist who had been standing by stepped up and gave the patient something to relax him. Kilgore looked up sleepily and asked how long he could safely be kept under.

"As long as it takes," the kindly doctor replied. "Not to worry. You're in good hands."

A three-dimensional hologram of Kilgore's brain appeared, rotating slowly above his head. It looked like a bowl of moldy noodles, black and ugly with growths.

"Count backward for me from a hundred," the anesthesiologist intoned, slowly depressing the plunger on a syringe that was inserted into an IV.

Kilgore lost consciousness. Tiny drills were brought out and probes, with long leads attached, were inserted into his skull. When completed, his head bristled like a pincushion.

Everyone stepped away from the table. The only sound was the whir of cooling fans.

"Start!" Stein ordered.

Two hours into the procedure, a worried assistant left his computer station and approached his boss.

"Problem?" Stein asked.

The small, dark, intensely capable man frowned. "Sir, no progress. The Organ Grinder appears to be stuck. It keeps going back and forth over the same layer of tissue again and again."

"Are the vats dispensing the appropriate carbohydrates, lipids, acids and proteins?"

"We've already had to refill one of them twice."

Stein put a reassuring hand on his technician's shoulder. "Then the device is doing its job. And ve must do ours. Be patient, my friend."

The computer operator returned to his work station with his face still clouded in concern.

Day became night and night became day again. Cyd and Alex sat on the floor with their backs against a wall, alternately waking and dozing.

Stein walked by and they looked up. The inventor shook his head and kept walking.

Another day passed and then another. On the morning of the fourth day the original staff had just returned for the start of their shift when the Organ Grinder shut down. The procedure was complete.

Kilgore lay motionless on the operating table as the probes in his head were carefully removed. Stein sat heavily in a chair next to where Cyd and Alex were sitting against the wall. He hadn't slept the entire time and looked exhausted.

"Is he alive?" Cyd asked, struggling to sit up.

"Technically."

Alex rubbed at his eyes. "Did it work?"

"Time vill tell."

"You don't sound that optimistic," Alex said.

"It's the scientist's job to be skeptical."

***

The doctors were unable to wake the patient, and it was decided that he should be moved to the intensive care unit next door. Alex and Cyd followed along behind Kilgore's gurney as he was transferred.

Too tired to sleep, they collapsed into chairs in the hospital's waiting room and stared into space. Stein came out through the double doors to the intensive care ward where he had been checking on his patient. They looked up and started to speak.

The scientist shook his head and kept walking.

"Alive?" Cyd asked, calling after him.

"I vill call you if there is any change. Get some rest."

Alex stood as Stein went out and offered Cyd his hand.

She smiled up at him weakly. "You go on."

"Stein said he'd call. Sitting here won't help."

"I promised Kilgore. You don't have to stay."

He hesitated, sighed and sat back down. A faint trail of exotic perfume caused him to look back up again as a newcomer entered the waiting room and seated herself in a chair across from them. A Chinese woman. Elegantly dressed in designer clothes and wearing expensive jewelry. Middle aged. Faded beauty that was not yet entirely faded.

The woman took a cigarette from a gold cigarette case and lit it.

Alex held up a finger. "Sorry."

"Don't you just hate these international flights?" she said in clipped but passable English, dropping the cigarette on the floor and crushing it out with a spiked heel. "You would think on your own airplane you could at least get some sleep."

"Where did you come in from?" Cyd asked. She had the feeling the woman was made out of pieces of glass that would cut you if you touched them.

"Hong Kong." She started to light another cigarette and changed her mind. "Ambrose Kilgore. You know him? They tell me he hasn't awakened yet."

"You're . . ."

"His wife. Yes. You look surprised."

"Not . . . not at all," Cyd managed.

"He never told us he was married," Alex said.

"You sound American," the former Miss Universe China remarked. "Americans are so naïve. Without one of us at your side it is often difficult, if not impossible, to become a billionaire."

Cyd was confused.

The beauty queen gave her a disdainful look and was about to make another veiled reference to China's inexorable march to world domination, when a scream, far away and growing louder by the second, came from inside the intensive care ward.

Alex sat up straight, his medical instincts on high alert. A patient was in trouble and nobody was doing anything about it!

The scream went on, rising in intensity until it was loud enough to wake the cadavers in the morgue downstairs. A swarm of activity could be seen through the glass in the double doors to the ward. A nurse rushed into the waiting room from the hall outside leading a pair of beefy uniformed security guards. Alex reached to stop them and ask what was going on. The guard shook off his hand and disappeared through the doors.

Cyd stuck her fingers in her ears. The howl was demonic.

Then, as suddenly as it started, it stopped.

Minutes passed. The two guards came back out. One of them had a torn shirt. Alex stood and blocked their way. "I'm Doctor Farmer. Was that Ambrose Kilgore? The patient from the lab? Is he alright?"

"Stark raving bozos, you ask me," the beefier of the two guards said.

The other, the one with the torn shirt, was breathing hard. "Shot they just gave him, he'll sleep until Yom Kippur."

Stein rushed in as the guards were leaving. He had apparently only gone as far as his lab when he left earlier. Cyd came to her feet, and he indicated they could follow him.

"This is Kilgore's wife," Alex said to Stein's retreating back. "I didn't catch her name."

Stein stopped and turned.

"Jia Li," the Chinese woman said. "Jia Li Kilgore."

Stein gave her a formal nod. "I'm the one you spoke to earlier on the phone, Mrs. Kilgore. Come with us, please."

They entered the ward as Kilgore was being wheeled out of his curtained cubical. He lay on his back on a gurney staring up. Cyd looked down at his comatose figure and a cry of alarm escaped her lips.

"Medically induced coma," the attending physician informed them. "All we can do for him now."

Alex bent to look. He was as appalled as Cyd.

Kilgore's eyes were wide open and a silent scream, horrible and ghastly, was frozen on his face. Whatever he was staring at in the prison of his mind looked like he was on a guided tour of hell.

Cyd noticed that his wife was unmoved by her husband's condition. "How can you be so . . ." she began, trying and failing to sound understanding.

"Cold?" Jia Li sniffed, turning to leave. "An end is just another beginning. I must go. I have another assignment waiting."

Cyd and Alex joined Stein to watch as Kilgore's gurney was wheeled away.

"There are common side effects to every procedure," the scientist shrugged. "Madness apparently being one of them in this case."

## Chapter Twenty-Eight

### MAZEL TOV

The first crop of Cannastar had been harvested and the second planting was in the ground. There was more demand for the lifesaving herb than Cyd and Alex could possibly supply, but they made certain that Senegal received its fair share. Albert Dado was President Dado now and he had his hands full trying to set his country right. Nonetheless, he had taken the time to send Little Boy and Juliette his congratulations on their impending nuptials along with a gift: elaborate, matching Senegalese wedding costumes made from acres and acres of billowing pink cloth.

Juliette had been planning her wedding for nine months and she wasn't going to let anything spoil it. Dado's gift might have been appropriated for a couple getting married in Africa, but she was fairly certain, if she and Little Boy were to show up in traditional Senegalese garb for a traditional Jewish wedding, they would be laughed out of town. Her solution was to have their pictures taken draped in pink splendor and sent to Dado. She was then free to wear the beautiful white wedding dress she had picked out for her actual ceremony.

Cyd and Alex were on their way to Tel Aviv in their motor home to attend the wedding. Alex, unfamiliar with driving a vehicle the size of a city bus, was gripping the steering wheel and staring intently out the windshield in an effort not to run over the tiny cars that kept darting in and out in front of him.

"I read that Kilgore's death is being reported as a heart attack," Cyd said. "Probably because there isn't a medical term for 'Scared to Death'. The article didn't make any mention of the Organ Grinder."

"Good." Alex blew his horn at a Japanese sedan that had just cut him off. "Stein might have lost his funding for his project, but at least he didn't lose his reputation." He slowed to let a car that was tailgating him go around. "What did you think about Jia Li selling her husband's seventy percent stake in our Cannastar farm to the Israeli government? I hear she got an astronomical price for it."

"I'd rather be in partnership with Israel than her," Cyd smiled. "At least, I trust Israel. They're practically running everything as it is, anyway."

Alex fished in the side pocket of the door, pulled out an envelope and handed it to her.

"What's this?

"Open it."

She peeked inside and gasped.

"Our share of the proceeds from the sale of our first Cannastar crop."

"Alex, this is a fortune! With two crops a year, what are we going to do with all the money?"

"We'll figure something out."

She tucked the check carefully away in her purse. "Can you believe that Chinese woman turning around and *giving* Stein her seventy percent share in the Organ Grinder? Why would she sell the Cannastar project, and then do a thing like that?"

"Maybe it was a thank you present for killing her husband."

"Maybe it was a gift to humanity from the bottom of her mercenary little heart."

"My guess is she didn't want her name associated with the thing that left Kilgore staring at something that would make the devil himself piss his pants."

"Karma's a bitch," Cyd sighed.

They were approaching the outskirts of Tel Aviv, and the heavier traffic was making Alex nervous. "You know," he said, moving cautiously into the slow lane, "it's going to take years of clinical trials and years of perfecting before the medical community will accept the Organ Grinder, let alone certify it safe enough for public use. I've been thinking. How would you feel about using our Israeli Cannastar profits to fund his research from now on?"

Her face lit up and she clapped her hands in delight. "Love it, love it, love it!"

\*\*\*

Juliette found that trying to plan a wedding in the Holy Land was about as simple and straightforward as trying to organize a two-thousand-mile Tour de France bicycle race. Fortunately, she had converted to Judaism for her first marriage, so that wasn't a problem. Nor was the budget; she could afford a royal wedding. Securing a venue, however, was another matter. Every place she called was booked out for nearly a year. Finally, Bait Al Hayam, just south of Tel Aviv, had a last-minute cancelation and she grabbed it. A seaside wedding! How utterly grand!

The real nightmare began when she tried to work with all the independent contractors. Between language barriers and differences in communication styles, she was getting nowhere on the phone. Videographers, photographers, florists, caterers, hair stylists, seamstresses, bands, DJs and rental companies all seemed to want to communicate via dozens of texts and Facebook messages without ever making a commitment or settling anything.

She wanted to scream!

## The Organ Grinder Factor

After multiple trips to the Rabbinate to submit all the proper forms and documentation to get married, she was still getting the runaround. She had yet to choose a Rabbi to perform the ceremony. Nearly three hundred guests were flying in from Paris and trying to find first class accommodations for them all was like trying to find water in the desert. Every hotel she spoke to was either full or wanted to gouge her. There was the Shabbat Hatan or Welcome Party to schedule. There were wedding itineraries and insider information about restaurants and local points of interest to print. There were goodie bags to select and order.

She was ready to elope!

Then someone suggested a wedding planner. She found a marvelous one that had organized dozens of weddings at Bait Al Hayam. They spoke fluent Hebrew, French and English. They would handle every detail; she needn't worry about a thing. The wedding planner proved to be a godsend, and her life became beautiful and wonderful and grand once again.

The big day arrived.

The weather was perfect, not a cloud in the sky. The outdoor Chuppah, or wedding canopy, was draped in white and dripping in flowers, and through its open sides you could see the beautiful sandy beaches, foamy surf and soaring skyline of Tel Aviv. After the ceremony, the guests would enter a vast, gayly decorated hall with windows that looked out on the sea where tables were set for the wedding feast.

The orchestra had already arrived and were taking their places on the stage above the dance floor. Juliette's guests from France, plus another two hundred or so of Little Boy's friends and associates from work, were sitting in white chairs tied with white-ribboned bouquets. Those that couldn't find chairs were standing shoulder to shoulder behind the chairs.

The bride and groom stood under the Chuppah facing the rabbi and the sparkling Mediterranean. Perfectly matched, the tiny pair could have been the bride and groom atop their own wedding cake. Fat Man stood to one side of the groom looking like a somber whale. Cyd and three other bridesmaids were lined up on the bride's other side wearing form-fitting dresses that looked to have all been cut from the same exotic pink cloth. A small African boy, dressed exactly like the groom in a matching blue suit and red tie, and wearing the same wedding yarmulka on the back of his head, stood directly behind the happy couple holding a ring owned by the groom.

The ceremony proceeded.

At the end, Little Boy joyfully stomped a glass with his right foot.

"Mazel tov!" the assembly roared in congratulation.

Hours later, the dining, drinking and dancing showed no signs of letting up. Cyd and Alex came off the dance floor trying to catch their breath, moved outside the fray and stood watching the raucous celebration. They were both a little drunk.

"You look pretty in pink," he said. "Where do you suppose Juliette found material that looks like that?"

She heard his cynicism and grimaced. "Don't ask."

Juliette appeared out of the crowd coming toward them with Momo in tow. A drunken wedding guest impeded her progress and raised his glass.

"L'chaim!"

The bride smiled politely and kept coming. Momo rushed ahead and hugged Cyd and Alex for at least the tenth time that day.

"Doctor Boss, Nurse Boss! Guess what *mère* just told me? She said she and *père* are going to adopt me! I'm going to be their son forever!"

Alex rubbed his head in the old familiar way. "You haven't told me yet how school is going?"

"Momo best boy in math and science class!" he boasted. His face fell and he seemed reluctant to go on. "Hebrew hardest to learn."

"Is it still going to be Doctor Momo?" Cyd asked.

The boy's enthusiasm came back. "Doctor Momo *Shaviv*."

Cyd smiled at Juliette. "Mrs. Shaviv must be very proud."

"Mrs. Shaviv," Juliette replied, "needs to sit down before her feet fall off."

"Where's Little Boy?" Alex asked.

His bride gestured vaguely across the room. "Ashraf is off somewhere getting drunk with his friends."

Cyd and Alex looked. They didn't see Little Boy, but they did see his best friend Fat Man. He was talking with the only woman at the wedding who was anywhere near his same size. They had been standing in the same position for over an hour looking into one another's eyes. Sensing that they were being stared at, they looked up.

Fat Man saw his friends smiling at him and smiled back, then took his new acquaintance by the hand and eagerly led her toward them through the crowd. "Everyone," he announced, arriving with the enormous woman in tow and beaming broadly. "I would like you to meet Janethon Silverstein. Ms. Silverstein has just asked me to marry her."

Silence. No one dared speak.

"What did you say?" Juliette asked at last with forced brightness.

"I said I'd ask you for the name of your wedding planner."

Janethon gave them all a chubby-cheeked grin.

"Mazel tov!" Momo cried.

The gathering darkness failed to dampen the spirits of wedding guests, and only seemed to liven them. Cyd and Alex sat exhausted at an empty table, its white tablecloth stained with food and wine. Watching with some concern, they saw the frightened, laughing bride and groom hoisted precariously into the air in chairs and carried around the room while friends and family clapped and danced around them to the tune of 'Hava Nagila'.

Cyd turned away and looked out the window at the Chuppah where the night wind was flapping the white drapes and blowing the flowers away. "I spoke with Otis."

Alex leaned closer to hear her above the noise.

"He says we're no longer criminals. He says, with everyone using Cannastar whether the government likes it or not, the charges against us have been dropped. Apparently, it's safe for us to come home."

"That's a relief."

"I'm tired, Alex. I need a rest." She paused and went on. "Israel doesn't need us to run the Grow anymore. They'll be good shepherds if we turn it over to them. We'll still get paid, and we can still fund Stein's Organ Grinder research. Our work is done here."

His eyes lit with humor. "I didn't think you were the domestic type."

"Neither did I. People change."

They fell silent.

Cyd looked out the window. "I'll go then."

"I? Not *we*?"

"There is no we, Alex. Unless you're willing to keep your promise to me, I'm going home alone."

"Promise?"

"If you don't remember, I'm not going to remind you."

"You mean when you sent me away to Bethlehem to pray? That promise?"

"When I sent you away because I didn't want you to watch me die. And yes, that promise."

"How could I forget?"

Again, they fell silent.

"I thought you had changed your mind."

"I thought you had changed *yours*."

He frowned. "So, it's settled then."

"Settled?"

"It was settled from the moment I met you. It's settled for as long as I live, and for as long as whatever happens after that. I love you, Cyd. I'd marry you if you wanted a wedding that looked like the one we just witnessed."

"Even if you had to wear one of those silly looking beanies and stomp on a glass?"

"I'd stomp a hundred glasses."

Tears filled her eyes and she kissed him wildly.

"One will do. I wouldn't want you to hurt your foot."

## Chapter Twenty-Nine

### SUNLIGHT

Montana's cowboy heart and western soul was in the song the band was playing. The haunting sadness in the joy of living, the endless pleasures in the simplest of things, the fullness of life in the vast and empty land that stretched to the mountains and surrounded the outdoor wedding of Cyd and Alex—it was all in the music. The big Montana sky was Cyd's Chuppah, the river that ran through her property was the Mediterranean backdrop to her ceremony, the forests and fields that surrounded the pasture where her wedding party gathered were her decorations and ribbons.

Horses looked on from a nearby pasture as friends and neighbors took their seats in the two hundred or so wooden folding chairs that had been set out on the uneven ground. Ranchers from all around had come with their wives and children to see Cyd marry her doctor. Maybe it was the indescribable mixture of pride and humility in the stoop of their shoulders, maybe it was feeding cows and pulling calves into the world at 3:00 a.m. in forty below zero weather, maybe it was the indefatigable love of God and country that so informed their lives. Whatever it was, the ranchers stood out in the crowd.

Friends who had risked everything to help Cyd and Alex bring Cannastar to the world had come. Otis, Eloise and their son Elton had flown in from Arizona.

"We're illegally legal now, man," the rotund Cannastar farmer announced proudly when Alex picked them up at the airport. "How about that?"

## The Organ Grinder Factor

Clarence Big Foot, the gregarious, ponytailed Native American who favored loud Hawaiian shirts, and his tall, retired-ballerina wife Mary, had driven over from their home on the Flathead Indian Reservation. Without their help and support, Cyd and Alex would never have been able to make their first Cannastar Grow a reality. They got out of Mary's new Range Rover, and Clarence pulled Alex aside. "I want to see you and Cyd alone after the ceremony," he whispered.

Betty Little Horn was there, or rather everywhere. The former farrier was Cyd's permanent ranch manager now and ran a successful quarter horse breeding business on the side. Cyd had given her the land to build a small log home not far from the big log house she had grown up in—the house she nearly lost before Clarence and Mary paid off her mortgage.

Betty had organized Cyd's wedding down to every detail. "Damnedest thing," the calloused horsewoman declared. "Seein' you as a bride almost makes me want to cry."

"Thank you, I think," Cyd replied, turning so Betty could zip up the back of her sleeveless white wedding dress.

"Kinda fun puttin' the whole thing together. Maybe I'll go into the business. Have people out here for a real Montana ranch weddin'."

"You want to be a professional wedding planner?"

"What's that?"

Betty's herd of mares was startled when the band struck up Mendelssohn's Wedding March and bolted across the pasture with their foals trying to keep pace. Everyone turned expectantly to watch Cyd coming down the aisle between the rows of chairs on the arm of their towering, ponytailed friend in the Hawaiian shirt.

Alex stood with the minister watching in wonder as she arrived.

"You know," Cyd said, taking her place beside him and smoothing the dress she was unaccustomed to wearing, "if you hadn't wanted to marry me, I already had my singles ad written."

He looked straight ahead, amused at her making conversation at a time like this. "Let me guess. 'Beautiful woman seeks handsome man for terrifying adventures in places nobody else wants to go.' "

"More like, 'Moody homebody with absolutely no domestic skills seeks doting doctor who can't cook either.' "

He turned with an adoring smile. Seeing her standing there in her white satin dress with flowers in her dark hair made his heart feel like it would burst.

"You really do look beautiful in that dress."

"And you look handsome in your suit."

He glanced down. "I'm never taking this off. I'm wearing it full time from now on."

"Even to bed?"

"Let's not get carried away."

She gave him the most amazing smile. "Oh, but I am Alex. I am totally, utterly, completely carried away by today!"

Tears filled his eyes. "Me too."

A wedding photographer snapped a picture of them at that moment. It would be the one they would keep always, and generations later when visitors saw it hanging in the Historical Museum in Helena, they would stop and stare and wish they could have lived in that time and been that much in love.

The minister cleared his throat. "If you two are quite done . . ."

At the conclusion of the ceremony, the bride and groom kissed, and the fiddle in the band struck up a lover's waltz. The couple walked back down the aisle and out onto a makeshift dancefloor set up in the middle of the pasture. Gradually, the wedding party joined in until the wooden platform sagged and creaked with boots and vests, and ladies in their Sunday best, all spinning and turning in three-quarter time.

The barbeque was so good there was a permanent line for seconds, iced kegs foamed with frothing beer, and the sound of popping champaign corks sounded like target practice. Cyd and Alex came off the dance floor happily flushed. They were passing a picnic table and marveling at the mountain of wedding presents piled on it when Clarence walked up.

"There's the happy couple," the Silicon Valley millionaire smiled, pulling them aside to talk more privately amid the festive noise and laughter. Other than a few new streaks of gray in his black ponytail, he hadn't changed a bit since the day Alex first met him after he and Cyd had crossed the Bob Marshall Wilderness on horseback and arrived at his house in a state of rain-soaked exhaustion. "Mary and I couldn't be happier for the two of you," he added, moving them a little further away and looking around to make sure they were alone.

Cyd thanked him and asked where Robert was. "We invited him," she said, searching the crowd, "but I don't see him anywhere."

"My son is down in Chile."

"He okay?" Alex asked. He had loosened his tie and unbuttoned his collar and was feeling more comfortable now. "It's earthquake central down there."

"He's fine. Sends his congratulations. Says he should have married Cyd when he had the chance."

"His loss, my gain," Alex grinned.

Clarence gave Cyd a loving look. "At least Mary and I have not lost a daughter."

Cyd stood on tiptoe and kissed his cheek. "What's Robert doing down in Chile of all places?"

"Geological studies. Chile has been having more earthquakes than usual lately. Big ones that last longer."

"Bigger than the 9.5 one they had in 1960 that went on for ten minutes?" Cyd asked.

"The daily ones are in the 5.0 to 6.0 range," Clarence replied. "Locals are so used to them that they practically ignore them. What they can't ignore are the ones in the 7.0 to 8.0 range that keep happening on a regular basis. It's these monster quakes that are causing the phenomenon."

"Phenomenon?" Cyd didn't want to seem impolite, but this was her wedding day and she was far too happy to worry about earthquakes six thousand miles away.

"Strange lights that appear out of fissures in the ground and disappear again the minute the earthquakes are over."

"Where?" Alex asked. "Not in the towns, I hope?"

"High up in the Andes and beyond the coastal mountains. Locals are calling them *Los Ojos de Dios*—The Eyes of God."

"Maybe it's just people moving around in the dark with search lights," Cyd suggested.

Clarence shook his head. "They're more like elongated slashes. Intense beams of light too big and bright for even stadium lights. They appear, turn the night sky into day, and go out again as quickly as they came on. There have been any number of sightings. Robert has seen them twice himself. The Chileans are afraid to go anywhere near where they show up."

Cyd looked longingly in the direction of the dancing. "Why?"

"They're afraid of what God might see if they get too close."

"Sounds perfectly reasonable."

Clarence ignored his sarcasm. "The earthquakes have caused major upheavals in the strata and exposed significant deposits of valuable minerals. Robert has been hired by one of the big mining companies down there to map the affected areas and try to determine the feasibility of recovering what's been unearthed. He tells me they could be looking at enough lithium alone to build lithium batteries forever."

"Is there a reason you're telling us all this?" Alex asked.

"I'm getting to that."

*Please,* Cyd thought.

Clarence lowered his voice. "There are legends on cave walls down there that predate recorded history. They tell of a race of alien giants that lived in Chile with an unlimited source of energy. Men who had bulbs that glowed, machines that moved without horses, chariots that flew without wings. Those mysterious statues you see out on Easter Island, two thousand miles off of Chile's coast, supposedly represent whoever or whatever these people were."

"Okay," Cyd said slowly.

"Chilean songs and stories over the centuries speak of alien giants who had the power of sunlight."

"Sunlight," Alex repeated with growing interest. "Are you saying some tribe of ancient extraterrestrials held the key to fusion energy? To the thing that powers the sun?"

Clarence shrugged. "Who knows?"

Cyd's eyes widened. "A free source of unlimited energy. How incredible would that be?"

Clarence scratched the back of his neck. "Don't suppose the two of you would be interested in making a trip down to Chile to check it out? I'd be willing to fund the expedition."

"Why can't Robert check it out?" Alex asked. "Finding out why a bunch of ETs left home, forgot to turn out the lights, and weren't concerned about the electric bill might be more interesting than staring at a bunch of rocks all day."

"He'd like nothing more. Robert is beside himself with curiosity over this. Thinks something really important could come of it, but he's down there to do a job. He doesn't have time to go trekking around in the mountains for months trying to prove a legend is true."

Cyd turned to Alex in protest. "We talked about coming home to start a family," she stated firmly.

"We just got back," he agreed in a voice that lacked enthusiasm. "I promised Cyd I'd open a practice and try my hand at being a country doctor. Looking forward to it, actually."

The old restlessness stirred in Cyd and her resistance began to weaken. The more she thought about it, the more intrigued she became. "Whatever is powering those so-called lights might be a better solution than trying to run the world on windmills that freeze and kill birds, on batteries that need to be recharged with electricity that comes from fossil fuel, and on electrical grids that won't support a fraction of the people driving electric cars once everybody has one."

"The oil and gas industry might not be too happy about fusion energy either once they realize it's going to put them out of business," Alex noted. He saw that Clarence and Cyd were watching him. "Just saying."

"I'm sorry," Cyd said, trying to hide her enthusiasm. "We can't. I can't."

"Understood," the big Native American smiled affably. "Forget I even mentioned it."

# Coming Soon!

## STEPHEN STEELE
### THE TROUBLE WITH MIRACLES
### BOOK THREE
# THE FUSION FACTOR

*An unlimited source of free energy forever.*
*A force so powerful it can turn the earth to space dust in a heartbeat.*

Alex Farmer and Cyd Seeley seek the ancient secrets of fusion energy in a thrilling journey that ranges from the high deserts and active volcanos of the Andes, to the lava caves beneath the mysterious statues on Easter Island.

Fusion energy, magnificent in its power, can create a pollution-free world, or turn it to space dust in an instant. Cyd and Alex fight to keep the miracle of endless free energy from falling into the wrong hands.

A tale of mystery and suspense, *The Fusion Factor* is a sci-fi thriller that will keep readers turning pages late into the night.

### For more information
### visit: www.SpeakingVolumes.us

# On Sale Now!

## STEPHEN STEELE
## THE TROUBLE WITH MIRACLES
### BOOKS ONE AND TWO

 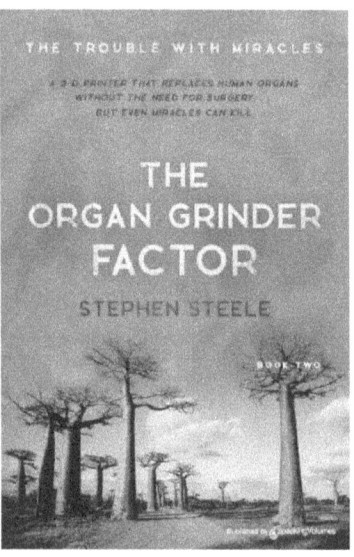

**For more information visit:** www.SpeakingVolumes.us

# On Sale Now!

## CHRIS JORDAN
## RANDALL SHANE SERIES
### BOOKS ONE AND TWO

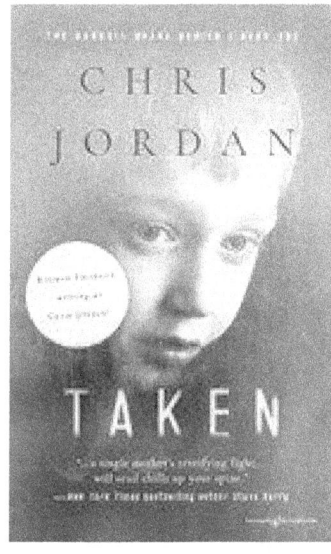 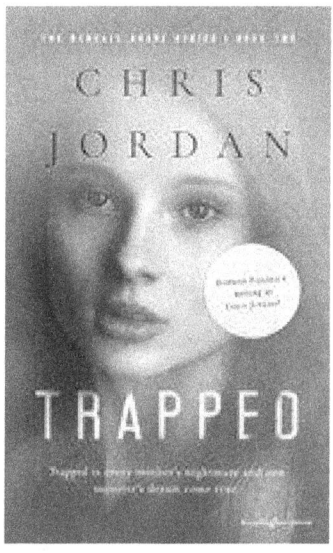

**For more information visit:** www.SpeakingVolumes.us

# On Sale Now!

## MICAH S. HACKLER
## SHERIFF LANSING MYSTERIES
### BOOKS 1 – 9

**For more information
visit:** www.SpeakingVolumes.us

**Sign up for free and bargain books**

Join the Speaking Volumes mailing list

Text
# ILOVEBOOKS
to 22828 to get started.

Message and data rates may apply.

CPSIA information can be obtained
at www.ICGtesting.com
Printed in the USA
LVHW052253220723
753203LV00009B/169